I0777720

Witch Tree

Also by J.E. Marriott

WITCH BOOKS:
Witch Bottle

THE CHAMELEON SAGAS:
Chameleon
Castrum Lucis

MAGIC, TEA & WITCHES:
Maud and the Tea of Dume

STAND ALONE:
The Witchlets of Witches Brew

Witch Tree

J.E. Marriott

Wyrdwood,
Canada

THIS BOOK IS PUBLISHED BY
WYRDWOOD, OTTAWA, ON, CANADA

Issued in print and electronic formats.
ISBN 978-1-988332-14-7 (pbk.)
ISBN 978-1-988332-15-4 (ebook)

First trade paperback edition July 2017
Second trade paperback edition February 2024

Dedication

For all those who feel their Ancestors
next to them and still walk
the path of old ways.

Chapter One

June 19th 1656,
Boston Common, Massachusetts

For a summer day, it was strangely overcast and heavy. Humid and dank as a large storm brewed, out past the harbour, and was creeping inland towards the watchful people of Boston. Summer storms led to many things: roused passions, ships wrecked against the shore, and the fear of unholy things coming forth and stealing souls. It was not a good day for hanging a witch by all the portents. The frogs knew it too, as they croaked loudly from the nearby pond, giving an eerie chorus to the whole proceedings.

A large crowd had gathered on the common grounds to the west of the Charles River and past the Ropewalk. Despite the ominous weather, the crowd was jubilant. Catching evil in their midst and bringing it to justice made them elated; all except for two souls standing by and watching in horror at the events unfolding before their very eyes.

The old woman's bony hand clutched at the young boy's shirt-clad shoulder, digging her fingers into the material and into his thin flesh underneath, pressing almost to the bone. They both stood and watched the woman in front of them as she was forced to climb the ladder leading up the trunk, to the sturdiest branch of the old tree. A thick rope was placed around her neck by the hooded man who had followed her up the ladder. He threw the rope over the gnarled old branch and then climbed back down as the woman stood there alone, balanced on a rung several feet above the ground. The dark haired woman was offered a hood but refused it stubbornly.

"Thou shalt all see thy evil of this act," The woman said bravely, jutting out her well sculptured chin in defiance.

Her voice remained strong despite the wild

emotions that must have been coursing through her body. The woman who stood precariously on the ladder was the mistress of the old woman and the mother of the small boy who stood watching, both with eyes wide in horror.

After a few moments, the charge of Witchcraft was read to the crowd and the ladder was quickly and unceremoniously jerked away, and the woman's full weight was suddenly taken up by the noose.

The woman struggled vainly against the tightened rope around her neck as she hung from the old tree and was brutally strangled in front of the large crowd of self-important men and their clucking wives. It was unfortunate that her neck had not broken instantly with the initial drop; now she would suffocate in gruesome agony before the world that had so cruelly condemned her, and before her horrified boy.

No one noticed the house cook and the small, dirty kitchen boy in the assembled crowd of merchants, whores and drunkards. In fact, the wealthy and self-important leaders of the town congregated at one end of the crowd, keeping separate unto themselves from all the worthless wretches. They didn't even look back over their shoulders at the crowd of peasants, who stood behind them, as they all watched one of their own gurgle her last breath, unable to say goodbye to her secret and illegitimate son.

The old cook continued to watch as her mistress looked out over the crowd of fifty or more people. She did so several times in her agony, perhaps looking for the boy. The cook hoped so for his sake.

Fighting against the intense pain, Ann Hibbens desperately searched the crowd with the last of her blurry vision for her lover. She hoped he would save her but she could not see him, so cursed his name over and over again with her fading breath. At long last, she felt the darkness creep behind her eyes and the incredible pain in her throat, chest and head began to ebb as her pitiful struggles became weaker and less frantic.

The last thing she saw were the eyes of her accusers gleaming with their black deed and their looks of smug satisfaction betraying their dark hearts. The men and women stood proud amongst the wealthy elite of Boston, believing their reputations unblemished by this execution and their world vision righted. So the bigoted and uneducated leaders of the town nodded in satisfaction as if an agreed deal had been struck and maybe one had, but not one they would ever conceive nor understand until it was much too late.

The old woman held the boy more firmly against her as her mistress succumbed to the terrible punishment. The men of judgement, in their presumed wisdom, had deemed this fitting for the wealthy widow. Did she not freely, and, some would say, shockingly, speak her mind too loudly? Of course she should hang for witchcraft! Finally, after the sentence against her was denied the year before, they could dispose of this troublesome woman.

The boy didn't sob hysterically, like the cook had seen with other children whose parents had been hung. No, the boy, barely in his tenth year, watched as silent tears tumbled down his face.

Although his mother had never acknowledged him in public, in private she had shown kindness to him on several occasions and he'd become fond of his 'upstairs mother'. He reached up for Sarah's hand and found it gripping his shoulder. He hadn't even realized it was there. He knew deep inside that he would be safe with her, his 'downstairs mother', for she was more of a mother to him in so many ways.

"'Tis alright, Benjy, thee wilt stay with me as my son, just as ye folk know ye to be," Sarah said under her breath as she leaned down to talk in his ear. She patted the boy on his wet cheek and gently turned him, guiding him by his shoulders. She walked him away from the gruesome scene of the end of his mother's life even before her body was taken down, to be pronounced dead by the surgeon.

The boy heard the Hangman call for the cart to remove her body and take it to the burial field.

"What wilt become of her now?" Benjamin said, glancing back over his shoulder at the now still body of his mother laying on the soil of the common ground with the rope still tied around her neck. Her head lolled to one side, her skin a faint blue, her tongue hung out of her mouth hideously swollen and dark in colour.

"She wilt be buried 'acourse. Mayhaps on unhallowed ground too, unless she paid for a plot and a dispensation, thy knows 'tis what 'appens with declared witches," Sarah said as they walked back through the hot and humid streets of Boston towards the mistress's old house. *It be the master's house now*, Sarah thought to herself. "We must a'be preparing for ye new master's arrival."

The mistress, Ann, had sent to England for her son whilst awaiting her sentence, and during that difficult time she had drawn up her will. She'd put her affairs in order the best she could while rotting in her cell. At least her money had helped a little in the end.

"Who wilt we serve now?" Benjamin said as he stepped over a small but stinking puddle, which a thin and starved looking dog was curiously sniffing at.

The summer storm overnight had drenched everything and made the streets muddy and full of puddles, but the midday heat of the beautiful June day had evaporated much of the water and the air felt thick with it.

"'Twill be thy master 'acourse, thy mistress's son wilt be arriving to take on ye house and lands as is his right."

"What is he like? Ye new master?" The boy said and looked up at Sarah, his tear stained face grubby and pale.

"As a grown man, I knowest nay, but as a wee boy he was... a'oddity, to be sure," Sarah said. Her heart sank and pounded at the dread that grew in her belly, reminding her what a nasty boy Jonathon had been.

He was the youngest son of Ann, with the eldest being John and the middle child being Joseph. He had been at school in England when his mother had run away with her two servants and a lover for the New World without a backward glance at her old life and her children.

"We wilt just 'ave to do our best to maketh 'im be welcome, aye?" She said and chewed her lip with worry. She was not looking forward to meeting with him again now. She hoped he had matured with grace, but deep down she doubted it.

Benjamin nodded but wasn't really

listening. All he could think of was his other mother being thrown into an unholy grave to rot away alone. He wanted to know where exactly she was laid so he could visit her and tell her of his day. Just like he used to when she was of good humour and willing for him to come upstairs and sit on the floor at her feet in her private chamber.

He made a decision there and then: he would talk to everyone in town until he found out where she lay and then he would sneak out and secretly visit with her whenever he was able to escape his duties. This thought made him feel less lonely and sad, and he knew he would be talking with his mother again soon.

Chapter Two

Present day, BookCon,
Los Angeles, California

Amy looked up from the book she was reading aloud and closed it just as the audience burst into applause. She smiled at the fans and looked around the room as the announcer nodded, giving her the cue to leave the stage.

"Thank you," Amy said as her fans continued to clap.

The announcer, a smart looking young woman, walked on to introduce the next guest. "Thank you, Amy Grey! The New York Times bestselling author of "Witch Bottle!" The woman said and clapped as Amy stepped down off the stage with a wave to the audience. "Amy will be signing books in Hall B in 30 minutes, so don't miss your chance to get your book signed!" She paused for the applause to begin to fade," And now our final guest for the evening, please put your hands together for the team behind this year's favourite TV show..."

Amy left the auditorium and headed to the Green Room for a chance to grab a drink and a bite to eat, before heading to the large room known as Hall B to sign books for the next couple of hours. The air changed next to her in an old and familiar way as she turned down the quiet and deserted corridor heading to the Green Room and Erda appeared by her side.

"Thy has a talent for tale-spinning a crowd, 'twas exciting to watch thee and my blood did warm in my veins." Erda said and smiled.

Despite Erda wearing her normal clothes, that of a 17th century Wise Woman, (though she would describe herself as a Cunning Woman should she be asked) no one batted an eyelid at her whenever she escorted Amy around the event. Their plan was decidedly simple, as most things are that deceived the eye. Erda might be a Spirit and Amy's great Grandmother many times removed, but she could also be corporeal when she desired. Between them they had hatched a plan that meant Erda could travel on the book tour with Amy, by pretending she was a character from Amy's book Witch Bottle. Indeed all she had to do was be herself– for she was the Erda of the story and a ghost from the 1600's. This whole plan greatly amused both Amy and Erda. Fans loved an author who brought one of the main characters from their book with them on a book tour. No one could even comprehend the truth, never mind think of it when they looked at Erda.

The security guard, who stood quietly by the Green Room door, nodded as the ladies approached and, recognizing them, politely opened the door and stood to one side.

"Thank you," Amy said.

"Thank thee," Erda said with a huge smile.

The security guard smiled and nodded as they entered, he was used to the strange antics of the famous, he didn't even seem to regard the pair as unusual in the slightest and closed the door quietly behind them.

The Green Room was the entire presidential suite of the hotel devoted to the relaxation of the guests of the Con, where one could sit side by side with TV and movie stars and share a bottle of wine or a pot of coffee with all of them. Some were a little aloof but most were charming and approachable. Amy had enjoyed many a fine conversation with stars from various TV series' and superhero movies. She had met famous people who were in front of the camera and behind it, including well known directors. She'd even been asked by an A-List director if her book had been optioned yet, meaning they were interested in turning it into a movie. He had ended the conversation with the comment 'my people will call your people' and a massive smile as if he could already see the money piling up in his bank account. Amy tried hard not to get too excited and would wait to see if anything came of it but deep down inside she was squealing with excitement.

As it was the end of the final day of the event, very few people were in the Green Room now and Amy grabbed a cup of tea and a plate of food from the never-ending buffet. She collapsed onto one of the four big leather sofas to relax for the next half hour, grateful for the break. Amy and Erda talked about how they were looking forward to going home. Amy was particularly looking forward to sleeping in her own bed once again. There was just something about hotel beds; they never seemed to be as comfy nor as relaxing as one's own bed, she had decided.

Thirty minutes later and for the last time, Amy sat at her table in Hall B ready to sign hundreds of books and meet her fans. The publisher had staffed and organized the room, and the queue of excited readers waited noisily on the other side of the entrance door. It stretched down the entire corridor and into the main vending hall. The queue was two rows deep and almost blocked the entire corridor. Most people had one or more copies of Amy's books. Not just the new best seller, but also her children's books that she had written years ago, before she had changed genre and now wrote horror and mystery tales. The fans were all chatting excitedly, desperately hoping the door to the room would open soon. The door itself was flanked by two security guards and was firmly closed at present.

"If you are ready, Amy? It's time," the young female assistant said.

Amy looked up at the woman and then over at the table near the door where her books were also on sale. A wise precaution by her publisher in case the fans hadn't brought their own. It was manned by three assistants who all looked like summer interns and rather young to Amy's eye.

In between their table and Amy's lay a roped off pathway that led from the door and split into two lanes, one to the table to purchase a book and then onto Amy's table, and the other wormed its way around the room up to Amy table only.

The exit line was a straightforward path from Amy's table down the side of the room and out a second doorway which also had a security guard standing next to it. Amy had been signing in this room once a day for the last three days and she had seen how well the set up had worked. The people moved through the room like a snake making its way around a maze.

Taking a deep breath, Amy said, "Ok, let's do this one last time." She smiled up at Erda who stood next to her in all her 17th century glory. Erda would sit down later but she preferred to stand when the people first entered as she somehow felt less trapped by the wall of people when she did. She hadn't been prepared for so many people crowding in one spot and it had seriously unnerved her at first. She had never enjoyed the feeling of being trapped or closed in.

Part of the plan that Amy and Erda had conceived was that Erda would also sign as the character of Erda Miller, of course. For appearances sake Erda didn't actually sign her name; she simply put an X on the page. The fans loved it and often asked Erda as many questions as they did Amy.

Of course, if a fan lingered too long there were members of staff hovering to usher people through quite quickly, and no one was allowed to monopolize either Amy or Erda's time too much as this enabled more people to get their books signed.

With a rush of frenetic energy, the crowd burst through the now opened doors and streamed down the roped lines. Amy hardly took a breath before the member of staff directed the first fan to Amy's desk.

"Hello." Amy said and smiled as she took the book from the Goth teenager in front of her. "What's your name?"

"Beth. Err... hello," The young woman said shyly, her cheeks flushing instantly.

Amy wrote a quick note to Beth on the title page of the book and passed it back to her.

"Thank you, Beth," Amy said with a friendly smile.

"Thank you. You're awesome!" The words rushed out of Beth's mouth and she blushed even more.

"Well, thank you, Beth. So are you," Amy said and grinned. She felt like hugging the girl to reassure and show her she was just a person like any other.

Amy had encountered this reaction many, many times over the past year and it still felt weird to her.

All these people seemed to look upon her as something special, but she was just a person who had written a story, even if the story was true and they never knew the truth of it. Amy knew she would never really feel comfortable with all the attention, but on the other hand, she loved meeting her readers and seeing them so happy. She decided that she might not like it, but it was satisfying in an odd way.

Erda also smiled at Beth as the girl moved towards her along the table, still blushing from her initial outburst. Erda placed her requisite X mark in the book, below Amy's signature.

Beth grinned and breathlessly said, "Thank you," she picked up the book and clutched it to her breast like a prized possession as she moved on from the table and was gestured towards the exit by a member of staff.

Another reader approached the table, this time a middle aged lady with very long, natural-looking and rather glorious red hair.

"Hello." The lady said with a huge smile on her face. "I loved Witch Bottle. I've also read all your children's books; my kids love them!" She said with a distinctive English accent.

"Hello, I'm so glad you enjoyed my books," Amy said and held out her hand for the woman's book to sign. "You sound like you come from the UK, too."

"Yes, I'm from Nottinghamshire," the woman said and beamed as she handed her book over.

"Ah, yes, I know it well. Been there many times." Amy nodded, opened the book to sign and looked back up at the woman. "Who shall I make it to?"

"Oh, can you make it to the Cooper clan? That'll keep everyone happy."

"Of course!" Amy said with a laugh and began to write a short comment in the book. "Do you live here? In L.A., I mean?" She asked while still writing.

"No, Hubby and I are just here on holiday, and, when I saw you were here signing books, I just had to come."

"Well, I'm glad you did. Have a great holiday and thank you for coming," Amy said and smiled as she handed the book back to the woman.

"No, thank you!" The woman grasped the book and moved along to get Erda's signature. "It's so clever to be able to meet a character from the book," she said to Erda.

"'Tis my pleasure to meet thee," Erda said as she made her mark.

"Thank you," The woman said and grinned widely as she left the table with her book. She now had happy memories of meeting the author and one of the main characters of her favourite book. She couldn't wait to tell her husband, who had been waiting patiently outside, all about it.

The rest of Amy and Erda's evening passed in a similar vein; comments were exchanged with the fans, signatures were added, and people made happy.

At long last, the final evening of the BookCon was over and Amy and Erda returned to their hotel room. Erda was none the worse for wear from the work. She sat herself down in the chair by one of the beds. Amy, however, collapsed on her bed.

"That was fun but I'm so tired and I can't

wait to get home to my own bed," Amy said.

"Aye, t'was entertaining," Erda said and smiled, happy that she had gotten to share this experience with Amy and with a slight shimmer she returned to her natural state of being, that of Spirit. She was now partially see-through as you would expect any ghost to be.

"We just have to fly home tomorrow and then you don't need to be corporeal any longer. Does it drain you when you are? Holding your corporeal form for long periods of time, I mean?"

"Nay... nay drain exactly. More constricts, like a fly within a stoppered whisky jar. I can move but 'tis nay freedom."

Amy sat up and shuffled herself until she was sitting with her back against the padded headboard and placed the pillows so they cushioned her aching back. "Hmm... I see, that kind of makes sense," Amy said and massaged her right hand, "Ouchy. My forearm and hand are so achy from all that signing. I think I'll have a nice, long bath and then a late supper from room service."

"Aye, 'tis wise. I shalt leave ye be to get

thine rest and wilt be back on ye morrow for our journey home and then thee can return to thy herbal and magickal studies," Erda said and promptly vanished into thin air.

"Bye." Amy said to the empty room and smiled to herself, looking forward to having Erda teach her more of her knowledge. She was pleased that Erda had enjoyed the flight out and had been able to experience all these new things with her. It was nice to teach *her* things for a change.

Just the return journey to go, and then they could relax. After all, there were two in her party as guests of the Con and the same, as far as her publisher knew, travelling to and from it. Everyone seemed to think Amy had hired an unknown actress to play the part of Erda for the duration and so, to keep the story going, they had to be seen together, even on their travels during the book tour.

They couldn't risk the world knowing that Erda was a ghost who could travel to any place or time whenever she wished. The fans may have all loved Witch Bottle but no one needed nor should know that the events in the book were true and had actually happened during the past year. If they did, Amy was sure all hell would break loose in more ways than one.

Amy wearily climbed off the bed, her aching body complaining loudly, and headed for the bathroom and a long, warm soak with some rather delightfully smelling bubble bath that was kindly supplied by the hotel. All the while, her mind was filled with the excitement of going home and seeing the renovations and improvements being made to her little cottage in Canada while she was away on the tour; all without Erda's knowledge.

"What a surprise it will be," Amy said to herself and the empty hotel room and turned on the hot tap. The room began to fill with a comforting fragrance and warm steam as Amy smiled to herself, undressed and climbed into the blissful water.

***

Amy stood and watched helplessly from high up on a nearby hilltop as the town of Morton Creek was battered

23

and destroyed by a swirling storm whose black clouds possessed huge, sharp teeth which swooped down, snatched up people and crushed them. These terrible apparitions chewed on them until they were ash, and the particles floated back down to earth on the now barren soil that was once her hometown.

Amy moaned pitifully in her sleep, rolled over and sank back into fitful dreams.

Chapter Three

Pre-dawn, October 31st, 1665
Boston Common, Massachusetts

The young man stood at the edge of the common land and determinedly looked across it and all around him the best he could in the dim moonlight. There were no other lanterns and no one was afoot. It was as empty and as still as a grave.

This was not a surprise after all. It was midnight and, thankfully, a full moon.

The blue-grey light fell upon the coarse grass of the common ground, lighting up the rough terrain and highlighting the dung piles from the animals that grazed there daily.

The young man had been in this place over the years many, many times before but he had purposefully waited until this night to do what had to be done.

By the light of the moon, he made his way across the expanse of the common toward the old tree. He kept looking around him to ensure no one was abroad at this early hour and in sight. He knew he would only have a few hours before the good folk of Boston rose to their daily lives and for the hundredth time he wished he wasn't alone in this endeavour, but there was not a single soul alive he could trust this night. Dropping his canvas sack to the ground, he pulled out his axe from it and stood holding the heavy weight of the sharpened tool in both his hands.

At nineteen years of age, the young man stood tall; he was wiry in physique, but strong from his years of service, first as a kitchen boy and then later as a stable hand. Now, his long hair was tied back, although it was unruly and always endeavoured to escape its confines, and his chin was covered in light stubble. At last, after much planning, he was here.

He let the axe swing down to one side as he listened to the frogs croaking from the nearby pond. He raised his other arm and with his pale hand he brushed his wild hair away from his pale blue eyes. His hair that had not remained tied was already stuck to the back of his neck with the nervous sweat as he mentally prepared himself for the job at hand. He knew that once he started his mission he could not stop until it was finished, no matter what, even if he had to take the life of anyone who tried to stop him. He knew there was a chance he would be discovered because of the noise he was about to make, and also because of the noise the animals on the common would make once he started. It was truly a dangerous act he was about to commit for so many reasons, none of which, if he was caught, would save him from swinging at the end of a rope at the hangman's pleasure.

With a deep breath, the young man clutched the axe again in both hands, drew it up and back over his right shoulder and then, with all his might, brought it down to bear upon the large branch that was at a right angle to the trunk of the tree. The thick branch had stood dead these past three years and was now bare of leaves. There was a dull thud that echoed around him as the axe blade struck the tree.

Over and over again he chopped at the branch until it fell to ground, its old twisted length, which had hung many a criminal, snapped in two as it crashed to the ground. Quickly and efficiently the young man chopped up the fallen wood into manageable sized logs to the sounds of the disturbed cows mooing their alert to each other. He knew he didn't have much time before he was discovered and moved as fast as he could.

He had to stop and wipe his brow as the sweat of fear and exertion had begun to sting his eyes. He looked around himself furtively for any sign of movement. He heard a horse snort but recognized the noise and softly whistled. A chestnut stallion trotted out of the shadows at his call, pulling a small wagon behind it. The horse came to a stop near the man and nuzzled his shoulder in loving recognition and acquaintance.

"Good lad, Thunder. Thy be a'standing still for I'm to be putting some weight in ye cart behind ye," the man said quietly to the horse as he stroked its long nose and patted its neck affectionately for a brief moment before returning to his task.

He began to lift the chopped logs and place them as quietly as he could in the back of the wagon.

It took several trips back and forth but at last the task was done. He took a cloth rag from his pocket and again wiped his face and neck of the cooling sweat now covering it.

Stuffing the cloth back in his breech's pocket, he eyed the rest of the hanging tree and its other branch that was now used for hangings having replaced the one he had just chopped down when it died.

He had no use for the rest of it and turned his back on the remains left of the monstrosity in the centre of the common.

He looked around him again and listening hard, there was no one awake nor had the cockerels called the dawn yet.

Grabbing the spade from the wagon bed, he rushed over to the tree and worked as fast as he could, digging away the dirt from the trunk of the tree and its roots.

This time he worked like a man possessed.

He did not have time to stop and wipe the sweat from his forehead, which was now flushed from his efforts.

The dry summer soil of late August stuck to him, leaving a gritty layer of grime over his skin like lamp oil spilt on water.

Hacking away at the roots, he finally broke free a piece as he heard the first cockerel crow and knew the bakers and pie makers would be awake and preparing for the day's batches of food.

The light around him had changed too: the light of the moon was now mixed with the eerie pre-dawn light and the young man knew he only had moments until the coming dawn would expose him to one and all.

With a final effort he grabbed his tools and the root and threw them into the back of the cart which rocked with the extra weight.

With one last look around, the young man spotted the point on the horizon where the sun would rise at any moment and hoped he could escape quickly enough.

He swiftly covered the chopped wood and root with a large dirty canvas that smelt of horse dung and jumped up on the wagon.

He turned Thunder around and encouraged the horse to move as fast as possible to get them both off the common land and out of sight before the good folk of Boston could see what he had done.

He knew that destroying the city's property was a hanging offence and couldn't help but smile at the irony of it all.

Chapter Four

June, Present Day, Canada

Amy closed the strong oak door firmly behind her and leaned against it, exhausted. Finally, she was back home after the book tour and the two back to back conventions that had been included in it.

She let out a deep sigh and closed her eyes, taking a moment of peace for herself. There was just something about this old stone-walled, wood-panelled cottage that relaxed her the second she was inside it. She had always felt this way about the place, even when she had visited it when she was much younger and it was her family's summer home. Before they had all tragically died and she had made it her permanent home. Somehow she felt closer to her parents and her brother here than she did anywhere else in the world.

"Oh, thank the Gods that's over. As much as I love meeting the fans, it's bloody exhausting living out of a suitcase for weeks on end, moving from one signing to another, one city to another," she said to Erda as she removed her bag from her shoulder and hung it on a hook by the door. She shuffled off her sandals and left them where they fell, and stood, gratefully, with her bare feet on the cool flagstones of the floor.

Despite the heat of an early morning in mid June, the cottage was cool at present, but Amy knew it would heat up soon and she would be very grateful for the AC her father had fitted in his time as the owner of the family cottage. It was still the same system, but Amy had renovated and modernized it before she had left for the book tour. She reached over to the control unit between the door and the coat hooks and switched on the AC to the automatic setting she knew she would need once the heat of the day built more and finally penetrated the thick stone walls. She glanced at the small screen and it said the internal temperature was 19 degrees, but outside it was already up to 28 degrees and it was only 8:26am, the timer told her.

Sighing, Amy grabbed her two travel bags, walked into the lounge and threw them one at a time on her large, squishy sofa ready to unpack later. "Still it was fun, even if I'm really tired," she said and stretched her back. Plane journeys and taxis made her cramped and uncomfortable, it was nice to be able to move freely again.

"Aye, 'twas grand to see and do such things with ye," Erda said and smiled.

Amy looked at Erda. The young woman, who was a distant but direct relative, looked healthy in her corporeal state, her strength having never waned once while they were away on tour.

I guess when you're dead there is no way you can be tired, Amy thought to herself.

"I enjoyed spending the time with you too but now I'm dying for a cuppa," she said and began dragging her tired body toward the kitchen to put the kettle on and make some much needed tea.

"Oh!" Amy said as she walked through the low doorway into the kitchen. She looked at the new staircase, which had replaced the old hatch and ladder at the far end of the room. The beautiful wooden stairs now led up through the new entrance into the attic.

"What troubles thee?" Erda said as she came in behind Amy, now back in her ghostly, almost a wisp of smoke, natural state.

Amy eyed Erda but was not bothered by the sudden change. She had seen it many times before and it no longer startled her. "The workmen finished the new stairs, I had almost forgotten about it all with feeling so tired and my brain not being in. I wonder if they finished everything upstairs too."

"Would thee like me to take a look for ye, whilst ye makes a brew?" Erda said, helpfully.

"Nope, I want to see for myself, but can you stay here until I call you? I have a surprise for you and I want to see if it's ready first," Amy said and began to move towards the new wooden staircase that matched perfectly with the old door frames, panelling, and beams on the kitchen ceiling. *So far so good,* she thought to herself, pleased at the work that had been done while they had been away.

It seems her confidence in the carpenter friend of Bryer's, who he had recommended, was well earned and she was glad she had taken his suggestion. The thought of Bryer Burnett and his lovely body was enough to distract her for a moment. She had found a great deal of happiness in her exciting and relatively new relationship with him and couldn't wait to see him again. *First things first,* she thought to herself and laid her hand on the newel post at the foot of the stairs.

"Oh, aye, I shalt stay... but a kindness for me? Thou art too generous, Amy," Erda said with a delighted look of surprise on her face as she watched her many times removed great granddaughter look at her as she stood on the bottom step of the new kitchen staircase.

"I'll call you if it's ready," Amy said and began to climb the wooden stairs up into the attic.

As the room above slowly came into view, Amy smiled to herself utterly delighted and excited by what she now saw. Her mind recalled what the old attic had looked like, a simple and partially boarded room full of boxes and a small dirty and slightly rotten window, giving it not nearly enough light. The old trusses had always been exposed and she used to be able to see some of the insulation and the wiring for the single light bulb that had hung loosely from a roof timber. It hadn't resembled much of a room before... but it did now, now it was something really rather special.

"Okay, you can come up now, Erda," She said and waited excitedly for her friend to appear.

Unusually, Erda walked up the new steps, seemingly enjoying the slight delay of actual walking instead of just appearing in the room, like she would have done before she knew there was a surprise for her. She decided she wanted to see the room how Amy had first seen it, one step at a time. As the room came into view, Erda was completely taken aback in surprise by the view.

The once unwelcoming room that spread the entirety of the cottage was now an almost perfect replica of the cottage she herself had lived in once many years ago. Amy had seen the cottage, when Erda had travelled into the past with her to explain how Erda had become Spirit.

The new attic now had a floor that was wooden boards with a rag rug in the centre, all four walls of its rectangular shape were wooden panelled to match the rest of the cottage. The old window had been replaced and under it sat an old cot bed. Next to the bed was a 17th century style wardrobe and a small side table with an oil lamp on it. Another window, of the same size, had been added on the opposite wall and next to that was an enormous and ancient looking armoire with many small cupboards, shelves and drawers.

Erda gasped when she saw it and rushed up the last of the steps. As she stepped onto the new flooring she found her eyes were drawn away from the beautiful furniture and over toward the right-hand wall. The old chimney on it had been opened up and a new, stone fireplace inserted with an old fashioned grate, and, by it sat an old wooden rocking chair with a patchwork cushion and blanket draped over the back of the chair.

"Amy..." Erda squeaked out, her voice contorted by the rush of emotion she now felt.

"I hope you like it. They have done a wonderful job of doing what I asked. I know you don't sleep but it seemed wrong not to have a bed in here somehow. Anyway, there is plenty of room over near the cupboards for you to make your potions and unguents. I also have an oak table coming in the next week or so to fit in next to the armoire. I had them put in the fireplace, as I know how much you like to sit by the fire watching the flames. I have seen you do it so many times downstairs at my fireplace," she said and smiled as she came to stand by Erda, "I tried to get the feel of your old cottage, I hope I did manage to... even if just a little. Do you like it?" Amy said looking hopeful, her hands clasped before her in nervousness.

"There art nay words for it... 'tis...'tis a marvel to behold." Erda stood looking around the room taking in every perfect, wonderful detail.

"You can now fill it with all the herbs, books, pieces of equipment... whatever you like and need for your magickal old ways. This is now your home too," Amy said, smiling a deep, happy smile.

Erda started to become corporeal as she moved closer to Amy. Tears of joy and gratitude ran down her pale cheeks and by the time she was at Amy's side, her flesh was as solid as if she were alive. "Mine eyes betray my heart-felt thanks to ye," she said as she took Amy in her arms and gave her a very solid and grateful hug. "I hath a... home again," she whispered throatily into Amy's hair.

Amy returned the hug and for a moment there was nothing else in the world but the two of them embraced in happiness.

A joyful glow could be seen on Erda's face as she pulled back. "I hath nay home in ye four-hundred years since my death, a'part from thy bottle but 'tis of nay comfort. I thank ye greatly."

"You are most welcome. I wanted you to know you have a home, with family, whenever you needed it. And you must also know, that it means you are not expected to stay here with me always, just that you have a place here to use as your own and are welcome when you do," Amy said and felt the warm glow of satisfaction and happiness spread through her chest, making her smile, and, for a moment, making her exhaustion evaporate like mist in the early morning sunlight.

For the rest of that day Amy pottered about her lovely cottage unpacking from the trip and settling back into her favourite place in the world.

The following night, Amy sat opposite Erda by the unlit fireplace in the attic, which had instantly become Erda's favourite sitting spot. She was at present trying to memorize the Runes and their meanings from the drawings and descriptions Erda had put down on paper for her. However, there were two sets of names for each, the old English and the old Germanic. "So your Grandmother taught you the ways of the Saxons and Northmen?"

"Aye, Alma was of ye blood through her father and proud of it she was, her mother was a Cunning Woman of ye wild fens to ye east of England. Ye wisdom and arts I pass to thee, art ye mixture from those two blood lines as 'twas taught to me. Their blood runs in thy veins too, Amy." Erda said proudly.

"I had never thought of having Viking blood in me and early Britain too, it's an interesting thought and incredibly fascinating to learn about my ancestor's lives. You know, you should write all your knowledge down or you could recite it to me and I could write it down in a journal of sorts."

"Dost thou mean a Grimoire? Hmm...'tis dangerous to keep such things even these days, people nay have ye sense nor ye training to be careful and respect such things, power within them wilt do much harm."

"But what if the general public thought it was fiction and only the wise knew it was real and had substance, then it would be a wonderful teaching tool unlike any other."

"Aye, but how dost one know a wise man from a fool?"

Chapter Five

August 19th, 1656
Boston, Massachusetts

The boy peered from behind Sarah's ample backside to get his first look at the new master, a legitimate son of the late lady of the house. Finally, and after much delay, the new master had arrived from England to take over his mother's estate, now that the mistress was dead and buried.

Benjamin had been scrubbed from head to toe in a tub by the fire this very morning, indeed all the household staff were clean, in their best Sunday clothes and their hair newly brushed as they anticipated the master's arrival.

Benjamin's skin still tingled from the

scrubbing his foster mother, Sarah, had given him. All the while she was instructing him on how to behave around the new master and telling him how different everything would now be for all of them. He had looked at her face and thought she seemed very worried, but when he asked her, she had brushed him off with replies such as, "Dinna ask so a'many questions, boy" or "It's nay for thee to worry thyself about, Benjy."

Sarah stood watching the coach arrive amidst great plumes of dust from the overly dry soil. It had been a hard summer so far and the grounds of the house created so much dust that it got in every nook and cranny of the kitchen, not to mention all the other rooms of the house. It was a never ending and near impossible task, during the summer months, for the servants to keep it clean, but today it was different: the house had been cleaned ruthlessly for the new master's arrival.

The old cook watched as the coach pulled to a stop outside the main entrance. Squinting through the dust cloud she nervously looked for her new master. The dust finally cleared to show a fully grown man wearing the finest clothes Sarah had ever seen and the sourest expression.

Jonathon Moore, a man of barely twenty years, stood proudly and looked about him at the property and the six members of staff imperiously. "Fetch me brandy, I die of thirst and am weary," he said to nobody in particular.

One of the housemaids rushed inside to do his bidding.

"Master Jonathon, it be lovely to see thy sweet face again, it hath been many a long year since last..." Sarah said as he marched past her.

Jonathon didn't even acknowledge the cooks existence, never mind reply or even look at her when he stalked into his new home with a look of disdain on his face.

"I travelled so far and long for this? 'Tis a goodness mother had other properties or journey wouldst be for naught," he said to himself, not caring who heard his words.

Sarah watched as her new master walked down the wood clad hall to the main room of the house, known as the keeping room. She could hear him shouting at any and all staff in hearing range how hot and stuffy the house was and for them to open the doors to let God's clean air in. Her instincts prickled at the man's arrogance and lack of interest in his staff. He most certainly was not like his mother in that regard, but then she had remembered him as a willful spoilt child when she, the Mistress and her chambermaid had left his father. The mistress had illegally remarried very quickly to an unsuspecting wealthy man by the name of William Hibbens and, leaving her children behind her, she had fled England to accompany her new husband to the New World. She also remembered her mistress used to say that 'in ye New World, all cares of thy old life were washed away by wind and sea 'til thy newly formed life appeared on ye shores of ye new land'. Sarah smiled sadly to herself. There was no doubt about it... she would miss the mistress greatly.

Pushing Benjy back towards the kitchen she quickly and purposefully moved away from the proximity of their new master and vowed to herself to stay as far away from him as possible at all times. Thankfully, being just the cook she could do that more than any of the other servants.

She was now even more worried about their future than she had been before. Their place in the household and in the employ of Master Jonathon was definitely not secure, not in the least. He could easily sell everything and go back to England, and then where would she and the boy be?

"I thought ye scrubbed me 'til it 'urt for ye new master to like me but he nay looked upon us, mother Sarah," Benjy said and they entered the overly hot kitchen with its permanently lit fire and small, thick glass windows. The room was filled with shelves, pans, drying herbs, baskets of bread, vegetables and apples in preparation for the master's arrival.

A large table stood in the middle of the room covered with the bread, fruit and vegetable baskets but also a brace of pigeons and another of ducks waiting to be hung. As ever the kitchen never stopped work and Sarah prepared what the boy would need for plucking and gutting the chicken before it was roasted on the spit which he would sit by the huge fire and turn until it was done.

"Aye, well, we dinna want tay bother thy master with such nonsense right now. Get thee to ye yard and catch a chicken for thee master's supper," Sarah said as she placed her newly cleaned apron around her waist, tied it at the back and then set forth to prepare a welcome supper for the master.

****

Jonathon lounged in the sedan chair by the great window of his mother's house. He looked around him in disdain. It was not that the house was unfit for his company: it was the fact that his mother had left him for this place and never once invited him nor his two brothers out to visit. She had taken up with another man too soon as was seemly after deserting his father, and so had disgraced the name of Moore, which had long and memorable lines of wealthy men and war heroes. Jonathon resented and hated his mother and everything she had done and touched since she had abandoned him thirteen years ago almost to the day. In that time, his poor father had died, some said of a broken heart, and the three boys had been left to maintain their father's estate despite the social disadvantage the scandal had wrought upon them. None of them were now considered suitable for the hand of the young ladies from the society families anymore, all thanks to his mother and her greed and lust for another man.

He was surprised his mother had been caught and tried as a witch though. He had thought her too clever by far to get caught. He knew she meddled in the Arcane Arts from what little he remembered of her when he was a child. One of the few memories he had, was of her and his father arguing about her ungodly interests and how dangerous it was for his father, who had now decided he would no longer allow it. He vaguely remembered his mother's stillroom that was filled with foul smelling potions, unguents, strange herbs and liquids as opposed to his aunts that was filled with beer, preserves, cakes, liqueurs and other delights.

He had learned from a very early age that his mother was different from the other mothers in respectable society in his home town and it scared him. He was told not to talk about his mother's stillroom and its contents to anyone, no matter who asked. He was convinced, of course, that she would have the same type of room here. He was not looking forward to seeing it and dealing with its strange and ungodly contents. *How would he dispose of it all without bring the suspicion of witchcraft down upon his own head,* he wondered. "To the Devil with you mother," he mumbled to himself and into his brandy.

The sooner I sell her belongings, including the house and her other lands, the sooner I can go home, he thought and smiled to himself at the inheritance he and his brothers would receive. Not that he would share it out equally, of course. They hadn't made this arduous trip, after all, and they would never know his greed.

He drank down the last of his brandy in one gulp, closed his eyes and let his mind find wonderful ways to spend all the money.

Chapter Six

Present Day, Ontario Provincial Police HQ,
Glendale, Ontario Canada

In the twilight, the sleek, modern and only two year old building stood looking out over the city of Glendale. The all glass wall reflected the lights of the city and those from the small park next to it. The building was located in the newly renovated area of town alongside several other new office towers and sat at one side of a large square with the park at its centre. Several lights were still on in the building, including those in the office of Detective Inspector Andy Withers, lead Detective of Homicide.

He sat in his chair, with his feet up on his

desk, chewing the end of his pen and wondering why the unsolved murder cases in front of him seemed so damned familiar. He almost felt like he was having a full-on déjà vu of this day, and, indeed, these horrific murders. He shook himself mentally.

He knew he had never ever seen anything like this in his entire police enforcement career and that, he admitted to himself grudgingly, was a fucking long time.

Too fucking long.

But still, a strange feeling of familiarity lingered just on the edge of his memory and his brain couldn't leave it alone. It was like picking a healing scab. He knew it would hurt or even bleed but the compulsion was too strong to ignore and so his mind kept flicking back to that strange feeling and he picked at it until he could stand it no more.

"Fuck this," he said and slammed the buff file he had been gripping so tightly, back onto his desk. He swivelled his chair round to look out of the large office window. The twilight had now faded and the view of Glendale city lights could be seen out of his 6th storey window of the new O. P. P. Office building.

Andy glared at the lights as if the longer he stared at them the more knowledge he would gain about this case, but it didn't work. All it gave him was a slight headache and bright dots in his vision. He sighed in frustration. The recent murders were weird and extremely violent. They disturbed him just a little bit more than his murder cases usually did and that pissed him off immensely. There was only a certain level of sicko he could handle and this person's level was just so much higher than that.

He sat for a while grumbling at himself and staring out at the city again. With an explosion of sudden movement, he snatched up his phone, found his junior partner's contact details and tapped his finger on the number. He heard Mitch's cell ring down the hall. "Time to go home, I'm sick of seeing the gruesome things this sick bastard is doing to his victims and I need a beer or several. You up for it?"

"Nah, sorry boss. The girlfriend is expecting me for dinner. Have one for me though.

G'night," Mitchell said, relieved his boss had called it a day while there was still time for him to get home before Louisa gave his dinner literally to her dog, again.

Hanging up, Andy stared at the phone for a few moments and mumbled under his breath, "Lucky bastard."

Leaving his office and making his way down in the elevator to the parking garage, Andy had to force his mind away from the disgusting autopsy photos with a shudder. His mind had a way of sneaking a peak at the images, indelibly staining his brain when he least wanted it to. He rammed his key into his car door, climbed inside and closed the door a little too hard, he sat there for a few moments contemplating where to go for alcohol. He didn't feel in the mood for company after all, so the usual local 'cop's bar' was out. He wanted a long drink in the peace of his own company.

At last, with his decision made, he reversed his car out of his parking spot and headed through the streets of Glendale looking for a takeaway and a liquor store. He was going to go home, eat some junk food and get stinking drunk tonight.

"Fuck it," he said just as the crack of lightning could be seen through his rear-view mirror and a roll of thunder rumbled around the distant hills of Glendale, promising that it was going to be a warm, sticky stormy night.

Andy arrived at his apartment building with his Indian takeaway and a bottle of scotch just as the heavens opened and torrential rain began to fall. By the time he was inside he was soaked through and his place was hot and empty. He stripped off his coat and threw it over a hook by the door. He checked his mail. There was nothing but bills and he threw the envelopes down on the counter. He picked up the TV remote and turned on a random sports channel. Kicking off his shoes, he sat on his sofa, not caring that his hair was still dripping wet. He ate his dinner straight from the cartons and drank the scotch from the bottle.

Soon the warmth of the food and scotch made him relaxed and sleepy and he snuggled down on the sofa and drifted off into disturbed dreams of carved up bodies and crazed old ladies as serial killers who seemed to get closer and closer to him until they were peering at his face barely inches away.

With a jump he awoke and he was covered in cold sweat from his nightmare. "Fuck me!" He said and tried to regain a steady heartbeat. He blinked, yawned and stretched the length of his legs fully over the end of the sofa. Sitting up, he rubbed his face and looked at his watch and saw that he'd only been asleep for an hour. It was still too early to go to bed, so he got up and cleared away the empty food containers and made himself a coffee with extra cream because he liked to treat himself when in this mood.

Returning to the sofa with the coffee, he spotted the book on the table, and, to wear his mind out, he picked it up and saved it from living a life of lurking on his coffee table for several more months untouched. It had been a gift to him from his sister and her family for his last birthday, and he'd always meant to get round to reading, "I guess it's time to have a look at you, my old friend," Andy said to the book, which had a cover of an old photograph of a Victorian busy street and the words 'unsolved murder mystery' blazed across it.

Sitting back down, he got himself comfy, with his coffee just at arms reach, and turned the book over to read the back cover. It was a mystery about a murder and suicide back in 1846, where millions of dollars worth of deeds, cash, along with a strongbox had also vanished from the scene.

The murderer apparently was the wife, Mrs. Elizabeth Ann Carr, who had stabbed her husband Phillip in the throat and then threw herself under a horse and carriage several streets away. No one knew why she did it. The couple were well known to be happy and in love, and as they could have no children of their own they did a lot for children's charities and were well loved by their society friends. They were even friends with the Bishop and had close friends at court. There was no explanation of why Elizabeth travelled several streets over to the rougher part of town before committing suicide, and when the house was inspected by the constabulary they found that Mr. Carr's strongbox with his papers, deeds and cash in was missing. Foul play, except his wife's, was not suspected. Had the wife taken it with her? Why then was she to commit suicide, and where did the strongbox vanish to?

There were just too many questions about the case and it instantly intrigued Andy as he dived right into the story. He rather liked real life murder mysteries. It was his job, after all, and he always kind of secretly hoped he would spot something the biographer missed and solve the cold case.

Eventually, he had read long enough into the night that he began to feel tired again and had to reread some of the lines of the text for them to make sense. He lay the book down on his chest to close his eyes for a little while, but all he could see was a sweet looking old lady with a knife in her hand standing over a cut up corpse. There was definitely no chance he could sleep with that image in his mind.

He forced himself to sit up on the sofa and decided to drink some more scotch to dull his brain. He then watched a replay of a curling match while desperately ignoring what his mind was shouting at him.

Chapter Seven

Amy stretched sleepily in her cosy bed. She yawned and looked around the room, happy to see her own furniture and belongings. She smiled to herself, pleased at the knowledge that she was home at last and could relax.

As her mind became more and more awake, she thought about her day and how she would spend it. She mentally made a list of things she needed to do. She would have to go into Morton Creek, the nearest town to her cottage and get groceries, pick up the mail and perhaps drop by Aunt Kath and Uncle Cy in their store to let them know she was home. *It will be nice to see them*, she thought.

Amy had known the old couple as her aunt and uncle for many years, since she first came out with her parents to this very cottage.

They were friends of her parents, and Kathleen and Cyrus MacArthur had been given the honourary title of being 'Aunt' and 'Uncle' to her and her brother, Richard, and she had never known them as anything else.

They had been absolutely delighted when she'd permanently moved into the old family holiday cottage and made her home in Canada last year.

Climbing lazily out of bed, Amy headed for the shower feeling much more like herself from her good night's sleep. After languishing in a long, hot shower she felt refreshed. She got dressed and was soon ready to get back in the swing of things at home. She had a book idea milling around in her head that she needed to get on paper and she was looking forward to more lessons from Erda. They hadn't done many, but what they had done, she had enjoyed very much

"Mornin'," Erda said from halfway down the new stairs leading from the attic as Amy entered the kitchen in search of a mug of tea and perhaps some toast, making a mental note to add bread to the grocery list.

"Oh, morning. Do you still like your room?" Amy asked and chuckled, already knowing the answer as she rummaged through the freezer for some frozen bread she could toast.

"Aye, 'tis wondrous," Erda said and stepped into the kitchen.

Amy filled the kettle, clicked on the Aga range's hot plate and placed the kettle upon it. "Perhaps we could find a safe spot for your bottle up there," she said and tried to imagine what it would be like to have one's Spirit magickally bound to a bottle and never being able to move on to whatever comes next after death.

Always having to exist while those around you aged and died, and could never escape the very hex that had put you there. "Hmm... there's a thought, what would happen to you if your bottle was ever broken? Would you be free?"

Erda tilted her head and thought about it for a moment. Frowning a little she became more corporeal and sat down at the old, wooden, kitchen table. After a moment, she said, "Nay sure. Mayhaps, I wouldst be attached to ye pieces or might my Spirit be shattered ye same? I truly nay knowest."

"Well, that's not a pleasant thought. Probably for the best if we never find out. Although...."

"Aye?"

"Hmm... what if... what if it would free you from the hex? That's also possible isn't it?"

"'Tis nay likely. Upon ye good many years I hath been tethered to ye cursed thing, I hath nay found a way to be free nor to destroy ye evil that doth connect us so eternally."

"Well, there are two of us now, perhaps we can work on it together and discover something new. Like they say, two minds are better than one," Amy said as she buttered her newly popped up toast and grabbed the strawberry jam from the pantry shelf.

"Aye, 'tis true, a goodly more things can be done with kindly assistance, but who are 'they' that sayeth it?" Erda looked at Amy with a puzzled look on her face.

"Huh? Oh, right. Yeah, it's just a saying, there isn't any 'they'.... per-say," Amy couldn't explain it more than that before her first mug of tea. Sitting opposite Erda at the table, she changed the subject and told Erda about the list of things she wanted to do today.

"Aye, mayhaps thou couldst fetch seeds for thy garden from ye garden... centre," she said as if it was not a normal thing to do. "'Tis a tad late to be a'plantin', true, but thee wilt get some eating out of it yet," Erda liked the thought of creating a garden once again, over the many years she had missed the feeling of her hands in the soft soil and the satisfaction of seeing food grow day by day. She had noticed how many of the modern folk did not grow their own food, and some didn't even have soil to till. The very thought made her feel disconnected again to this generation.

"How do you know about Gardening Centers? I'm pretty sure they weren't around in the 1600's," Amy said with a lift of her eyebrows.

"Nay, 'tis true. Only seed for barley and wheat 'twas to be purchased from ye general store but most folks hath land and grew food, nay like thy folks. I learnt of such wondrous places while following people of thy time. I ache for my hands upon ye soil and watched much of thy farmers lives."

"Oh, right. I still find it odd that you know some modern things but not others," Amy said and she sat back in her chair finishing the toast and sipping her hot tea.

"Upon many a'year, I wandered and didn't really watch, 'tis tiresome when naught can hear nor see thee. 'Twere sometimes as I tried to maketh notice with my descendants but more times failed and thy knows of ye bad case of..."

"Ahh... yes, hmm... that time you frightened someone and they ended up in the nut-house." Amy said, interrupting.

"In ye Asylum, aye." Erda looked saddened and obviously blamed herself for the poor girl's final days.

Amy suddenly felt guilty for her flippancy. "Who was it, if you don't mind me asking?"

Erda looked into to Amy's eyes, "Her name 'twas Eliza Sarah Grey, she was thy third great aunt on thy father's side."

Amy tried to think how far back that connection was, "What happened? You only told me she went... erm... mad because... of you, you said," Amy cringed at how that sounded.

"She nay went mad from me alone 'course. Her family thought she be tho' and they locked her away for it," Erda took a deep breath and slowly let it out. "'Twas I did it, make 'em think it. I tried many a'time to talk with her, like I did with you and she could nay hear mine voice but faintly, she could never see me tho'. She was different from her brothers and sisters, touched by witchcraft, some thought, and when she told her family of a voice in her head, being me, 'twere afraid she was bedevilled. They sent for a physic who looked upon her but to naught and had her put in ye asylum, there she did wither away and die."

"That's horrible, poor Eliza... what year was this?" Amy said frowning, thankful that meeting Erda last year had not sent her crazy, even if she thought it had in the beginning.

"'Twas the year of our lord God 1913. She was a woman without a husband of her own, nor children sadly at the ripe age of twenty and six years when her life fled from her."

"And you have been alone all this time since then? No others could hear you?"

"Aye."

"What about before her? I mean, have you ever been able to talk to someone else like you can with me?"

"In ye four hundred years I hath been Spirit, I hath been able to talk to people thrice and appear before two, thee are second," Erda said carefully.

Amy frowned again, something about the way Erda worded that reply made Amy's spider senses tingle. She squinted at Erda, "And the other person, who was that?"

"'Tis a conversation for another time," she said and avoided Amy's gaze. "I shalt make thee a list of seed and plants for eating and for making of healing receipts."

Amy mentally noted the change in conversation and was determined to return to the subject another time. She was intrigued by Erda's wish to not continue. Usually she was open about everything and had, as far as Amy knew, never concealed anything from her. "A list, right, good idea."

Erda became instantly solid before Amy's eyes and reached out to pick up the pen and notepad on the table. She carefully wrote a list of items in her archaic handwriting and passed the pad to Amy.

Amy looked down at the list and after a few moments she could read the names of the plants and seeds and admired Erda's writing.

"Your handwriting is lovely, who taught you to write?"

"My mother's brother was a scribe. He transcribed many books for ye church, he taught me every sennight whence he came to our home for supper upon market day."

"Sennight?"

"Each seventh day."

"So a week?"

"Aye."

"That was kind of him. I'd love to hear more about your... our... family and where you all lived and came from, sometime," Amy said and smiled.

"I shalt be pleased to tell ye," Erda smiled back.

Amy felt at ease with Erda again and felt that the conversation had relaxed back to its normal easy flow. Determined not to dwell on imagined hidden stories, Amy stood, put her plate and mug in the sink, and prepared to go to town for supplies.

She hoped to pop in and see if Bryer was about so they could set up a date or something... and perhaps... more. This thought made her grin naughtily to herself. She pulled out her phone from the pocket of her shorts and texted a quick message to Bryer telling him she was back home, about to head into town and could they meet up? Putting the phone back into her pocket, Amy felt butterflies at the very thought of seeing Bryer. She had a quick flash of how they had first met last year. He was the listing photographer for the Realtor that was going to sell her cottage before Amy had decided to live in it, and she had felt herself drawn to his good looks straight away. She had gone to his studio to do some new head-shots for her publisher and not long after they began dating.

The warmth of him spread through her body and left a tingling sensation full of need as her heart raced. Yes, she would be very happy to spend some time with him as soon as possible. She had been away on tour for just a bit too long in her opinion and she hoped he would text her back soon. She was pleased but a little shocked at how badly she wanted him.

****

Pulling the truck in front of the store, Amy climbed out and tried to see in through the front windows, but the brilliant sunshine reflected off the general store's glass to a blinding degree. Amy looked up at the bright blue, cloudless sky and at the sun that was beating down on her. Looking away quickly she blinked away the bright spots in her vision and checked her phone for the temperature. It said 32 degrees and later in the mid-afternoon it was expected to rise to 38 degrees.

"Wow," she said to herself. Despite having spent much of her childhood summers at the cottage, the sun still affected her greatly and decided it must be due to her British constitution. Amy pulled on a sun hat to protect herself from possible heatstroke and grabbed a bottle of water from the cooler on her passenger seat.

She didn't go to the general store first, instead she went into the ice-cream store, which was two buildings down on the same side of the road. She entered the store and queued up behind a couple with two young children who were having difficulty deciding which flavours to get.

The coolness of the store made Amy sigh with delight and she closed her eyes enjoying the feeling of the cool air on her bare arms and her rather white legs beneath her olive green shorts.

"Can I help you?" A softly spoken voice said, almost in Amy's ear.

Opening her eyes with surprise, Amy looked in the direction the voice had come and a small, bony woman of about sixty years of age looked up at her with the most engaging smile Amy had ever seen. It was the type of smile that simply glowed of happiness and satisfaction with life.

"Oh, yes, sorry. Can I have a medium tub of the pistachio and another one of the strawberry, please?" Amy said and moved around the family, whose children wanted a scoop of everything, to the far end of the counter where the woman had now gone.

"Certainly, my dear," the woman said.

Amy watched as the woman got two medium sized tubs out of the freezer, put them in a bag and rang up the amount on the register. Amy paid the lady, said thanks and walked out of the shop and back into the heat, which now felt like a physical wall of hell. Quickly, she took the tubs back to the truck and put the strawberry one in the cooler on the passenger seat, this time having come prepared.

Last year, she had done the same, one tub of strawberry for her and the other, pistachio, for Aunt Kath and Uncle Cy when she was about to visit them, but by the time she had gotten home afterwards her ice-cream had melted into a watery pink puddle in the bottom of the tub. Ice cream was too important to waste, she decided cheerfully.

As Amy closed the truck door, the sign for the mid-summer fair posted in the bakery shop window opposite, caught her attention.

"Next weekend, huh?" Amy said to herself and smiled. She remembered going to the fair with her brother and parents years ago and had loved it. She decided on the spot that she would still visit it. Sadly none of her family were alive now to enjoy it with her, but she would go and be accompanied by her happy memories.

Turning, she walked up the path and into the general store that Aunt Kath and Uncle Cy ran. It was an old time general store, and by general it literally meant everything was sold there if you could find it. The place was an Aladdin's cave of hidden nooks and crannies filled with everything from sugar to saws, from bird seed to bathroom tiles. If you could name it, you would find it or something just as good in there.

A familiar-looking, tall man in his thirties was serving an older man at the counter and there was no sign of her Aunt and Uncle. Amy waited patiently until the man moved away from the counter after finishing his purchase. Amy drew near and realized who she was looking at. It was David MacArthur, Cy and Kath's son.

"Dave! Hey, been a long time. How are you? I thought you'd moved away." Amy said, surprised to see him working in the store. Although they had played together as children, they hadn't kept in touch when he had left to go to college.

The prematurely balding man with dark blue eyes looked at her, confused for a moment and then Amy could see recognition spread across his face.

"Amy? Seriously? Amy Grey, what are you doing here?" His face split into a massive smile that made his eyes sparkle. He came round the counter and lifted Amy off her feet and whirled her around. "What the hell is the Frog'amy doing here?" He said and laughed as he put her back on her feet.

"Hey, just Amy now... no longer Frog'amy, I had to give up the frogs," Amy said with a laugh, she hadn't been called her childhood nickname since the three of them, her brother Richard, Dave and herself had played together, and that was many years ago.

"Damn shame, but it won't stop me, Frog'amy. Didn't know you were back. Staying long?" He said and leaned against the counter and turned the electric fans towards them both.

"I was about to ask you the same. Last I heard you had gone to college and vowed never to come back," Amy said and was grateful for the breeze in the overly warm store.

"Yeah, well, things change," he said. "I was sorry to hear about your parents, both of them in the fire like that... that's a real bad way to go," he said and suddenly looked ashamed for being so blunt. "Sorry."

"It's okay, Dave. And I agree with you," Amy looked away and quickly swallowed the hard lump in her throat, determined to not think on it and she looked back at him. "I would have thought your mum and dad would have mentioned it, but I've moved back to the cottage permanently, and I've been doing some restorations too," she said, as her smile returned.

"Nice, always did love that place," he said.

"You should come out sometime and see what I've done to it. Perhaps we can cook on the campfire and have some beer by the lake?"

"Sounds good to me," he said with a grin.

"I'll give you a ring. I was actually looking for your parents. Just wanted to let them know I was back in town and I have some of their favourite ice cream in the bag for them too." Amy held up the bag as if to demonstrate.

"They no longer work here, haven't done for a while."

"Oh? I didn't know. Are they upstairs in their apartment then?" Amy said, surprised that they hadn't told her they were retiring and handing over the store to their son.

"Upstairs? Hell no! We rent that out to a couple that wanted to come out from the city and 'downsize', whatever that might be. My parents are out at the house on Spruce Road."

"What? They moved? I didn't know! They should have waited until I came back, I could have helped. What number on Spruce Road?"

Dave looked at her oddly, "Right... erm,

1072, of course."

Not noticing his confusion in her surprise, Amy said, "Okay, thanks. I'll pop in on them later in the week as I have more errands to run now, but tell them I'm back and looking forward to seeing them, will you? Gotta go, I'll call you about the beer and food," Amy said as she made her way to the door.

"Sure thing. I'll bring the beer," he said and lifted his hand up and said bye to her.

Amy jumped back in her truck, put the pistachio ice cream in the cooler with hers and headed down the street toward Bryer's photography shop. She couldn't stop thinking about Kath and Cy moving so suddenly. She was sure they hadn't mentioned it before. *Perhaps I was too caught up with Bryer and the book launch to be around much,* she thought to herself feeling somewhat guilty.

Amy turned the truck onto Alexander Street and drove past the White Oak Bar where her and Bryer had gone many times for the great food and games of pool. She could see The Blinded Eye book store coming up on the left, owned by her best friend Maggie Moon. Finally, she pulled up to the curb, next to the book store and outside the store that said 'Burnett's Photography' above. A rush of nervous excitement ran through her as she quickly turned off the engine and leaped out of the truck forgetting her hat in her hurry.

Amy quickly strode to the door and turned the knob but it wouldn't open, it was locked. She peered in through the window and thought that perhaps Bryer was working on some of the police photos. He sometimes did this for the income and thinking he didn't want anyone to walk in on them like she had once done, he might have locked the door because of that. She pulled out her phone and pressed "dial" next to his name in her contacts and waited for him to answer. An automated message began to speak in her ear, "The number you are trying to call has been disconnected." Amy closed her phone. *Well, no wonder he hasn't texted me back, he must have got a new phone*, she thought.

Stepping back a few paces she was about to return to her truck when she stopped and actually looked at Bryer's store front. The windows were dirty and covered in dust and the display pictures in both windows were gone as if he had taken them down for cleaning or something.

The whole place looked barren and unloved.

Amy's stomach dropped as she stared at the store.

It was closed and it looked like Bryer, who also lived upstairs above his studio, hadn't been there in weeks.

She walked down the small alley between his store and the empty one next door and headed for the back door. There was a small sign on it. As she got closer she could read it and what it said made absolutely no sense to her. It stated that the store was 'For Rent. A commercial and residential property' and had a phone number underneath it.

Amy stared at the sign, her mind wouldn't or couldn't take it in. It made no sense at all.

Had he left town— left her?

Chapter Eight

1798, Hingham, Suffolk County,
Massachusetts

The old gnarled hands of the Scribe reached forward and snatched the book from its shelf, they carried it to the table and let it fall the last inch or so making a loud bang as the wooden boards protecting the book's contents hit the aged wood of the table.

Every object on the table rattled and moved a little with the sudden vibration. The hand pulled out the chair and lit the nearest oil lamp before sitting down at last in front of the book.

On the table next to the lamp and the book sat a pot of oak gall ink and a quill which was freshly tipped especially for this moment. The dark room around the simple table hovered on the edge of vision as the light from the lamp did not spread far, and the twilight, which had partially leaked in through the cloth-covered window, had now faded away leaving nothing but cold darkness in its wake.

The hands now opened the book with a lot more reverence than their touch had been a few moments before. They opened up the metal clasp and lifted the heavy and somewhat tattered wooden board that covered the front page. Inside, after a page of drawings and strange diagrams, which the reader knew by heart, the page of incantation sat in the dim light.

The Scribe intoned the words on the page with their eyes shut, knowing them from the many times they had been seen and said before. The words tumbled monotonously from the Scribe's mouth but on this occasion there was a sadness to them, a feeling of finality and an edge of anger and regret.

The words having been spoken, the Scribe now turned over several of the pages until they recognized their own handwriting from many years past. The pages flicked by, as the decades had done, until at last the Scribe came to a blank page. One of the old hands slowly reached out and with a fingertip gently touched the paper, stroking it and feeling the rough texture of it, the skin carefully moving over it, appreciating one last chance to make everything right— if they could.

With a deep sigh the Scribe picked up the quill, dipped it into the ink and began to write the carefully chosen words upon the page. The ink quickly soaked into the paper and spread slightly as the words flowed from the hand into the book, words upon words were placed in the correct order with the right intent upon each and every one of them.

The Scribe hoped it would be enough as they laboured for hours to recite the message, the hand ached, the back screamed in agony but still the Scribe wrote, knowing full well that the end was nigh and this was their last chance.

A terrible wind had gotten up outside. It howled around the old walls like wolves chasing the full moon. It rattled through the shuttered windows and whirled around the room making the oil lamp flicker in its wake.

The Scribe hurried, it was almost midnight and nearly time to leave this world forever.

With a sudden bang, the door flew open and the wild wind entered fully into the room. It whirled around making the ragged window hangings, the old straw on the floor and the long grey hair of the Scribe billow and dance on the air as if controlled by a crazed puppet master.

The roar of it deafened the Scribe as one hand firmly gripped the book to keep it on the table and the other finished writing his desperate last words.

"You can have me now, I am done," the Scribe said and stood by the table spreading their arms as if to meet a lover. The bedraggled grey hair and long filthy robes moved around the Scribe in waves like a great sea in a storm. Tears streamed down the worn, dirty face, but there was also a smile, one of sadness and resignation to the fate that was about to catch up with the Scribe after so many years.

With a crack of lightning and a boom of

thunder, the Scribe clutched each side of their head and screamed as scenes from their long life raced through their mind, expanding and searing as they went until finally the Scribe fell to their knees and looked down at their hands full of blood from its ears.

The pain increased until it brought on blessed unconsciousness and the Scribe's body crumpled to the floor as the wind sucked the life force out of the old scribe along with its soul.

A final blast of frigid air rushed around the Scribe and knocked the oil lamp over. The oil ignited all at once and spread over the floor, lighting the old dry straw and quickly spreading to the lath and plaster walls. In its hunger, the fire devoured everything in its path including the table, chair and the Scribe's now lifeless body.

Everything, that is... except the book.

****

Two hundred miles away, a healthy child died in its shocked mother's arms.

Across the ocean in England, on a ship

docked at harbour in the port of Portsmouth, an oil lamp was knocked over and the taper lighting it fell to the ground as the man died instantly and dropped to the wooden boards heavily like a sack of turnips. The fire quickly spread upon the ship, which was preparing to set sail that day for the New World. The old wood burst into blue and green flames from all the salt dried within its fibres. An intense blaze roared over the man's body as if in great anger, taking with it eighteen families bound for a new life and almost all the crew. Those that escaped the fire and jumped into the water found the tide at port stronger than usual and they all drowned to a man.

In Scotland, on a quiet farm in the highlands, a great storm engulfed the buildings, crops and animals, killing and destroying all in its wake as if to wipe everything on the farm from the face of the earth, including the family of six living there.

Back in Hingham, the Scribe's family; two sons and the last remaining female of the family, an aunt, succumbed to great hallucinations and much convulsing and pain. Finally, they died after ingesting an unseen fungus on their rye bread. St. Anthony's Fire was incorrectly blamed for their deaths.

Chapter Nine

Present Day

Amy had agreed to meet her friend Maggie for lunch, at Acker's Cafe, in Morton Creek. Although she was looking forward to seeing her for the first time since returning from her book tour, Amy was still anxious about Bryer. She had not heard from him nor been able to contact him on his cell phone or the shop phone. She had already been back to his place again but it was just as deserted as the last time, only two days before. She had also promised herself to drop in on Aunt Kath and Uncle Cy that afternoon and catch up on everything about their move. Amy was also looking forward to seeing what the new house was like.

Just before noon, Amy pulled up to the curb outside the cafe, which always made her smile to herself. It was the place where her family went for brunch every Sunday during the summer when she had been small and when they had come over to Canada from the UK every year for the six weeks summer holiday.

There is something so very reassuring in seeing beloved places from your childhood standing the test of time, she thought. Such things can make your heart sing, and that's exactly what it did to Amy, a wave of nostalgia filled Amy's heart and she felt drawn into the place as always.

Climbing out of the truck, she glanced up at the bright, blue sky. It was one of those days that her mum used to call the 'Canadian Sky' days because the sky had no clouds and seemed huge compared to the almost perpetually overcast in England. It was like a different and very beautiful world. Putting thoughts of her lost family and the grey of England behind her, she strode purposefully through the green door of the café, making the well-worn welcome sign swing with the movement.

Looking around the room, she saw Maggie hadn't arrived yet and Amy took the last booth at the window, next to the shiny leafed plants.

The cafe was made to be as homey as possible: the walls were painted a warm terracotta colour with wooden shelving displaying old fashioned wares such as oil lamps, antique hand tools and quilts. There were a few stools at the wooden counter, some free standing chairs and tables nearby. Over by the large brick fireplace, there were comfy chairs and coffee tables for those customers who preferred a more homey and comfortable seating area.

She noticed there were a few people in the cafe already and more continued to come in after Amy had sat down. It seemed that 'Acker's Cafe' was still the place to go for lunch. Amy looked at the menu on the table until a young, fair-haired waitress came over and deposited a glass of water with ice.

"Good morning," the waitress said with a smile, "I'm Rachel and I'll be your server today."

"Morning. I'm just waiting for a friend,

Maggie Moon from the book shop?" Amy said to the young woman.

"Oh, yes, I know Maggie. I'll send her over when she comes in and I'll come back for your order then," she said and smiled as she walked away to serve coffee refills.

Amy wondered if her childhood friend... well, not friend exactly, rather nemesis... Annabeth was in today. She had bullied Amy whenever she visited from England and she'd eventually taken over the cafe when Annabeth's grandfather had retired.

Amy suddenly felt like a shiver went down her spine and she knew someone in the cafe was watching her intently. She sipped her water and tried to look discreetly around her to see who it was. Her eyes were drawn to the table at the far back of the café but the waitress stood in front of the person and she couldn't see who had been watching her. She just knew it was from that direction. Amy looked away but with the corner of her eye she watched and waited for the waitress to move.

At last, the waitress did move on and Amy

risked a look in that direction and looked directly into the eyes of Detective Inspector Andy Withers. He was the cop who had brought down the horrendous and crazed woman that had been killing Amy's distant family members. It had been a sick plan to raise Amy's long dead and several times great Granddad from the grave. Amy couldn't help but shudder when she looked into his face as the memories of last year flooded her mind. She hadn't seen him since then and he looked about the same: a middle aged man being overworked by a job that most people simply didn't want to do. His face was no more haggard than before, a surprise considering what they had been through together, but, she was pleased to see, his eyes were still bright and intelligent and that was always a good sign.

Detective Andy nodded and turned his gaze away from Amy and he showed no real interest in her at all. Amy glanced at the person currently sitting opposite the cop, who was looking at her directly with the most amazing green eyes in his handsome, suntanned face. The unknown man also nodded at her but tipped his finger to his forehead in a friendly and respectful way and then turned back to talk to Andy.

Amy turned away from them, looked out of the window and frowned a little, she was very sure she didn't know the man Detective Andy was with and by the look on Andy's face, he hadn't looked enthused to see her. Perhaps he didn't want to think about last year either or perhaps he was just having another bad day. He seemed to have a lot of them, and they must be a hazard of the job.

"Hey there, lady!"

Amy's head spun round to see Maggie slip into the booth opposite.

Maggie's face split into a huge grin and she flicked some of her long curly red hair over her shoulder. "How was the book tour? Gods, it's good to see you."

"Maggie, hey. It's great to see you too. The book tour was great but tiring, and I'm glad to be home. How's business?"

Maggie, the owner of The Blinded Eye, a great little book store and the only one in Morton Creek, smiled at her friend. "Pretty good actually, thanks. Everything okay? You looked a bit worried when I came in.”

“Yeah, fine thanks. I’ve been trying to get hold of Bryer for a few days, have you seen him?” Amy asked her as the book store was next door to Bryer’s Photography Store and they were friends.

Maggie looked a little confused and frowned, “Not since he went to Toronto.”

“Toronto? Oh, I didn’t realise, did he find some photography work there or is he working with the cops again?”

“No,” Maggie frowned again. “He moved there with his wife, don’t you remember? Are you sure you are okay?” The concern in Maggie’s voice was obvious.

“His wife?” Amy’s throat closed and it was hard to swallow. Her mind whirled with incomprehension and she could feel her entire body throb with her quickened pulse from the shocking impact of Maggie’s words. *His WIFE!?* Her mind kept saying over and over.

“So ladies, what would you like?” The waitress said as she appeared beside them.

“Erm...” Maggie looked at Amy who

looked like she'd seen a ghost and said, "Can you give us a few more minutes?"

"Sure," The waitress said, smiled and moved on.

"I thought he was divorced." Amy said her voice sounding alien even to her.

"First I've heard of it. Anyway, they left a few weeks ago, heading for the bright lights of the big city. Didn't you know he was leaving?"

"No... I didn't." Amy said as the urge to cry from the disappointment, heart hurt and all the lies he had obviously told her.

Was it just to get her in bed? She wondered furiously.

"Oh, well, I'm sure you can find another photographer for your book stuff, in fact I think there is one in the next town over, but I bet he is not as good as Bryer though. Anyway, what shall we have for lunch? Anything you fancy?" Maggie said as if she had no idea she had just shattered Amy's love life into a thousand pieces.

Amy's mind whirled with anger and sadness.

Had it all been a lie? Had no one else known

about them? Had he kept it a secret because he was still married to his wife? Her own voice echoed around her mind and it had no answers.

"Amy?"

Maggie's voice penetrated the emotional shock that had wrapped itself around Amy like suffocating clingfilm.

"Just order me a club sandwich, I'll be back in a minute." Amy got up, and, on auto pilot, walked through the cafe, past the detective and his unknown lunch partner, and into the small ladies room at the back of the cafe. Going into a cubicle, Amy put the lid down on the toilet and sat on it, utterly stunned by the news.

The muffled noise of the cafe could be heard outside of the ladies washroom but Amy didn't hear it. She sat alone, unable to think for a moment.

"Well, shit," she said to herself through gritted teeth as anger began to boil in her veins and betrayal seared her heart. She breathed in deeply and let it out slowly and continued to focus on her breathing, trying to calm her wildly beating heart down to some sort of semblance of a normal rhythm.

Leaving the unused cubicle, she washed her hands, which felt hot and sticky, in the lovely cold tap water and stood peering at her own reflection. She looked white with high pink splotches on her cheeks. She continued to concentrate on her breathing as she dried her hands and looked back into the mirror.

"Well, fuck you and fuck that shit," she said to her reflection, although the words were aimed directly at Bryer and his lovely blue eyes. "Fucking shut up brain," she said out loud as an older woman walked into the ladies, looking at Amy as if she were nuts for talking to herself, which she was, of course.

Amy gathered herself together and would be damned if a man... like him, with no respect, was going to ruin her lunch with her friend.

Well Sod that, she thought with determination, and defiantly walked out of the ladies and headed back toward her table with her head held high and her mind focused on not tripping over.

Crossing the room, she noticed that both

the Detective and his guest had left. She vaguely wondered if the Detective was on another case. She supposed that he was always working on another case. It was the nature of his job after all.

Sitting back down at the booth with Maggie, Amy sipped her drink and looked up at her friend, and, choosing to ignore the whole idea of Bryer, she launched into a great telling of where she had visited and what she had seen on her book tour.

During this conversation their meals arrived and Amy found that, after all, she did have an appetite and ate ravenously as she told Maggie about the two conventions she'd been to and the famous people she had met.

"Sounds like you had a great time. It must have been great seeing all those places and the celebs," Maggie said and looked a little envious, "Now that you're back home, will you be starting another book?"

Amy nodded with a mouthful of her club sandwich.

"Will it be in the same series as Witch Bottle or another one of those children's books?"

Maggie had finished her last bite and wiped an errant spot of ketchup off her chin from her burger.

"It will be in the Witch Bottle series. Not sure of the story line quite yet, though," Amy said and placed her napkin on her empty plate. "That was good as usual. So do you have any book events sorted for autumn?"

"Actually, I wanted to talk to you about that. The cafe part of the book store has been doing well and it's bringing people in, so the book sales are also up."

"Oh, that's good news," Amy said. She loved the little bookshop and the cosy cafe at the back of it.

"Yes, I'm very pleased and I'm thinking of expanding and taking over next door, that way I can have twice the book space and a larger cafe. What do you think?"

"Oh, that sounds great, what a good idea. I love your shop and the cafe, such a nice feeling in there," Amy said.

"Anything else, ladies?" The waitress asked as she silently appeared by Maggie's elbow like a ninja and picked up their empty plates.

"Yes, coffee, black," Maggie said somewhat startled.

"Green tea, please," Amy said.

They both watched the waitress depart the table and then turned back to each other.

"Tell me honestly, no strings attached, how would you feel about being my partner in the newly expanded shop?" Maggie said, looking Amy directly in the eye.

"Oh, I..." Amy was stunned and rather speechless. She loved the bookshop dearly and knew Maggie was an excellent business woman and she replied without a second thought, "You know, I think I would love to!" She said with a huge grin.

A bookshop owner? It's like being a child again and having my dream come true, she thought. All she ever wanted in life from about the age of eight was to write books and own a bookshop.

"Oh, that is excellent news," Maggie said and sprung out of her side of the booth and gathered Amy into a hug despite Amy still being sat down.

Amy smiled and her hurt heart swelled with

happiness and the love for her dear friend.

****

Before returning home after lunch, Amy wanted to share the news about going into business with Maggie with her family. Well, her 'almost' family. Uncle Cy and Aunt Kath were the nearest thing to family Amy had left and so she headed out to the address their son had given her earlier in the week.

Driving down Spruce Road, Amy decided she loved the little wooden clad houses that were all painted pale colours. There was such glorious variety, too, including green, yellow, blue and white. Each had a small, open-plan garden with no fencing in between, flowers and shrubs surrounding most of the houses.

Following the house numbers, she finally came to a stop outside a pale yellow house with the number 1072 on the letterbox by the path. Parking the truck in the small driveway in front of the garage, she climbed out and looked up at the large trees that shaded the house. At this far end of

Spruce Road, several houses were on the edge of a small wooded area which gave a more secluded and quiet feel to the area.

Before Amy could even step up onto the small porch and reach the white painted door, it flew open and Aunt Kath rushed out with such a smile on her face it was as if she hadn't seen Amy in years.

"Oh, Amy, how wonderful to see you!" she said.

Amy was enveloped in a powerful hug which was surprising in its strength from such a small older woman.

"Aunt Kath, it's good to see you too," Amy sighed and let herself be hugged, since there is nothing better than the healing touch of a loved one hugging you.

"Come on in, we were just about to have some iced tea and ice-cream on the back porch," Aunt Kath said as she spun round on her heel and swiftly went back indoors.

The house was all open plan downstairs with the lounge and dining room taking up most of the first floor, the kitchen was at the back as were the stairs leading upward to the rest of the building. Following her Aunt through the house, who stopped only briefly to get a bowl and a glass from a kitchen cabinet, they went outside to the small back deck that had a marvelous view below of the town and the river beyond it.

It was a beautiful house and as pleased as Amy was to see that their move had been a happy one, the sight of Uncle Cy stopped her in her tracks. The once strong, healthy, wiry man was now looking decidedly frail and weak. He had an oxygen tank attached to a small trolley by him and a breathing tube fastened around his face that fed air directly into his nasal passages.

"Oh, Uncle Cy... what happened?" Amy sat on the white wicker chair by him and placed her hand on his arm.

"Amy, my dear... how good it is... to see you again," He said, his voice weak and whispery.

"Perhaps you could help me to get the ice-cream out, Amy," Aunt Kath said.

"Oh, yes, of course."

Amy followed Aunt Kath to the garage where they stored the big chest freezer and Amy swung up the heavy lid for her aunt to reach in for the big tub of ice-cream. "What happened? Last time I saw him he was fine, better than fine."

"You know he's had Emphysema for years but it has gotten a lot worse recently. The doctor..." Aunt Kath stood up straight and looked Amy in the eye, and tears began to cloud her eyes.

Amy swallowed hard, she had no idea he was ill and by the look of Aunt Kath it seemed that it was not good news, "What did the doctor say?"

"That... that he only probably has a couple of months," Aunt Kath's face crumpled and she burst into heart wrenching sobs.

Amy pulled the old lady into her arms as they both stood in the garage crying while the ice-cream began to melt and drip condensation onto the cement floor.

Chapter Ten

October 15th 1665, Muddy River, near Boston, Massachusetts

Benjamin Thomas loomed over the newly covered grave and looked about him and around the woods he stood in. There were no sounds except those of the night creatures in the woods and they would have gone silent if anyone was nearby.

The place was as silent as the grave... literally.

Wiping the sweat off his face, Benjy picked up the spade and lantern, and returned to the horse and cart. He placed them quietly in the back and took a few paces toward the river. He stripped completely naked and his white body shone in the moonlight.

Leaving his clothes on the bank, he quickly walked into the cold water and then dove in, ensuring all of him was submerged to rinse off the sweat and grime of digging the grave and also the blood that had splattered down his face and neck.

He came out of the water glistening from head to toe in the pale light of the quarter moon, and, although his skin bristled with goosebumps, he did not dress in the clothes he'd taken off. Instead, he walked back to his cart and opened the large chest which sat on the wooden boards like a squatting frog.

Pulling out the expensive and excellent quality apparel from the chest, he was going to dress himself in his victim's clothing. He would even brush his shoulder length hair and tie it back in exactly the same fashion as Jonathon, his half brother had done. The resemblance between the two men was uncanny now that Benjy had grown. Even their size and height had been about the same despite having different fathers.

Benjy had watched his half-brother every

day. Jonathon Moore had taken over his mother's house after the hanging and sold most of her other properties. These included another stable, a wheat farm and a wine merchant's home, all of which she had inherited from her late 'husband' when he died. Jonathon had used the monies gained from the sales to finance his lavish and wild lifestyle, but Muddy River he hadn't known about at that time.

He had bought all the best food, wine and female company the money could buy. He had been so obnoxious and uncaring about his staff that when Benjy's foster mother, Sarah, had taken ill with the smallpox, Jonathon had seen no need to spend money on a doctor and told the then twelve year old Benjy that she would recover. It was only a 'mild malady of the poor'. Sarah had died the next morning and had left Benjy alone with the master whom he now hated more than anyone in the world. That hatred and disgust had grown over the years just as Benjy had grown into a young man.

When Jonathon had gone through his mother's library, selling off her beloved and very expensive books, he discovered a secret sliding door in the bookshelf which was just big enough to hide a single book. It was Ann's secret journal. He had read the book and been in a foul mood for days after. Benjy had been watching from the hallways and doorways as he had since Sarah died. He had seen Jonathon find the book and heard him mutter the words 'Devil's whore' over and over again as he read the book late at night.

Jonathon, however, was so arrogant and full of his own self-importance that he never noticed the young man watching him from the shadows of every corner.

From the notes in the back of the journal, Jonathon discovered his mother's secret. She had another property but had disguised her name as A. H. Moore in her ownership of it. This angered him greatly. How dare she use the name of his father when she had already destroyed it with her ungodly scandal in England.

The property he found after a little detective work, all the while watched by Benjy, of course, turned out to be a small cottage in the woods by Muddy River.

It was the very river Benjy now stood by,

wet and naked as the day he was born and it was the river that would see Jonathon's timely death.

Requiring the utmost secrecy, Jonathon, having no idea who his companion was, had ordered Benjy to drive him in the old wagon out to the location.

In doing so he had made the mistake of dismissing Benjy as an irrelevant and unimportant servant who would be expected to not even comment on, never mind cause trouble from the knowledge of where they went.

Benjy, now being the head of the stable, was capable of driving the wagon and it was not unusual for him to do so with his master aboard. This is how Benjy and Jonathon ended up alone in their mother's secret place in the dead of night.

"Stay there," Jonathon ordered in a terse voice as he climbed down from the wagon. He threw his travelling cloak onto the seat, took the lantern from its place on the wagon hook and headed towards the old stone cottage on foot.

Benjy didn't say a word and looked around him the best he could in the pale moonlight and from his vantage point up on the wagon. The place was nice, he decided.

It was far enough away from the stinking streets of town that no noise followed them. He could hear the river was close by and the cottage was small and neat with a small porch that had a rocking chair on it. He liked it immediately. He felt a kinship to the place and he could imagine his mother being there, perhaps with him, and they could enjoy another life, one they could share together as a family, as they should have done for all these years.

The light from the lantern moved around inside the cottage and caught Benjy's eye. It was shedding a small amount of light out of one of the two front windows. The small glass panes of glass distorted the movement. It looked strangely like devils were dancing inside and perhaps they were.

A crashing noise came from within and Benjy jumped down off the cart and ran toward the door that was still slightly ajar. He peered around the door and saw that Jonathan had lit another oil lamp and was looking closely at the jars and bottles which were all lined up on a shelf along one side of the cottage and next to a wooden table and benches. Jonathon picked up a jar, read the label and threw it to the floor where it smashed. The contents, which looked like chicken hearts, flew in all directions and finally came to a squishy landing on the flagstone floor. The smell of vinegar and brine assaulted Benjy's nostrils.

"Lying witch! Devil temptress!" Jonathon ranted as he went through her things, smashing and breaking as he went. He upturned chests of clothes, the simple sort of a country woman, not the kind a townswoman of his mother's status would normally wear.

All the while, Benjy watched from the doorway as his beloved mother's things were torn apart and discarded as foul and ungodly, like she herself had been treated. The heat of his anger raised with every piece of damage Jonathon did, and, when Jonathon finally sat down on a bench exhausted, sweating and breathing loudly from his exertions, Benjy entered the cottage on the pretense of seeing if his master was safe. In reality, he could no longer be kept outside and see his mother's life destroyed and lost to him, not after Jonathon had already taken his foster mother

Sarah too. He could not bear to lose this last thing, this cottage and its contents, they were all he had now of a mother's love.

"Get thee away!" Jonathon growled at Benjy as he entered the cottage, angry at the disturbance.

"Nay," Benjy said and stood his ground against his master for the first time in his life. He couldn't deny it felt so good, so right at long last.

"Thee wilt do as I sayeth boy or thy wilt be flogged upon our return," Jonathan said and rose from the bench, puffing himself up in all his own perceived importance.

"Thy wilt nay lay thy hand upon me. Thee are nay worthy of her love, nor her money and her precious things," Benjy growled the words across the room. The depth of the ferocity he felt surprised even him, he stood with his fists clenched at his sides and he could feel his nails digging into his palms with the pent up rage.

Jonathon looked utterly stunned and stood with his mouth open, his mind could not believe he had just been spoken to in such a way, and by a servant of all things. "Who art thou to speak to me thus?"

"I...I am thy mother's son," Benjy said as relief flooded through his body at actually being able to voice it, finally, after all these years.

"Thee... thee is what? Nay, boy. Thou art naught but a cook's son. Leave me be and I shalt deal with thee upon our return," Jonathan dismissed him with a wave of his hand, sat back down on the bench and pulled his mother's journal from his coat pocket. The small, soft leather bound book flopped open on the table and he turned several pages quickly as if looking for something.

Benjy wasn't sure what to do now, he felt deflated and unimportant. Jonathan obviously didn't believe him. He watched his half brother read his mother's words which had been denied to him and the jealousy raged again, he clenched his fists again at his sides as he bathed in his own anger, relishing it and welcoming the heat of it like a good fire on a cold day.

Cursing his mother loudly, Jonathon grabbed up her book and threw it into the empty fireplace, stood up and brushed himself down from the detritus of his rampage and straightened his shirt and cuffs.

"Take ye oil lamp and burn this ungodly place to ye ground, then drive me back home," Jonathon ordered and walked past Benjy heading toward the door and the wagon outside.

In a flash of murderous anger, Benjy grabbed the oil lamp, followed his half-brother to the door and brought it down heavily on the back of his head. It smashed into a thousand pieces and spread the oil all over Jonathon and the floor. The man fell like a dead weight down onto the flagstones. The oil immediately ignited from the lit wick and spread so fast that Benjy jumped back in utter surprise.

Benjy grabbed a cloak off the hooks by the door and covered the fire with it, patting it down quickly and efficiently. He stood looking down at his half-brother in the gloom of the darkened old cottage, his eyes trying to adjust to the sudden change in light. He looked around for another lamp and saw one in the small room at the back that was, he supposed, his mother's sleeping room. Lighting it, he walked back through to the main part of the cottage to find Jonathon's body was gone, and there was no trace of him in the cottage. Swiftly, he looked about him and in his panic grabbed up a knife from the shelf of various kitchen utensils, expecting to be attacked at any moment but he wasn't... all was quiet.

Benjy rushed across the room knowing there was no way he could let Jonathon leave. He knew he would be caught and hung, just like his mother. Servants attacking their masters, it was not something Boston society would allow. He placed the lamp on the table as he passed it and moved to the door, gripping the door frame in sheer panic and tried to see outside in the pale moonlight. At last, he saw movement near the wagon. Jonathon had managed to crawl on his hands and knees, still of clouded mind from the blow to the head and the burns he had suffered. He was dragging himself toward the wagon trying to escape. Benjy ran over to his half-brother and before he knew what he was doing, he had grabbed him by the arm, pushed him roughly to the ground. Breathlessly, he suddenly knelt over him, looking down at his blood covered hands and the knife within them. Jonathon lay deathly still, with several stab marks in his chest and throat.

Benjy couldn't recall killing him, but his right arm and hand were completely numb from the force used and from the knife hitting bone over and over again, jarring the limb. Benjy dropped the knife and peered at Jonathon. He leaned forward to listen at his mouth, making sure he was finally dead this time.

He was. The life had fled from his broken body.

Benjy got up and staggered back, his brain in shock from what he had done in a blur of anger and self-preservation. His legs gave way suddenly and he dropped to the ground like a stone. He just sat there watching the still body of his half-brother under that pale moon. Not thinking, not plotting, just trapped inside the shock of his deed.

As time passed, he slowly came to his senses and realised he would have to act quickly. He grabbed Jonathon by the ankles and dragged him into the cottage and then left, closing the door behind him. He picked up Jonathon's cloak from the wagon's seat and put it around him and pulled the hood up. He and his brother were very similar in size and shape and he knew he could get away with anyone seeing him dressed as his brother, unless they came up close and saw his face, of course.

He climbed onto the wagon, turned it around and headed for home. He had decided the best course of action would be to collect all of Jonathon's personal items as quietly as possible, pack them and then leave before the household awoke. Everyone would think Jonathon had returned to England due to some debt troubles perhaps, or an angered husband of a wife he dallied with. All his plans would work if he could get into the house and pack everything and out again without being spotted. Thankfully, having grown up in the house, he knew his way around with his eyes shut.

****

Benjy easily succeeded in his deceiving task and he had managed to escape with most of Jonathon's possessions and clothing, without anyone waking and seeing him. He had made it appear as if his half-brother had left in a hurry. Relieved, he made his way back through the early morning hours to the cottage, and, with a spade borrowed from his mother's secret home, he dug a pit for Jonathon in the woods nearby. Dragging the body from the cottage to the pit, he rolled it in and heard a nasty crunch as it landed heavily at the bottom. The soil was shovelled back into the hole and leaves and branches scattered over the unmarked grave until it looked like nothing had ever disturbed the spot.

Jonathon Moore was buried by his half-brother without ceremony or even a word or a backward glance.

Benjy washed in the river, dressed in Jonathon's clothing and sat by his mother's fire reading her secret journal with a contented smile upon his handsome face.

Chapter Eleven

15th June, Glendale, Present Day,
Canada

Detective Andy stood leaning forward, without compromising the scene, to look at yet another naked, dead body. Despite the overhead light illuminating the body, the rest of the dark hallway remained dim and stank of piss, shit and gore. The stench soaked into Andy and he raised his hand to his nose and mouth. The rank odour had already reached the back of his throat and he swallowed down the bile as he tasted the disgusting air. There were times when he truly hated his job and this was definitely one of them. No one should ever end their days by dying like this. He looked around the hallway. It was a typical dirty place of a cheap apartment block in the roughest part of town. His eye roamed back over the body and ignored the glaringly obvious cause of death as he tried to take in other details of the young man and his tragic lifestyle.

From the holes and track marks on the deceased's arms, he was a junky and a heavy user. His face was dirty and the scruffy beard was unwashed, his greasy mop of dark brown hair stuck to his forehead and looked as if it hadn't been brushed, never mind washed, for a couple of months or more. The body lay crumpled in the corner and under the stairs amidst old newspapers, a blanket and used needles. Andy could only surmise the man was homeless and had spent some time here, maybe even lived where he died.

"So Lou, what do you have for me?" Andy said to his Forensic Officer.

Lou Chang was kneeling by the body. His small movements were making the white, plastic disposable suit he wore creak and rustle. He lifted his head and looked at Andy. "Looks like all the skin on his torso was removed, front and back, and on his legs. The genitals were taken too. The blade marks are sure and precise around the arms at the armpits but, obviously, the perp didn't require the skin off the arms... maybe because the victim was an addict? Who knows."

"Fuck me. Think this is like the other cases last year? Did the wacko take any organs this time?"

"No. The Coroner has already been and had a quick look, but he said he would confirm it at the autopsy."

"Right," Andy said, making a mental note to visit Dr William Chester, the Chief Coroner, and get a personal report from him.

At least that way he can explain all the medical crap to me, he thought.

"Of course..." Lou said.

"What?" Andy sighed, he had been in this game for a long time and knew when bad news was coming.

Lou looked Andy directly in the eye as he stood making his suit crackle again.

"Of course, the skin is an organ, it's the largest organ of the body..."

"Seriously? You think that sicko is really fucking back?" Andy said as a deep disgust and dread filled his stomach like a lead weight. He now could no longer deny the knowledge he had known deep down in his soul.

"Boss? You won't believe this..." Mitch said from behind Andy.

Andy turned to face him and looked at him expectantly. "What?"

"The patrol officer who was first on the scene, found the guy's wallet and reported his name to be Karl Hamilton," Mitch said, his eyes wide in amazement.

"Who the fuck is Karl Hamilton?" Andy said impatiently, not understanding the importance of the name.

"Remember the family tree that the records office sent over? He..." Mitch pointed to the body, "is the brother of Olivia Hamilton, the college victim killed in the hospital last year."

"Oh, fuck me. No... not again. Ah, shit. That's just fucking great, that fucking sicko is killing again," Andy leaned against the hallway's paint chipped wall and sighed. "Fuck," He said quietly, more to himself than anyone else.

****

Detective Inspector Andy stared at the whiteboard and he couldn't believe his eyes.

He had already rigorously and painstakingly examined every case similar to his cases from last year and the recent murder cases from his area along with those from the rest of Canada, the US and the UK. His colleagues had sent him their files and he had put the details up on the huge whiteboard. There were crime scene photos, names, arrows and comments written in his own hand. He had finally finished getting it all up and was now just standing back looking at it, coffee in hand.

"Fuck," He said as the he realised he was right, they were all linked. All the murders had been done by the same person or persons over the last seventeen years. He had a major serial killer or killers on his hands. The really clinching piece of evidence had come from Mitch, his 'techno whiz kid' partner, who had also been consulting with

121

the records office, and now three things had become abundantly clear: all the victims had body parts missing. There was absolutely no trace evidence of the perp at each crime scene, which could not be explained. And, probably the most important thing of all, the victims were related to each other. Yes, every single one of the sixteen victims were members of the same family tree. Some were more closely related than the others but still, related they were.

"Fuck," Andy said again just as Mitch walked into Andy's office. "Fuck, fuck, fuckety fuck. That's just fucking nasty. An entire family line."

"What you found, boss?" Mitch said and leaned against the desk looking at the whiteboard too.

Andy relayed what he had found to his partner.

"The paperwork just came through from the records office, your contact confirmed it's an entire family line as far as they can tell.

"Shit," Mitch said, as his face crumpled in utter disgust. "Why? Why would someone do that to a family, for God's sake?"

"Exactly."

"How are we going to catch him with no evidence and no leads?"

"No idea," Andy took a sip of his coffee, deeply wishing it was a shot of good, old and very expensive whisky. "How's your research going?" Andy noticed a file in Mitch's hand for the first time.

"I have something which may help, actually, if we're lucky," he said with a satisfied smile on his face.

Andy experienced, yet again, the sense of déjà vu of the entire moment from looking at the board to when Mitch came into his office. He shook his head trying to rid himself of the weird feeling but it lingered at the edge of his mind like a moth around a flame.

"You okay, Boss?" Mitch said as he peered at Andy's suddenly pale face. "We can call it a night if you want. It is getting late."

"No, I'm good. Just can't shake the feeling of... something... oh, I don't fucking know. Something is giving me a weird fucking feeling about all this shit," Andy rubbed his face with both hands and looked back at Mitch. "So what have you got?"

"Well, we have looked at all the usual suspects and they have all alibi'd out, every single one of them. I've also found some surviving relatives of the deceased, one or two are in our jurisdiction. I think we should give them some protection until this sicko is caught."

"Good idea, put a car on their homes around the clock."

"Will do, Boss." Mitch nodded and continued, "So... I began to widen the circle, you know the kind of thing the next round outwards from the usual suspects, and I tracked their movements at the times of the murders, although I can't tell you anything about the ones in the UK or US, the ones here have some common denominators and we have six names of people who are..."

"Connected?" Andy said hopefully.

"Well, not exactly... more... just around."

"In the wrong place at the wrong time, huh?" Andy said with a smirk. It was a common saying of suspects who don't want to be blamed for a crime.

Mitch nodded with a grin.

"Okay, give me the names," Andy picked up the whiteboard marker pen, moved over some paperwork that was hanging from a magnetic clip and squared off a section from the rest of the details with two quick lines giving himself a designated space in the right-hand corner and wrote down the names as Mitch called them out.

A chill of familiarity rippled down Andy's spine as he read the names back to himself silently in his head. Something about this weird-ass case and everyone involved in it, was creeping him the fuck out.

Chapter Twelve

Amy pulled her truck up outside The Blinded Eye book shop for her meeting with Maggie to go over the expansion plans. She determinedly refused to look at the shop next door, the one Maggie was taking over... the one she had visited, both professionally for headshots and privately to be with Bryer. It was where she could honestly say she had fallen in love with him.

"Bastard," Amy said as her eyes flicked oh so annoyingly of their own volition to the empty store front.

"Be at ease, Amy, thou shouldst be pleased to knowest his truth," Erda said as she appeared next to Amy on the truck seat.

"Shit! You made me jump. You need to be

more careful popping up like that or people will see you," Amy said and deliberately ignored Erda's conversation subject.

"Nay, only thee can see me thus." Erda raised a hand and indicated to her Spiritual self.

Amy nodded, "Right, they can only see you if you want them too. Yeah, knew that. Brain is not working today, better have some tea in the meeting or I shall daydream all through it."

"Thee want me to cometh?"

"No, I'll be fine. Thanks," Amy smiled at Erda, climbed out of the truck and by the time she had closed the door Erda had vanished.

Amy turned around to face the book store and began walking to the curb. A gust of wind blew in her face and she turned her head slightly against it and pulled her hair out of her face. She stopped dead still in her tracks staring across the road at the person looking in the deli window opposite, perusing their goods.

"It's not possible." Amy said and felt decidedly nauseous and dizzy. She gripped the nearby lamp post to steady herself as she stared at the person, willing them to turn around and willing them, with all her might, not to be the person she thought she was seeing.

Milliseconds ticked by but the time seemed like hours to Amy as she watched the person slowly turn round to face the street. The wind had lifted the silk scarf around the woman's neck and she was fighting to get control of it again in the sudden gusts.

Amy saw the face full on and stared, her heart crashing around in her chest, like a crazed bird in a cage. It felt like it would suddenly burst forth and be flung out onto the road several feet away from her with a loud splat. She saw the woman's face fully and she knew exactly who she saw, but her brain just could not comprehend the sight. "What the fuck?" the words tumbled out of her mouth and she was left standing with her mouth open.

Across the road, dressed in a summer dress, cardigan and silk scarf, looking very much a 1950's woman, stood Emily Carpenter. The very same Emily Carpenter who, last year, had been the serial killer that had made the evil Dr John Lambe rise from the dead by using parts of his descendants bodies to recreate a body for his spirit. John Lambe was not only Amy's many times removed grandfather, but also Erda's ex-lover, who had burnt her at the stake and had also been Emily's murderer. He had strangled her to death, once she had resurrected him, right in front of Amy and Erda. Thankfully, Erda's original Hex from her death had caught up with John and destroyed him but Emily... Emily was dead, very dead and had been for over a year.

But, no, she was standing there, very much alive, directly across the road.

"What the fuck?" Amy said again, her brain unable to come up with anything else to say.

Emily successfully managed to control her errant scarf and continued walking down Main Street as if nothing ever untoward had ever happened to her and she was just the slightly arrogant and classy Realtor everyone knew her to be.

Amy watched her walk away, her brain not taking in her surroundings. She jumped out of her skin and gave out a small startled cry when she felt a hand on her shoulder. Spinning round Amy came face to face with Maggie who had come out of her shop to greet her.

"Oh, Sorry didn't mean to make you jump. Hey, are you okay? You look like you've seen a ghost," Maggie's eyes searched Amy's face for a clue of why she was so pale and then they flicked to the area of the road that Amy had been staring at but it was empty.

"I... well, yes actually. I think I did," Amy said and looked back up the street for Emily but she was nowhere in sight.

My mind must be playing tricks on me. It's not possible, she thought and looked around wildly for Emily, afraid that she would sneak up behind her and kidnap her again for her hideous ritual in that disgusting basement. Amy shuddered and took a deep breath as she tried to contain the tide of panic that had washed over so quickly.

"You sure you're okay?" Maggie said, looking very concerned.

"Yeah, think so," Amy said, finally looking back at Maggie and giving her a weak, reassuring grin.

"Let's get you a cup of tea, that always

helps the British doesn't it?" Maggie said and laughed.

Amy grinned at her, but all she could think was if Erda could be a Spirit, couldn't Emily be one also? This thought terrified her deep down in her soul.

Inside, Amy excused herself before the meeting with Maggie and their two solicitors started and went to the restroom to collect her scattered thoughts.

"Erda?" Amy called softly, once she had checked she was alone in the room. "Erda, can you hear me? Come quick, I need you."

The air shimmered next to Amy and Erda appeared. "Are thee safe?" Erda said the second she appeared.

"Yes, well, I think so. Shit, I don't know." Amy said and began pacing, trying to make sense of everything in her brain.

"Nay understand thee. Are thee well?" Erda frowned with concern.

"Yes, just maybe losing my mind... again," Amy looked directly at Erda and remembered the first time she had seen her as a Spirit.

"Again? Speak thy truth and clearly for I am lost."

"I can't believe this myself but... I... just saw Emily walking on the street."

"Emily?"

"YES!" Amy said with a spike of anger. She breathed deeply for a moment and tried again. "Yes, it was Emily Carpenter. You know, she who caused all the trouble last year and tried to kill me and killed all those members of my... our family." Amy's voice rose several notes in panic by the time she finished speaking.

"Nay, 'tis nay possible," Erda said and shook her head.

"I swear I did. Could she be a Spirit like... like you?"

"Nay, her Spirit was nay bound to anyone nor anything before she departed."

"But, what if..." Amy began.

"'Tis nay possible I tell thee, her Spirit left. I saw it."

"How? How did you see it?" Amy said in surprise, she hadn't known this bit of information.

"When she died I saw her Spirit leave and...

float yonder and a'way. Spirits can see others, thee knowest."

"I didn't know but now I do. Handy, but still... how could I have seen her then?" The panic returned to her voice.

Erda shook her head. "I nay comprehend."

"Did she not die? What if..?"

Erda held up her hand to stop Amy, "'Twill be fine, I wilt go forth, look for her person and find what is a'foot. Thy be safe here with other goodly folks," she said and vanished.

Amy took in a deep breath, collected herself the best she could and returned to the shop's office for the meeting.

Only thirty minutes later, the contract was agreed upon and signed. The two local solicitors, obviously grateful for the work, left the bookstore soon after leaving Amy and Maggie alone in the office. Maggie sat back in her chair behind her busy looking but neat desk, and smiled. "This feels so right, don't you think?"

"Yes, you're right, it does. And the plans for the extension into next door..." Amy's heart filled with pain again as she thought of Bryer, she quickly and firmly pushed him out of her mind, "well, they are looking great," she said and smiled a genuine smile. She was truly looking forward to being Maggie's partner in the book store and café.

"Hey, I know what I wanted to ask you. You being into history and all that for your books..." Maggie said as she checked her watch.

"What?"

"There's an auction of books this afternoon in Glendale at the auction house. I have a thing for ancient books. Would you like to come with me? We could grab some lunch on the way and make it a bit a of a road trip, what do you say?" she said looking hopefully at Amy.

"I would love to, what a great idea and it would be good for a bit of research too. Let's do it," Amy grinned in relief, happy to get away from Morton Creek and the possible return of Emily Carpenter, for a while at least. She knew Erda would be able to come to her if she found anything out. Having a Spirit, and a somewhat witchy one at that, on your side was good for making one feel safe when alone. The fact that Erda could hone in on where Amy was at any given time, like a homing pigeon, also gave Amy a feeling of safety and she had come to enjoy their connection and how Erda watched over her.

****

Amy and Maggie wandered around the showroom at the auction house for a while looking at the collections for sale. The room was presently full of the contents of an estate sale and much of it was furniture from the 18th century, but the sales also included a book library divided into two lots containing forty or fifty rare books in each lot. The room was full of people from all walks of life: some were amateur enthusiasts, others were experts, one or two were constantly on the phone to the buyers they represented, conferring with them.

Some people seemed to just be there for the spectacle and seemed a little out of place, as if they had never been to an auction before, Amy was one of those people. She looked at every lot carefully. The beautiful furniture was truly exquisite and she'd particularly fallen in love with the writing desk that was full of little drawers and secret places. It reminded her of her desk at home which was a legacy from her father's mother and it was something she would never replace. Still, this desk had a feeling about it as if it knew great secrets, and that intrigued her.

"Beautiful, isn't it? It's like it knows a secret or something we don't," Maggie said next to her as if reading Amy's mind.

"I was just thinking the same thing," Amy said and smiled at her friend, "Found anything you like?"

"Oh, yes, lots. But I only came for the books so I'm trying really hard not to look too much at the other incredible things that would look great in my house," she laughed and led Amy through the showroom to the area with the rare book collection.

Maggie leaned over the roped off area to get a better look and then stood back up and consulted the auctions catalogue.

Amy looked at the two beautiful library cases, both identical, and each with a notice on a stand next to it giving the lot number and their names. No one was allowed to handle the books without a member of staff being there, and then only briefly, with gloves on, and under an expert eye. So the notice also said in a very courteous but no-nonsense manner. Amy peered the best she could through the glass of the case, first one lot and then the other. Her attention was drawn to the books on the second shelf of the second book case. The books in there looked somewhat older than the others and a little more tatty. A couple of them were even bound with archival wrappings to preserve their crumbling covers, or so the catalogue said, Amy now read as she looked at them. She wondered what marvellous tales hide inside them all. She had to admit it was tempting to buy them all just to find out.

As the auction was about to begin, Maggie and Amy walked through the showroom and into the plush auction room and took their seats. There were approximately sixty gilt and red velvet cushioned chairs in the room, which held its own pieces of art on the walls. It even had a chandelier above their heads that shone down upon them all brightly. At the end of the room was a raised area with a podium in the middle and on each side were pedestals and a small table showing some of the best pieces of the ceramic collection.

The auction began and Amy watched, utterly fascinated by the entire proceedings and was tempted several times to put in a bid, but she did not have a numbered paddle, so couldn't, thankfully. Maggie, however, did and Amy could see she was almost sitting on her hands forcing herself not to bid and saving her resources for the book lots.

At last, the two lots of books came up and the bidding started. It was slow at first but then got more intense as the minutes ticked by. Several of the bidders who had made a bid at the beginning of the lot dropped out as the price went too high for them and only three people were left bidding, one of them being Maggie. The other two Amy couldn't see, as one was a client on the phone with a broker and the other was a man who sat almost at the front of the room. All she could see of him was the back of his head or when his paddle rose up into the air increasing the bid every time one of the other two made one.

The assembled people began to gasp as the price shot up, well past the market value that Maggie had told Amy it would probably go for. It got to the point where even Maggie had to drop out, which made her bitterly disappointed. The last two were left to battle it out until the man at the front outbid the other by a huge amount and the first lot went to him. The room was filled with murmurs of surprise from patrons and collectors. The price he had paid was very high, even Amy knew that.

The auctioneer began the bidding on the second lot of books and again there was great interest. It seemed that this collection of books was very much coveted by most of the patrons. Amy was surprised, she had seen the item listing in the catalogue and nothing in the list of book titles and authors really stood out to her, but then she was no expert. Yet again, Maggie made her bids with the others, until they all fell away to leave four people this time. The price climbed steadily and once more the man at the front of the room continued to outbid everyone by a huge amount and won the lot.

The people were stirred once again into murmurs but were quickly silenced when the auctioneer began the next lot's bidding.

"Shame, you didn't get them," Amy whispered to Maggie.

"Yes, I really wanted them, too," she said, frowning, and sighed.

The auction soon ended and people began to file out, but Maggie remained in her seat and Amy sat with her, wondering why.

"Shall we go?" Amy said, not sure if they were allowed to stay in the room once the auction was over.

"I just want a word with Cabot," Maggie said, jumped out of her chair, made her way to the front of the room and towards the suited back of a man talking to an old, but very glamorous woman, near the podium.

"Who's Cabot?" Amy asked and quickly followed her friend. She watched as Maggie approached the man and recognised the back of his head: it was the man who had outbid her friend and everyone else for the two book lots.

"Congratulations, Cabot," Maggie said

from behind him.

Hearing his name the man turned round and Amy was surprised to recognise him. It was the man who had been speaking with Detective Andy over lunch in the cafe the other day.

Seeing who had spoken to him, Cabot's smile deepened as he said "Well, if it isn't Miss Maggie Moon. What are you doing here? Not shopping for your little book shop, I know."

Amy looked from one to the other. It seemed they knew each other and the undercurrent seemed like they didn't like each other.

"Your hammer price on both lots was well over the price expected, anyone would think you were desperate for the collection," Maggie said. Her voice rang with steel.

Amy looked at Maggie with surprise. She had never seen her act this way with anyone before. Amy stepped next to her friend and looked at the man she so obviously didn't like.

"Please do introduce me to your lovely friend, Maggie," Cabot said, turning his green-eyed gaze on Amy.

Amy felt a shiver down her spine. It wasn't one of dislike though: quite the opposite... it was one of utter lust. Amy blushed profusely and had to look away at Maggie as she felt she would melt under that gaze.

"This is my dear..." Maggie said the word dear as if it was a threat, "friend, Amy Grey. Amy this is Cabot Tanner, he owns this auction house amongst other things," she said mysteriously.

Amy, not sure at all of the hidden meanings in the introduction did the only thing an English person could do: she smiled brightly and remembered her excellent manners.

"How do you do, Mr. Tanner," she said, and held out her hand to him.

Taking her hand in his, he briefly nodded over it in a very old fashioned and courtly way and said, "Very well, thank you. It is a pleasure to meet you, and you must call me Cabot."

Amy felt the warmth of his skin as his hand lingered a little too long, and rather suggestively in hers. She swallowed the lump that had risen in her throat and replied, "Cabot. As you wish. So you own this auction house?"

"I do. This one and the eight others spread around the country. And what is it you do, Ms Grey?" He said and finally retrieved his hand from hers.

"I'm a writer," Amy said, unable to get her mind to work enough to create a longer sentence.

"Really?" Cabot's perfect right eyebrow raised almost to his also rather perfect hairline. "Surely you are not "the" Amy Grey, author of that enchantingly delightful book Witch Bottle, are you?"

"I am," Amy said, surprised he had even heard of her, never mind the book.

"Well, I would love to sit down and share a drink with you and that lovely mind of yours... sometime, if you would allow me the honour," Cabot smiled from ear to ear and his eyes lit up with a great passion.

Amy felt the skin of her face prickle and grow warm.

This man is dangerously charming and handsome, she thought to herself. She also saw in her mind, flashes of what she could do to him and he to her, which made her blush even more and she had to look away from those eyes again.

"Not today, Romeo," Maggie said tartly, "Goodbye, Cabot." She grabbed Amy's arm, whirled her around and basically frog-marched her out of the auction house and away from Cabot.

"Wow, you didn't tell me you have such... such... friends," Amy said as she climbed into Maggie's car still feeling a bit dazed by it all.

"That man is an arrogant, self-entitled asshole," Maggie said with venom.

"Maggie!" Amy said, surprised by the language.

"Well, he is, and I wouldn't call him a friend, more like a rival... we both... erm... have the same collection interests. You should stay away from him. He's notorious with the ladies and more than a little dangerous."

"Well, that's more than a little cryptic," Amy said as she watched her friend pull out of the parking lot and head home.

"I'll tell you more about it one day."

"I hope you do." Amy said and meant it. There was just something about him that made her gravitate to him, like the old fashioned magickal trick where the magician pulls his fingers away from the hypnotized assistant and she leans whichever way he moves. Amy spent the rest of the trip home thinking about her strong reaction to him and those incredible green eyes.

Chapter Thirteen

Early evening, October 31st, 1665
Boston, Massachusetts

Benjy sat in the corner of the tavern with a pewter mug of warm beer in front of him and watched as patrons entered and left. He was waiting for a certain person to enter. He had been told the person came here to drink and eat their meat pie sometimes during the week, and so Benjy had come each and every night hoping to see the man he was after. The tavern was warm and smelt of human sweat, meat pies, beer and wood smoke from the great fire that blazed in the stone fireplace on the far wall.

Everything at the house had gone to plan.

It was supposed that Jonathan had left under the cover of darkness as he did not want to be discovered by whomever he was hiding from. And, as Benjy had thought, the rumours were circulating that Jonathan had been forced to sneak away from his new home because of gambling debts or even an enraged husband. After a few days people stopped looking for him and carried on with their life without the master of the house to disturb the now smaller daily workload and a sense of calm had filled the place. The servants all continued to maintain the house just in case of his return, but all were much happier and relieved now. Benjy felt satisfied he had got away with the murder of his half brother Jonathon. He could now return to his original plan, and for that he needed Jabez Mort, the man he was patiently waiting for at this very moment.

A crowd of people came into the tavern, and, for a moment, his view of who entered was obscured by the number of people. His eyes fiercely flicked from one person to the next, until their gaze fell upon a small but well built man in a cloak, with his hood up against the weather. He had separated himself from the newly arrived and rowdy crowd and sat himself at an empty table. He was obviously not from the area due to his Moorish looks. The man ordered beer and food and then threw back his hood to reveal very dark curly hair, olive skin and dark eyes which looked around the room until they saw Benjy watching him from the far table. The man nodded and beckoned Benjy with a simple flick of the hand and then he looked away to watch his beer being delivered to his table.

At first Benjy was taken aback. How did this man know him from any other man there, and why did he call him over? Did he know he was looking for him? Benjy wondered and frowned, the man's look had been hard and it had made Benjy uncomfortable. Still, he was here to meet him so meet him he would. He rose, picked up his beer and walked over to the man's table.

"Doest thee answer to ye name of Jabez Mort?" Benjy said.

"Aye. How may I help thee?" Jabez said and looked up at the young man, squinted his eyes as if measuring Benjy's soul and watched him carefully.

"I understand from... a friend... thee may help." The last thing Benjy was going to do was reveal that Jabez's name was in his mother's journal.

Benjy had returned to the cottage after the 'search' for his master had ended and everything had settled back to its normal pace. He had sat and reread her journal from end to end and he now had more time to study all the things it described within, including the spells, curses and hexes. He had not been surprised to find out his mother actually was a witch. In fact, it excited him and even more so when he committed to memory all her writings and thoughts from the book, it made him more connected to her. He knew she had shared this knowledge with none other, for the times were too dangerous for such foolish trust. This made him feel special again and worthy of her love.

"Mayhap I can assist thee. Wouldst thou sit?" Jabez offered the bench beside him.

"I thank thee," Benjy placed his beer tankard on the table and sat down wondering how to have this conversation in public.

"Thou art Ann's son, art thee?"

Benjy stared at the man, unable to read anything from his expression nor those deep dark eyes.

"'Tis truth, how doth thee know?"

"She kept it from thy world but nay from me, we were brother and sister of a sort. Thee hast come to me for something... dark?" Jabez whispered the last word and looked about him.

"Why... how doth thee know what I hath come to thee for?" Benjy was again surprised by the foreign looking man.

"First we shalt eat and talk of... such things that others talk of and then we shalt go elsewhere and talk of things thee came for," Jabez said. He then said his thanks to the skinny girl who had just brought his pie over and he ordered Benjy pie too, without even asking if he wanted some.

For the next hour they ate and drank and made small talk of plagues and wars but not of witches and spells.

Benjy began to relax next to the stranger.

If he hath been mother's friend then he shalt be

mine, he thought confidently by the end of the meal.

"Come, we leave," Jabez said and drank down the last of his beer. He stood and walked to the door without looking to see if Benjy had followed him or not.

He had, of course.

The two men walked down the darkened streets, stepping over puddles, manure piles and rotten vegetable leaves left over from the market. They walked the length of several streets and turned left or right until Benjy wasn't exactly sure on which side of town he was. At last, Jabez stopped outside a large, newly built warehouse, which was double the size of a great barn. It sat by the rough dirt road, next to a river, and a small but respectable house had been built close to it.

Benjy wondered if the river was the same one that ran past his mother's secret cottage and tried to think about it in his mind by creating a map of sorts.

Jabez opened the door of the house and stepped over the threshold.

"Come," he said and held the door open

for Benjy to enter. He led the young man down the corridor and into a room with a large fire already burning in the fireplace. Jabez sat in the larger of the two wooden chairs, both of which had padded cushions on the seats, and told his servant, who had silently appeared at his side, to bring the brandy. He then looked at Benjy and nodded to the other chair near the fireplace in an invitation to sit.

Benjy felt strange sitting on the chair in the house of a man who obviously had some money to his name. Normally, he was never allowed to sit in his master's presence and certainly not in a chair. A bench was good enough for a servant in his world, and the sensation of the soft cushioning felt odd to him.

Once sat, he looked around the room and at its modest but rather tasteful furnishings and embellishments.

"What doth thee want of me?" Jabez said getting straight to the point as he looked at Benjy directly from the opposite side of the roaring fireplace.

Benjy looked around for the servant who

would reappear any moment.

"Fear thee not, my servants art loyal unto death," Jabez said ominously.

"Thy name was in mother's journal, as was mention of thy Hangman's Regret, it was some sort of recipe..."

"I knowest of it." Jabez raised a black eyebrow, "but dost thou?"

"Mother wrote a note for mine eyes only in the back of her journal. She asked when I grew to seek you out and get thee to help with it, if ye case against her went badly."

"Ah, thy mother did speak thus to me before they took her to her death. She wanted thee to know thy power and thy heritage."

Benjy frowned at him, not truly understanding him but willing to do whatever his mother had wished of him.

"Hath thee found all thy needs?"

"Yay, they art hidden and safe."

A glass of brandy appeared on the small table next to Benjy and he looked across to see another on the table next to Jabez's seat. He looked around for the servant but they were so fast he just caught a glimpse of a small, dark skinned child disappearing through the doorway, as silent as a mouse.

"Thee wilt drink thy brandy and then fetch thy ingredients to me. We shalt begin at midnight."

Benjy clutched the glass and drank down the brandy in one swallow, the burn of it making him cough and splutter.

Jabez laughed quietly at him and picked up his own glass to make a toast, "thy Hangman's Regret... so it shalt be," he said and sipped at his brandy slowly, appreciating the flavour as it slipped down his throat, caressing it like a woman's gentle touch.

Benjy recovered himself and smiled as the excitement buzzed through his veins, making him feel very alive.

****

Within two hours, Benjy had arrived back at the house with a full wagon and everything the journal had told him to bring. He climbed down, but before he could reach the door of Jabez's house, it opened and Jabez came out wearing his hooded cloak.

"Come," Jabez said and led the way to the large wooden warehouse next door, pulled open the two large entrance doors, and warmth and light flooded out into the night. They temporarily blinded Benjy and made the horse take a side-step in surprise which made a frightened noise in its throat.

Benjy comforted his horse and tapped the reins on the horse's back, encouraging the dark brown stallion to move forward, bringing the wagon into the building. When they were far enough away from the doors, Jabez closed them and walked around to the front of the wagon, just as Benjy climbed down. He patted the horse and looked all around him.

"I wilt show thee where thy ingredients can be placed," Jabez said and walked away from Benjy who was left standing with his mouth open. He had never seen anything like what was before his eyes now and he wondered at it all with the wide eyes of a child.

The building looked like a barn on the inside, with its wooden walls and stalls sectioned off, but that is where the similarities ended. In one stall, there were large piles of rags with big cauldrons full of torn rags, in another, more of the same, the next had more of the big iron cauldrons that looked like they held boiling water and they were suspended over a huge fire pit.

Benjy had no idea what he was looking at and quickly followed Jabez toward the back of the building and through a doorway. This room was different from the rest. It was filled with tables full of jars with liquids and dry plants in them. There were even a few books on a shelf behind and on one table in the middle of the room was a pile of newly made paper. Benjy had never seen paper so large before. It was about four times the size of his mother's journal, which was only the size of his hand. He walked over to the pile and carefully placed his hand on it. The paper was spongy and soft.

"Stop!" Jabez shouted and rushed over, "'Tis worth more than thee can imagine."

Benjy quickly removed his hand, "What art

thee doing here?" He looked round like an amazed child.

"'Tis where I make paper for books. I hath orders from ye Latin School and Harvard College. And, to my joy, there also be a print shop being built upon ye roadside wanting my work to make books too," Jabez said proudly, knowing full well he was the first to make paper in all the towns in New England.

"How dost thee know the way of it?" Benjy said impressed at the man's knowledge.

"I visited Paris and learnt ye ways of making paper from rags there, but 'tis my mother, who was Spanish, learnt ye way of Amate. 'Tis ye art of making paper from bark and she taught me thus," He said holding a piece of thin paper that was quite different from that on the table.

Benjy's mind boggled and he stared at the object in front of him unable to comprehend it. He never imaged paper could be made from rags, never mind from part of a tree.

What a deeply strange world this Jabez Mort lived in with such amazing knowledge and wisdom. Benjy admired him and desperately wanted to be a part of that world.

"Fetch in thy ingredients upon this night and we shalt begin." Jabez said excitedly, the glee on his face obvious.

At last, he would be able to create the Hangman's Regret and see the ungodly power for himself.

Chapter Fourteen

1846, New York City

The room was almost dark, being lit by only a couple of candles, and the corners were filled with darkness and the unknown. The flickering light from the slight breeze made it seem as if creatures were dancing in the recesses of the room.

The Scribe picked up the freshly cut goose feather and shaped the tip, and, once pleased with the result, laid it back down on the wooden table next to the bottle of oak gall ink and a wood handled knife. The Scribe removed the cork and poured some of the ink into a small bowl and then re-corked the ink bottle. Taking the sharp knife, the Scribe made a small cut on their thumb. They squeezed the appendage and allowed the blood to drip into the awaiting ink. Once the blood had stopped flowing, the hands turned toward the book which sat squat and fat, full of old pages and long forgotten people. One hand lovingly caressed the wooden boards that served as the cover, protecting both the contents and its magickal purpose.

The hands opened the book and carefully turned the centuries-old pages with their ink that had darkened over time, as oak gall ink does, until at last they found a blank page.

The Scribe picked up the quill, dipped it into the bloodied ink and wrote at the top of the pristine page: "The pen is mightier than the sword," and chuckled darkly to them self.

For a moment the Scribe paused, knowing full well the consequences of unguarded wording and then began to write their own desires upon the page, each word crafted carefully and each letter soaked into the unusual paper making a reddish-brown mark on the page.

The Scribe described every action and

reaction to their needs in minute detail as one missed conclusion or misdirection could cause the entire endeavour to fail, or worse, horribly backfire and create much danger for the Scribe. When the writing had been finished to the Scribe's satisfaction, they sat back and let out a breath which they didn't realise they had been holding, and swallowed hard. Their heartbeat was pounding and their breath came quickly. Although they had done much magickal work before, this was the first time they had written in the book since it had come to them.

Soon everything would begin to shift and change and the Scribe would have what they wanted, and there was an ecstatic smile on the Scribe's face.

Now the world and time would conform to the Scribe's will.

They now held control over everyone in the past, the present and the future, it was a heady feeling. The Scribe thought about what they had written of their vision directly onto the pages. They gently lay their hands upon the book and waited.

Far away, in a house by the sea, a woman lay awake in an ornately carved bed by her loving husband who was sound asleep. She had lain as such since retiring for the evening and had pretended to sleep when her husband came to bed. As soon as her husband began to snore, she reached under her pillow and pulled out one of his hunting knives. The full moon that seeped in through the gap in the heavy curtains glinted off the blade as she jumped up, straddled him and before he could awake and react she thrust the sharp metal into her husband's throat just below his Adam's apple. She pushed the blade through his neck until she felt the skin at the back of it pop as the blade burst through.

The man vainly struggled for his life as he gurgled and slowly drowned in his own blood, the warm red mess spreading itself over the white sheets and soaking into the blankets, pillow and mattress.

The woman held the blade in his throat and gripped his body between her knees as the last of his bucking strength left him and he went limp beneath her. Only then did she release him from her grasp, leaving the knife embedded in his throat. She climbed off the bed and for a moment looked at the corpse of her beloved husband by the light of the moon. There was no expression upon her face: not glee, nor sadness. It was utterly blank and even her eyes seemed lifeless.

Seemingly in a daze, the woman went downstairs, pulled on her evening coat and went to her husband's private study. Unlocking a drawer in his desk, she removed a large, tin full of paper money and land deeds, and calmly left her once happy family home.

****

The man arrived at his hovel tired and hungry. He had been scouring the streets and the market area for scraps of food that had been cast aside. He had done well this evening and had found a limp cabbage, two soft carrots and a perfect turnip which must have rolled off a barrow unseen by the vendor. It may not be much, but at least his family would eat for the next few days, and that was all that mattered.

Just as the man reached out for the doorknob of his battered and broken door, a woman stepped out of the darkness next to him, making him jump. The man instinctively reached for the knife in his belt, but upon seeing the woman who was dressed as a lady of society and holding a box in both hands, he stopped himself.

The woman looked him in the eye and placed the tin box at the man's feet, but did not say a word. Turning slowly she walked away.

The man stared at her and then down at the tin box. He could see her hand prints still on it, and as he peered closer he saw the imprints were made of blood. He looked again in the direction she had gone, but she must have turned the corner for he could no longer see her. Thinking for a moment and worrying what might be in the strange, bloodied box, he picked it up, feeling the weight of it in his hands. Looking around him to make sure no one saw him, he entered his shabby home bewildered by the sudden and peculiar event. His mind could find no reasoning for such an occurrence.

The woman reached the street and waited.

She knew a horse-drawn cab would be along shortly, as this was the main thoroughfare between the wealthy homes and the brothels, taverns and gambling houses. Her wait was not a long one and she watched as a cab soon appeared at the end of the street. Pulling the short barrelled gun from her deep coat pocket she shot it into the air, making the horse panic and break into a gallop despite the efforts of its driver. As the cab came almost level with her, she threw herself onto its path and was crushed beneath the horse's hooves and killed instantly. Her murder-suicide made the newspaper and it became a huge mystery as to why she did it. She and her husband had been very happy and extremely popular in their social circle.

The poor man, whom the woman had given the box to had quickly moved his family far away from their hovel and the poor area of town. He elevated their station with the money and the property deeds, which she had signed over to him, from the strange, quiet lady, and soon he had several businesses and a shipping company that transported items from the West Indies to the Americas. Within his lifetime, the family became one of the wealthiest families in the land and had a hand in most of the trading, legal and otherwise, with all the other international shipping companies, but none were larger than his.

He had so many questions, not least of which was how she knew his name to transfer the properties.

They never did know why the woman gave them all the money and deeds nor why she had done the terrible things she had done. One thing the family always remembered: the money had truly been blood money and her husband and the woman herself had paid for it.

The newly elevated family were very pleased it wasn't them and they also went on to build a hidden criminal empire from it.

It was a very different life from the one they were going to lead before everything changed.

Chapter Fifteen

Present Day

Amy finally returned from her visit to the auction. Maggie had driven them back to the book shop and had been preoccupied the whole journey back. Amy didn't mind the quiet journey. It gave her time to reflect on Cabot Tanner, the wealthy, handsome man with the most amazing eyes. She felt like a teenager again, mentally drooling over some good looking guy and she forcefully put him to the back of her mind once she was back in her truck and on the road home.

Seeing Morton Creek again, and the spot where she was convinced she'd seen Emily the serial killer, she couldn't wait to get home and talk to Erda and just hoped that she found out something. Even if Erda proved Amy to be crazy that would be better than actually finding out Emily was still alive.

Which is impossible, of course. Right? she thought, trying to convince herself it actually was.

Amy found Erda up in her room in the attic and she had been busily filling it with bottles and plants. There were bundles of herbs drying upside down from the rafters and also on the shelves on the wall opposite, the place was beginning to fill up with old-looking books with the occasional new one dotted in amongst them. Amy couldn't imagine how and where she got the books from, but wasn't surprised. Erda was a resourceful Spirit after all.

Erda was sitting in her rocking chair by the fire, peering thoughtfully into the empty fireplace, the day being entirely too hot for a fire.

"This place is looking great!" Amy said as she climbed the last two steps of the stairs and walked over to the new chair on the opposite side of the fireplace to Erda. She had decided to buy another chair as she knew she would be spending much time sitting and talking to Erda here, so she might as well be comfy when doing it.

"Thank thee," Erda said but didn't look up and her voice sounded quieter than usual as if she was deeply distracted by something.

"Are you okay?" Amy asked and sat down.

"Aye."

"You don't look it, or sound it, are you sure?"

"Aye... what would thee do if I tell thee Emily, that devil's woman, is alive?" Erda's head turned toward Amy and her eyes looked directly into Amy's.

"I... what? Why? Is she? Fuck. No. She can't be... we saw her die!" Amy said and sprang out of the chair and began pacing back and forth. "But... how?" she said and stopped to look at Erda.

"Nay knowest yet. What wilt thee do?"

"Do? Erm... shit... I, well we, no, I, of course... I will go to the cops and get them to arrest her," Amy said as she sat back down. "Yes! I will go to see Detective Andy and 'cus he knows about her... from before... well, yes, he can arrest her."

"Aye, wise," Erda nodded.

"We must do it now, before she kills again or... oh god, what if she comes after me again?" Amy stared at Erda, paralysed by the fear as it crawled up her spine and strangled her mind until no more thoughts could be formed.

"She will nay get in thy house, I hath been warding it with all ye charms and blood protection I can muster from my memory. My Alma was very good at such things. Nay evil and dark may pass my thresholds."

"Thank goodness for your dear grandmother, because if she hadn't taught you... well, I don't like to think about it." Amy's mind didn't want to think about how unprotected she would feel without Erda's wardings and so she forced herself not to think about it. She turned her mind to the current problem.

"Just how the hell did she survive? Are you sure she's real and not a ghost?"

"Like I a'fore mentioned she is nay Spirit. She be like thee, full of blood and bone."

"Oh god." Amy slumped in the chair. She

felt like all the air and her very bones had been sucked out of her body, leaving her breathless and limp.

"Hmm..." Erda said to the fire.

"What?"

"Mayhaps there be something else a'foot."

"Something else?" Amy said, sounding horrified. "Like what?"

"Hast thou noticed a strangeness upon ye air, such that thou feels things are wrong but thy nay knowest why?"

"No, well, not really?" Amy said and thought for a while "But..."

"Aye?" Erda tilted her head in enquiry.

"Well, it's just that a lot happened when we were away on the book tour... I mean, normal things, but now I think about it, they all seemed to happen at once. Yeah, but that's life isn't it, don't they say that bad things come in threes?" Amy laughed a little and thought it sounded like a nervous laugh. Then she frowned because the more she thought about it the more everything seemed strange, kind of off tilt, like... well, like, what... she didn't know exactly.

"'Tis true some things come thrice, tell me as sure as thee may be what happened whence we returned?"

Amy listed off the small and what she had originally presumed to be innocent changes of a normal life as Erda listening intently to every word.

"Agreed, these are expected each on their own but together mayhaps not. I wilt think on it all," Erda said and, once again, looked back into the empty grate of the fireplace.

Amy watched her and knew it was how she did her best thinking, even if she herself couldn't see the attraction of it. She understood it more when there was a fire as she also found flames entrancing and often stared into them, but an empty grate? Maybe it was a 17th century thing.

"Right. So...about Emily? What shall I do?" Amy said as she nibbled her lip and frowned.

"Thee should tell Detective Andy, so he knowest ye truth."

"Hmm... not relishing that conversation one bit," Amy said and sat looking gloomily out of the attic window at the beautiful blue sky of summer.

****

To distract herself and put off calling Detective Andy, at least until she had got her brain around what was going on, Amy decided to spend some time in the garden with Erda. She found her in the herb garden removing weeds and tending the plants, "Hey, the garden is looking lovely, you definitely have green thumbs."

Erda, who was kneeling on the ground, looked at her soil-covered hands and thumbs, "Nay, mine thumbs art brown with soil," she said, frowned and looked up at Amy.

"You're so literal. No, it means you have the ability to grow green things, plants, shrubs etc.," Amy said with a smile. She always found it amusing when the difference in the English language over the last four hundred years brought unique conversations like this one.

"Why wouldst growing green things maketh my mine thumbs a'coloured?"

"Just one of those sayings."

"Ye hath a lot of ye strange sayeths, dost thee nay?"

"Yes, I guess we do. Never really thought much about it until you came along."

"Aye, well. Sit thee and I shalt teach thee a charm my Alma taught me upon her lap."

"Oh, that would be great," Amy said with a smile and sat on the grass, at the edge of the herb garden, and looked expectantly at Erda.

"Ye must remember this great charm, so thee can use it for a'many things. 'Tis the Nine Herbs Charm, so listen with all thy heart." Erda rubbed the soil off her hands, sat back on to the ground and arranged her skirts around her.

"Ye Nine Herbs Charm is used to treat thy wounds against nine poisons and many dis-eases. 'Tis what thee calls in-fek-tions now, I doth believe.

"Remember, Mugwort,
what ye maketh known,
What ye arranged at ye Great proclamation.
Ye were called Una, ye oldest of herbs,
Ye hath power against three

and against thirty,
Ye hath power against poison
and against dis-eases,
Ye hath power against ye loathsome foe roving
through ye land.

And ye, Plantain, mother of herbs,
Open from ye east, mighty inside.
Over ye chariots creaked,
over ye queens rode,
Over ye brides cried out,
over ye bulls snorted.
Ye withstood all of them,
ye dashed against them.
May ye likewise withstand poison
and dis-ease and ye loathsome foe roving
through ye land.

Stune is ye name of this herb,
it grew on a stone,
it stands up against poison,
it dashes against poison
Viper's Bugloss it is called,
it attacks against poison,

It drives out ye hostile one,
it casts out poison.
This is ye herb that fought against ye serpent,
It hath power against poison,
it hath power against dis-ease,
It hath power against ye loathsome
foe roving through ye land.
Put to flight now, Venom-loather,
ye greater poisons,
Though ye are ye lesser,
until he is cured of both.

Remember, Chamomile,
what ye made known,
What ye accomplished at Alorford,
That never a man should lose his life from dis-ease
After Chamomile 'twas prepared for his food.

This is ye herb that is called Wergulu.
A seal sent it across ye sea-right,
A vexation to poison, a help to others.
It stands against pain, it dashes against poison,

A worm came crawling, it killed nothing.

For Woden took nine glory-twigs,
He smote ye adder that it flew
apart into nine parts.
There ye Apple accomplished
it against poison
That ye loathsome serpent would
never dwell in ye house.

Chervil and Fennel, two of much might,
They were created by ye wise Lord,
Holy in the Tree as He hung;
He set and sent them to ye seven worlds,
To ye wretched and ye fortunate,
as a help to all.
It stands against pain, it fights against poison,
It avails against 3 and against 30,
Against foe´s hand and
against noble scheming,
Against enchantment of vile creatures.

Now there nine herbs hath power
against nine evil spirits,
Against nine poisons and
against nine dis-eases:

Against ye red poison,
against ye foul poison,
Against ye white poison,
against ye pale blue poison,
Against ye yellow poison,
against ye green poison,
Against ye black poison,
against ye blue poison,
Against ye brown poison,
against ye crimson poison,
Against worm-blister,
against water-blister,
Against thorn-blister,
against thistle-blister,
Against ice-blister,
against poison-blister,

If any poison comes flying from ye east,
Or any from ye north, or any from ye south,
Or any from ye west among ye people.
Woden stood over dis-eases of every kind.

I alone know a running stream,
and ye nine adders beware of it.

May all ye weeds spring up from their roots,
Ye seas slip apart, all salt water,
When I blow this poison from you." [1]

"Wow! I have to remember all that?" Amy said.

"Aye, each and every word I didst speak. I shalt say it again showing ye each of ye herbs and I shalt explain ye making of ye charm anon." Erda stood up, ready to take Amy to each of the nine herbs that she had ensured where planted in Amy's garden when she had planned it out.

"Ok, but first, I'll record you on my phone, otherwise I will never remember it," Amy said and withdrew her phone from her shorts pocket, found the recording app and tapped it to start.

"How wilt ye get it out of thy phone?" Erda said, intrigued.

"I will just play it back over and over and it will help me to memorize every word. I'll show you when we are done."

"Aye, thy must," Erda said, and continued to repeat the charm, saying each part of it next to the relevant herbs so Amy could put the name to the actual plant.

"What's Stune?" Amy said.

"'Tis lamb's cress, aye?"

"Ah okay," Amy said remembering that is was something to do with the watercress family. "Wergulu and Viper's Bugloss? Never heard of those either."

"Wergulu is Nettle and Viper's Bugloss is ye Blueweed. Now I tell thee of how to prepare and use this charm. Take ye mugwort, plantain open from the east, stune, viper's bugloss, chamomile, nettle, apple, chervil and fennel, and old soap; pound ye herbs to powder, mix them with ye soap and ye juice of the apple. Prepare a paste of water and of ashes, take fennel, boil it with ye paste and wash it with a beaten egg when you apply ye salve, both before and after. Then sing thy charm three times on each of ye herbs before ye prepare them, and likewise on ye apple. And sing thy same charm into ye mouth of ye man and into both his ears, and on ye wound, before ye apply ye salve."

"How wonderful. Thank you, Erda. Truly

fascinating. Does it work?" Amy Said.

"Aye, if thy adds a little of thy own magicks," Erda said with a knowing smile.

Chapter Sixteen

Several times Amy had called Detective Andy's office, but each time his answering service picked up her call and each time she hung up without leaving a message. She sat on her patio looking out over the garden, which Erda had been working on since they had returned from the book tour. She was already eating some of its produce, thanks to Erda's green thumbs.

Can ghosts have a green thumb? Amy frowned and wondered.

The garden now had four sections: the lawn area with a new deck, and on it were chairs, a table and a large, shiny BBQ. There was also the now overflowing vegetable garden, a herb garden and an expansion to the old orchard where the new fruit trees would be planted once they arrived from the nursery.

Putting her cell phone down on the table and picking up the glass of iced tea, she sipped it enthusiastically, enjoying the taste and the cool liquid sensation as it slipped down. The morning was warm and before it really heated up, Amy wanted to visit Maggie and the bookstore to see how the renovations next door were coming along. Amy's heart sank with disappointment and sadness when she thought of the store that had once been Bryer's. She still was amazed at how he had dropped her without even a word of goodbye and she missed him terribly, but she knew she had to let him go and move on with her life.

Breathing in deeply and then letting the air out in a sigh, Amy picked up the phone again to ring Detective Andy one last time. This time she decided she would leave a message for him. She waited for the beep.

"Hi, Detective Andy..." Amy's brain stalled. She had no idea what she was going to say. How do you tell someone that a person has come back from the dead or something to that effect?

"Erm... I just saw, well, yesterday, I saw..." *Oh get a grip*, she thought. "The murderer, Emily Carpenter, is still alive. I saw her on Main Street here in Morton Creek. You need to arrest her before more people die," she said and hung up, pleased with herself for doing the right thing and her civic duty.

"Didst thee tell thy friend, Andy?" Erda said suddenly by Amy's side.

"Shit!" Amy said and sat bolt upright in her chair.

"Art thee well?" Erda said, her eyebrows puckered in concern.

"Yes. Oh, damn it. I forgot to leave my name, now he will think it is some loony calling him," Amy stared at the phone still in her hand. "Hmm... " she said, wondering if she should call him back. "Nah... another message really would make me sound crazy, wouldn't it? He will work out who called him simply by me mentioning Emily's name. I think," she said more to herself rather than to Erda. However, she remembered just how profoundly the case had disturbed him before and she didn't envy him listening to her message.

"Aye," Erda said and sat next to Amy at the table. "I wilt be making a partitive unguent. It wilt be ready anon. Thinking thee and I shouldst visit yon night and see how Emily doth survive."

"Are you serious? You want us to take our Spirits back to that horrible night that nearly killed me and Bryer, again?" Amy said as fear rippled down her spine at even the mention of it.

"Aye, 'tis ye only way to knowest of her fate."

"But... crap, I know you are right, but I really don't want to see all that again," Amy rubbed her forehead. She was beginning to get a headache.

"Sadly, 'tis needed. But thy wilt be safe as Spirit, thy knows this."

"I know... I know," Amy said and finished her drink in two large gulps. "I need a real drink before we do that. When will it be ready? The unguent, I mean?"

"I must gather ye herbs and melt the wax... 'twill be ready shortly."

"Right, well... first, I'm off to town to see Maggie and get a stiff drink over lunch. We can do it when I get back," Amy said firmly and walked into the cottage, grabbed her keys and headed out towards her father's old truck, putting all thoughts of what they must do tonight out of her head, at least for a while.

****

The doorbell rang as Amy walked into the book store. She loved visiting her friend and now business partner in the store, as it felt so calm and relaxing in there. She loved the wooden bookshelves that overflowed with stories, the coffee shop at the back with its warm colours, as well as the small nooks you could drink your coffee and read a book in. Indeed, she loved everything about the place.

"Hey, didn't expect you today."

Amy whirled around and smiled at Maggie who was standing next to a cardboard box with a box-knife in her hand.

"Thought you might like to come to lunch

with me.”

“Oh, what a good idea. Just let me finish this box and I’ll get Rob to take over for me.”

Rob, the young man who had been working with Maggie for the last couple of months, had recently left school and was filling time and his bank account before going off to the Henry Dale University in a few weeks. He was a tall, spotty youth with a generous laugh, kind heart, and a genuine love for books.

“Sure, no worries. I’ll go for a wander amongst the books until you’re ready.”

With a nod and a grin, Maggie bent back over the box to cut the tape with the knife, her red wavy, long hair falling down from her shoulder like the velvet curtains that swished across a stage at the end of a play.

Amy walked slowly down the left side of the store, eyes flicking from one title to the next, taking in book cover images and names, delighting in the thought that she now owned fifty percent of the place. Her slow paces suddenly stopped as her eyes caught sight of a certain book. ‘The Complete Witch’s Handbook’, the title read in big bold letters, by Michael Hornsborough. Her interest was piqued, and she slid the book off the shelf. She glanced at the large pentagram on the cover, opened the book and flicked through a few of the pages wondering if the subject matter in it was anything like the wonderful things Erda was currently trying to teach her. A few pages in, she could see that it wasn't the same at all, and put the book back on the shelf.

She continued to look along the same shelf until she spotted 'The Cunning Ways' by J. T. Burgess. Pulling it out, her heart lifted when she saw the cover showed plants and herbs, a couple of animal skulls and a subheading that read: 'Folklore and Country Remedies'. Opening it, she peered inside, feeling like she was looking at a book full of secrets. Her heartbeat raced, as her eyes flicked down the list of contents seeing that this was more like what she was after and similar to what Erda talked about. She smiled to herself and resolved to buy the book on the spot.

"That is an excellent choice," A smooth voice said from behind her.

Amy turned and stood stock-still, trying to

believe her eyes.

There, standing right before her, was Cabot Tanner in all his sexy glory. He was groomed to perfection, as if he was attending a function in high society and not lurking in a small bookshop in a small town in the wilds of Canada.

Well, as wild as Morton Creek got, her brain reminded her as it tried to think of something to say. "Oh, hello again," was all that came out of her mouth.

"Hello," he said and smiled a perfect and most charming smile. "Again."

He had made the word 'again' feel like it was the Fates that had connived to bring them together once more.

"Yes, um..." Amy said and tried hard to pull herself together. "Have you read it?" She blurted out. *Of course, he hasn't! Are you crazy? What would a man like him, a man who had everything, or could have everything he wanted, be doing reading a book on the old ways?* her mind answered ridiculously astonished at her idiocy.

"Actually, yes, I have and it's probably one of the best in the field, as it were," he said and narrowed his eyes at her. "More importantly, are you going to read it?"

"I erm... yes, I was thinking about it," Amy said and glanced down at the book and then back at him. The break in eye contact helped her to get her mind back on track, and, when she looked back up at him, he didn't seem quite so radiant as she first thought. He seemed just a little too perfect, a little plastic even.

"Oh, really. I wonder for what purpose. Perhaps it is for research for another novel?" He said as those hypnotic eyes looked into hers.

There it was again, a pull in her torso like he had tied a rope about her waist, holding the end and it was pulling her towards him. Amy blinked and the pull was broken again.

"Something like that," she said a little haughtily, disliking the feeling and walked past him to the counter where Maggie had been watching the exchange with a deep frown on her face.

"You okay?" Maggie asked, not bothering to lower her voice.

"Yup," Amy said, placing the book on the

counter and determinedly tried not to look over her shoulder at Cabot. "I want to buy this one."

"Oh, that is a good one. I didn't realise you were interested in the Cunning Ways," Maggie said, "but I should have guessed really after your last book."

"Yes, it seems my... my ancestors practised the art, or so I am made to understand," Amy said, feeling not quite sure how to say it without saying she lived with the Spirit of her ancestor who was a Wise Woman and a practitioner of those Cunning Ways. Not knowing where to look so that she didn't have to peer into Maggie's eyes and let her see she was hiding something, Amy looked back at Cabot who was standing and looking inside a book and definitely not looking at her. However, she got the distinct feeling he was listening to their conversation and she quickly looked back at Maggie who had been watching her the whole time. Amy felt very conspicuous and uncomfortable suddenly.

"You don't have to buy it, you are an owner here now. I'll just write it off," she said with a reassuring smile.

"Thanks," Amy said and smiled at her friend, feeling once again relaxed and comfortable with her.

"You're welcome. I'll just tell Rob we're off and get my purse."

Amy watched her friend go through the door marked 'Private', which led to the storeroom and Maggie's office.

Within a moment Maggie was back and she put her arm through Amy's and walked toward the door without another word.

Amy had to force herself not to look back to see if Cabot was watching them but she knew deep in her soul he was.

****

"Gods that was good," Maggie said as she leaned back in her chair, wiped her mouth on the napkin and placed it on her empty plate.

"Yes, it was," Amy said and took a swallow of her red wine. She was only having one glass, as she was driving, but she was enjoying it so much she wished she could have another. *Perhaps I'll nip to the booze shop on the way home and stock up again,* she thought to herself as her eyes roamed the motley crew in the bar.

The White Oak bar was one of those places that looked shabby, but the staff were friendly and the food was excellent.

"It was a surprise to see Cabot here," Amy said, "in town, I mean. Does he come to Morton Creek often? I wouldn't have thought it was his kind of place, not up-market enough for him."

"Yeah, he has a cottage out by the lake. When I say cottage I mean mansion, of course. He is a bit further up the lake from your place, I believe."

"Oh, wow. Had no idea he lived out here, thought he would have some fancy place in Glendale or one of the bigger cities."

"Oh, he does. Apparently, he has several places in several countries," Maggie said with a tone of distaste.

"There's really something about that guy you don't like, isn't there? Care to share it?"

"Nope, not over a pleasant lunch like this, perhaps one day over a bottle of good scotch."

"I knew you were my kind of friend," Amy said and laughed, delighted that her friend loved a good scotch as well as a glass of red just as she did.

Maggie laughed loudly. She was one of those people that never 'hid her light' as they say, she always laughed and talked with gusto and smiled often.

Although Amy's British upbringing had made her more shy of being bold in public in such an unguarded way, her friendship with Maggie helped her to relax those polite rules a little. Although they had been drilled into her from a young age, now she found a great freedom in the way Maggie made her feel and act.

"A few friends and I are having a bit of a party on Saturday. Would you like to come?" Maggie said with a smile. "I think you will like meeting them; they're a fun group and they are all dying to meet the famous author who is now my business partner."

"Oh, how lovely of them, but somewhat embarrassing too. I would love to come though, is it somebody's birthday?"

"No, it's the Summer Solstice and we

always have a party on it," Maggie said and peered at Amy as if gauging her reaction to what she said.

Amy saw the look and wondered at it. "Sure, I would love to."

"Good," Maggie seemed pleased with her answer. "It's at my place, I'll text you the address and time."

"Okay, great. Actually, I'm looking forward to seeing your place, we've been close friends for a few months now and I've never seen it, probably because you work too much," Amy grinned, "I'm really rather nosey when it comes to homes. They can tell you so much about a person. I have often wondered what the 'book lady's' home would be like even before we became friends."

"Full of books, of course." Maggie grinned. "It's small but I love it."

"It's important to love where you live and want to go home to it every day. I adore my place and I'm so glad I didn't sell it after all," Amy said.

Maggie checked her watch. "Damn, better get back. Don't want to leave Rob alone too long. I know he has Laura in the café, but still, she will be busy too," Maggie said and rooted in her bag for the money to pay for her half of the bill.

Amy held up her hand.

"Hey, don't worry about it, I'll pay. I invited you to lunch, remember?" she said with a smile and picked up the bill before Maggie could argue.

"Oh, ok thanks. So I'll see you on Saturday?" she said, stood up, and hugged Amy goodbye.

"Sure will," Amy said as she hugged her back.

She waved goodbye as her lovely friend walked out of the bar with a smile upon her face. Amy paid the bill and returned to her truck and ran some errands.

Picking up a few groceries, a crate of wine from the local liquor store and a bottle of something special for the party, Amy drove home slowly as she mentally prepared herself to use the unguent that Erda would have made by now, to visit the past and that terrible night once again.

A deep, dark feeling of dread spread along Amy's spine.

She would rather do anything, absolutely anything in the world right at that moment, rather than go back in time and revisit that horrendous night once again.

Chapter Seventeen

Wednesday, 31st October,
Last Year, Canada

It felt like Amy had closed her eyes for only a millisecond, when she began to open them and blearily refocus.

The Partitive Unguent still smelled in her nose. The mixture smelt odd, but it was a pleasant smell of gardens and cut grass, of sweet herbs and green growing things. The unguent was made of melted wax and several herbs that had been crushed and mixed into the slowly hardening wax. Erda had smeared the greasy ointment across Amy's brow. Amy had felt the warmth of it upon her face and found it comforting, like a mug of hot chocolate on a cold winter's day. It had made her warm and relaxed and she soon drifted off as if to sleep while she lay on her bed, and then she fell into the blackness. An odd thought occurred to Amy: she could still smell the unguent on her body but now she was no longer in her body and was Spirit with Erda. *How can I still smell it? Amy wondered.*

Amy's mind cleared quickly, as did her vision, and she saw her corporeal self dimly in the semi darkness. She was sitting tied to a chair with a blindfold on, less than three feet away from her. It was an usual and particularly strange thing to see yourself doing something in the past and also be observing oneself at the same time. It made Amy dizzy for a moment.

"Art thy well?" Erda said from beside her, her voice not lowered as no one could hear nor see either of them in this form.

"Yes, just a little lightheaded."

"Aye, 'tis right when faced with thyself."

Amy watched her other self as she struggled with the panic that rose in her from being kidnapped and tied up in a strange room.

Amy remembered the feeling of helplessness and fear as she sat there waiting for god knows what to happen to her. Her stomach lurched at the thought of it, and she wasn't sure she could go through all this again.

The three of them, Erda and the corporeal and Spirit Amy, heard a door creak open and a light switched on. Footfalls could be heard on what sounded like wooden steps. They came closer and almost overhead. The Amy who was bound to the chair continued trying to shout for help despite the revolting gag that was shoved in her mouth. The Spirits watched as she was blinded by the bright light when her blindfold was suddenly ripped off, pulling some of her hair with it. She winced, blinked several times, and tried to focus her pupils, which reacted sluggishly from the drug she had been given when abducted. Slowly the blurred image began to coalesce as her vision cleared.

"There is no point making all that fuss, no one can hear you."

The bound Amy stared at the person before her, unable to believe her eyes, nor contemplate the truth of it.

Emily Carpenter stood over Amy, all five foot three inches of her, she was, and looked like, a frail old woman well past retirement age. Her grey hair was neatly coiffed as she stood in her pretty floral dress with her Chanel style jacket over it.

Amy just gaped at her unbelievingly.

"I still can't believe it was her, she looks so... so incapable of such horrors," Spirit Amy said to Erda.

"Aye, evil doth come in all shapes and sizes," Erda said as she calmly watched the events unfold.

Emily grinned. It was the most frighteningly evil smile that either of the Amys had ever seen, it was the smile of a psychopath. Emily took a step closer and yanked the foul gag away.

"Help! Help me, someone!" bound Amy shouted as soon as her mouth was free.

The hard slap that made Amy's face sting and her eyes water, came from Emily so fast that Amy just didn't see it coming.

"I told you no one can hear you, so stop making that horrendous noise and have some dignity," she said as she walked behind Amy.

"I think we shalt move forth a little," Erda said and reached out for Amy's hand just inches from hers.

Spirit Amy's vision blurred and the scene raced forward like some demented fast-forward on a TV, until it suddenly stopped.

"Time to give you a front row seat, I think," Emily said as she dragged Amy's chair round to face the opposite direction, making a horrendous wood-on-cement scraping noise as she did so.

Spirit Amy and Erda looked across the room at the thing they had both been determinedly ignoring until now.

Bound Amy's eyes nervously swivelled as the chair moved around. Deep in her heart, she expected to see instruments of torture and pain, but what she really saw stalled her mind so completely that it could no longer function properly. Her drowning mind only decided to fixate itself on the fact that the old woman was much, much stronger than she should have been, almost inhumanly so.

"There, what do you think of our masterpiece, quite beautiful, isn't it?" Emily said, her voice rang clear and proud.

In front of them all, on an old wooden table, was a partially skinned, dead body.

It was also a body that had been opened up to expose all of its internal organs. As the smells of both the body and the chemicals, combined with the horrific sight overloaded her senses, bound Amy instantly vomited on the floor, narrowly missing her right shoe. She spat the last of the vomit away and looked back up. Sadly, her eyes couldn't help but refocus on the hideous thing before her. She could see that each of its organs had been stitched into place, however, and what made this image worse, was the glaring fact that the body had only small amounts of skin on it. They were sewn together also, like a skin suit which did not cover the whole body. The rest of it was just muscles, bones and the newly added organs.

"This has been my life's work, and,

although it's taken several years to collect the parts from the various sources, my final creation is a thing of beauty, is it not?" Emily gloated over her repulsive creation with the look of an old master appreciating their latest painting or sculpture.

"Fuck me, you are insane," bound Amy said. Now comprehending the enormity of the woman's crimes, she knew now that many people must have lost their lives for this monstrosity worthy of Frankenstein himself, and, what made it even more revolting was that Emily was talking about it as if she has just restored an old classic car from parts found at a junkyard.

"Of course I'm not," Emily said, "No insane person could accomplish all this," Emily gestured with her hands towards the gruesome thing that resembled a body.

"Please move us on, I can't see it all again," Spirit Amy said, her voice a little higher and her throat tighter than normal as the fear and loathing of the situation slowly infected her like a creeping fog over land.

Erda did as Spirit Amy wished and once

again images whizzed past and stopped again. They watched in subdued horror at the scene before them waiting for the right moment, for the very reason they were there.

A groan drew bound Amy's attention back from the thing on the table to Emily and her weird ritual, or whatever it was, around the corpse. She was no longer chanting, and a low groaning emanated from her lips, and then she began to violently shake. Amy had no clue what was happening as she watched horrified, wondering if Emily was having a seizure of some sort. Finally, the shaking stopped and Emily panted, desperately out of breath, and she clutched the edge of the table for support. Recovering her breath slowly, she hobbled around the table to the work bench, picking up the strange glass jar.

Bound Amy noticed that Emily was trembling now, her hands shaking, and she didn't look as strong as she had just moments ago, as even her walking was more laboured.

Emily clutched the jar to her breast like a prized possession and watched the corpse intently, and, although her face looked tired and haggard, the look of absolute awe on it was unmistakable.

At first, bound Amy couldn't see what Emily was looking at, as she was seated and had less of a view. In front of their eyes, the corpse of patchwork organs began to knit together, literally. Incredibly, the incisions and sutures vanished one by one as the body sealed them together, as if they had never been separate items. Then, the three of them, Erda and the two Amys, watched in horror as the body began to grow its own skin from the sewn patches covering parts of it.

Spirit Amy shuddered and felt the bile rise in her throat and then remembered she was there without her body and the need to vomit was only in her mind.

A terrible feeling crept over bound Amy, what would happen when it had all of its skin? And, by the looks of it, that wouldn't be long now, as the skin had grown over most of the body except for the chest area and the face like ice slowly hardening toward the centre of a pond.

The skin on the face began to grow over the red muscles and the white bones. Emily leaned forward and pressed the mask in her hand, which was attached to the bottle, to the newly formed lips and nose. With a click of the valve, a hissing noise could be heard, and then what sounded very much like a sharp intake of breath by the corpse. Emily took the mask away and was smiling a most wondrous smile, "Welcome, my friend," She said as the corpse began to breathe deeply and noisily.

Bound Amy's brain stalled once again due to utter shock at this new development. *How could it be breathing? It was a corpse*, she thought and she just stared at the abomination in front of her eyes.

At that moment, a second Spirit Erda appeared silently next to Amy and watched the events unfold with her.

"Wait! This is not right!" Spirit Amy said.

"Aye, 'tis nay right. 'Tis an abomination of nature."

"No, I mean, this is not how it happened. Before you arrived Bryer was here under the spell she cast on him and she shot him, remember?" Spirit Amy said with a look of puzzlement on her face.

"Is thee sure? He arrived a'fore me?" Erda said suddenly looking at Spirit Amy.

"Yes, definitely. I remember every little detail about this night, like I could ever forget this crazy shit."

"Something else is a'foot then," Erda said, frowned and continued to watch herself and the other Amy.

After a few noisy breaths, the re-animated corpse sat up and looked around the room with a gleeful, maniacal look upon its face.

The newly reanimated corpse turned its handsome head and looked around the room. Firstly it looked at Emily, then at bound Amy and finally at the Erda from that time. Its eyes lingered for several moments on her but he did not see the future Erda nor Spirit Amy.

There was an utter and complete silence in the basement, not a single word was murmured, and no one moved an inch.

The naked body on the table then did the last thing anyone ever expected, it burst into laughter. It was the deep, rich, joyous laughter of the insane, and Emily joined in as if the corpse had just told a remarkably funny joke that only they understood.

Both sets of Amys and Erdas looked at their respective other halves horrified.

"Holy shit," bound Amy said.

At last, the corpse stopped laughing and just sat there on the table with a huge, satisfied grin on its rather attractive face.

For several more moments, every one continued to look at each other and they still said nothing. It was as if time had stopped entirely, as if the universe itself had refused to continue with such a grotesque miscreation within it.

Finally, the corpse, which was no longer a corpse, looked back at the original Erda, again it smiled but this smile was a cruel and evil one, and it said, "Thy curse is finally broken, thy ruttish hedge-born scut!"

"Thy mouth is still as foul as thy corpse, John." The original Erda said, seemingly unmoved by the whole bizarre event, as if all the clues and strange warnings from her instincts had now clicked into place in her head. She oddly didn't feel alone, it was as if someone else was in the room with them and it somehow gave her strength.

"It's about time you bloody showed up,"

Bound Amy was able to say at last, and somewhat angrily to Erda.

Erda looked deep into Amy's eyes but said nothing to her.

Bound Amy looked again at the once-corpse-now-alive-man who had managed to climb easily off the old table as if he had known and used this new body his entire life. He, apparently, didn't mind being utterly naked in front of everyone as he showed no inhibitions nor embarrassment in the least. Amy realised, with a shock of recognition so great that another frisson of fear ran through her tired body, she was now actually looking at Dr. John Lambe, Erda's former lover, murderer and also Amy's own, many times over great, grandfather. Amy's mouth dried up as she looked from person to person trying to reconcile what she was indeed seeing.

Is this all real? Or am I dreaming? she wondered.

"Thy hex nay longer corrupts me. Many years I doth but try inhabit others. Alas whence I take full control, a'body withered thereupon rotted as thy curse foretold. Thence a kindly thought bid me welcome whereupon our search began a'new." He held out his hand to Emily and, taking hers in his, he kissed it gently.

Emily smiled sweetly, as if to a lover, and passed him a man's pair of trousers and a shirt. She appeared uncomfortable with his nakedness, even if he wasn't. "Remember, your promise, John," she said as he took the clothing from her.

"Aye, Mistress Emily, we shalt come to thee," he said and stroked her cheek gently with an indulgent smile upon his face.

It would have been a nice scene between lovers, if it hadn't been so nauseatingly disgusting, bound Amy thought.

John examined the clothing and put it on slowly as if he didn't have a care in the world. However, the zip on the trousers puzzled him for a while, until Emily reminded him how it worked. They had obviously shared many things together over the years, while his soul resided in her mind, and modern fastenings must have been one of them.

"You, you are the killer of all those people!" bound Amy blurted out, horrified as the thought dawned on her. She wasn't sure whether she spoke to John or Emily or both.

John looked over at her, "Aye, whilst my abode 'twas within Emily, we hath achieved many things of such a wondrous nature."

"What hath thy truly done, John?" Erda said, frowning at him.

"Thou shalt be proud by my cleverness, 'tis all to do with blood," he said with an imperious wave of the hand and paused, as if his brilliance needed to be coaxed from him by fervent acolytes waiting upon his every word.

"May I?" Emily said.

John thought for a moment, "Of course, my loverly," he said, convinced she would make him sound even more impressive and he could then listen to her words and bask in his own glory.

"The illustrious Dr. Lambe could not, unfortunately, hold himself in another body and push out their Soul, without the body decaying, as he said, and, when he chose me, that glorious February day many years ago in England, he found I had some knowledge of the arcane arts too. Between us we worked out that, although he was trying to be whole, he was going about it the wrong way. We formed a partnership and began our heroic search."

"Thy sayeth thy searched a'fore, what pray tell dost thou search for?" Erda said, unfazed by the ridiculous hubris.

"Search for what?" bound Amy said at the same time as Erda and frowned, she felt rather puzzled by all.

"For blood, my dear," Emily said to Amy and smiled at her in a kind way, as if she were a young child asking the simplest of questions. "You see, when his Soul fully possessed the other bodies, they essentially became him again and the curse was triggered, but we came upon a better idea. What if the blood was Erda's? Would the curse then refuse to be triggered because she was the one who had created it in the first place? She had certainly not directed it at herself, of course. So, we decided we would use parts of her bloodline to build a body of her DNA, and, if it was pure enough, his Soul would mix with her blood and the curse would not touch him. He would then live to carry on his glorious and very important work."

"Wait? What?" bound Amy stared at Emily.

"These devils hath killed members of my family, thy family, Amy, just so he couldst return."

"A little succinct but essentially, yes," Emily said, nodding.

"Holy fuck! You killed members of my family just for the spare parts? To build...you?" Amy stared at John, "Jesus Christ! They were your family too. Abigail was your daughter. Do you not feel anything, you bastard?"

"Sweet child, thou art too sentimental. I needed, so I took, 'twas always such," John said as he moved closer to Amy and took her face roughly in his hand. "Thou art lovely, thy sweet breath giveth mine life, gratitude." He swiftly closed the distance between them and kissed her hard on the mouth.

Amy struggled to pull her face away, both sickened and revolted by him and his touch.

Erda stepped forward. She was ready to do something, anything, if he hurt Amy.

John released Amy as quickly as he had

grabbed her and he stood by her with a smug grin on his face.

Amy turned her face away from him, not wanting to see the evil that lived in his eyes.

Emily pulled out a gun from her pocket, raised it and pointed it at bound Amy.

"No!" Amy screamed at the sight of the barrel inches away from her face.

John spun round and took a step nearer to Emily. He quickly and easily knocked the gun from her shaking, gnarled hand.

It startled her and she blinked at him. "But John..." Emily said.

"I shalt complete my own bidding now, dost thou comprehend?" He took a step closer to Emily, "'Tis time for thy due, come hither, my loverly."

"Oh, yes. Yes, please, make me young and beautiful, take away this aged, painful body and the wrinkles, just as you promised," She said as she came into his arms, her voice rising in pitch as her excitement and ecstasy grew.

John held her close and caressed her grey hair, whispering sweet things in her ear and promising many delights of the flesh. All of a sudden, he grabbed her by the hair and pulled her head back and she glared at him, suddenly frightened by his strength. Placing a single hand on her throat, he squeezed it hard until the life fled her body and he dropped her to the ground like an unwanted rag doll. He looked down at her vaguely, and then his eyes quickly flicked away, his interest now permanently lost.

"There... see, she died," Spirit Amy said with satisfaction.

"Aye," Erda said.

They both stayed by the back wall of the basement and waited and watched the scene before them.

The original Erda of that time stood completely still. She said and did absolutely nothing except watch John rather intently.

Bound Amy tried to calm herself and took some deep breaths. She gulped the air in quickly but all that did was make her slightly dizzy. She opened her eyes again and looked at Erda, "Do something for God's sake," She couldn't believe she was just going to stand there and watch.

"I am," she said simply.

"Naught thou canst do, Erda. I am upon ye earth again, whole, thy blood hath healed me. Thou are but Spirit, thou canst achieve naught," he said, realizing he had the upper hand at long last.

Erda moved forward and walked around the other side of John, forcing him to turn around to watch her.

Her eyes flicked to Amy and back at John, while she asked him what he planned to do next and, of course, he was more than happy to boast about his plans. In fact, he explained in great detail how he would find acolytes to teach the Arcane Arts to and then he'd make more children for his grand legacy to continue, gaining wealth and prestige as he went through the years until he was in a position of great power. He had obviously thought this through, plotting away, long and hard, while living inside Emily.

Without warning, Amy felt the ropes on her wrists loosen and finally she was free. She glanced over and saw that original Erda had worked some kind of magic and spelled her ropes to loosen. She looked over and saw the gun laying on the cement floor. She carefully and quietly stretched her arms down and untied her legs from the chair, trying not to move too fast or make any sound so as to not attract John's attention.

"Enough of thy useless chatter," John said to Erda.

Erda remained stock-still, continuing to watch him carefully.

The now unbound Amy, finally regaining the feeling back in all her limbs, tried to leap for the gun at the same time as John heard her, turned and did the same. They struggled with it and the gun went off, narrowly missing Amy's upper arm by millimeters. John, being the stronger of the two, wrenched it away from her hands and pointed it directly at her.

Amy gasped, staggered back and put her hands to her ears which were painfully ringing from the gun being fired so close to her.

"I must taketh my leave of thee, for ye present," John said with an ominous tone to his voice. He turned and quickly moved aside a shelving rack to reveal a hidden old door, obviously Emily's emergency exit.

Erda still remained unmoved and she continued to watch John.

"For God's sake Erda, don't let him get away," Amy cried, desperate for Erda to do something, anything and do it now.

John turned the doorknob but it was locked. He rushed back to Emily's inert body and rummaged in her dress and jacket pockets, and, finding an old key, he stood and staggered, apparently dizzy for a moment.

The three Spirits and corporeal Amy watched him without moving, two of them knowing what was coming and mentally bracing themselves. Spirit Amy's hand slipped into Erda's hand and squeezed it tightly.

John shook his head and frowned. He was now having trouble seeing as well as standing. "What doth thou think thou hast done?" he said fear beginning to creep into his voice.

Everyone watched in silence.

"Thy foul-toothed devil's whore, what spell hast thee cast upon me?" He staggered over to Amy and held the gun to Amy's head.

Amy froze as the barrel of the gun pressed into her flesh just behind her ear and she stared balefully at Erda, her heart pounding crazily in her chest. Surely Erda wouldn't let her die, would she? She was family, after all.

There was absolutely no sign of emotion on Erda's face. She seemed not to care in the least.

"Retract thy spell or lose thy child," John said.

Amy, terrified, looked up at John who now looked distinctly ill, the pallor of his skin had changed from a healthy pink to a sickly grey colour and he was sweating profusely.

Gripped by some mysterious pain, John abruptly collapsed to his knees, gasping. He waved the gun shakily in Amy's direction but groaning in agony, dropped the gun and clutched at his torso.

Amy watched as the gun skittered away in the opposite direction to her.

Erda, at last, moved. She came close to John and looked down upon him, "Thou ought to hath knowest, John. Thy way to remove a'curse 'tis to make the one who sayeth it, taketh it back. Thy killed me a'fore thou couldst do that."

"Sayeth now, I beg thee." John gasped out, pain creasing and distorting his face.

"Thou gave me no mercy nor my family, thy shalt hath none," She stood and watched him writhe in agony.

The second Erda, who was still standing by the wall holding Spirit Amy's hand, leaned forward and frowned deeply.

"It hath changed again... for 'twas ye occasion upon Detective Andy arriveth, was it nay?"

"Yes! You're right, it was. What the fuck is happening?" Spirit Amy said.

The original Erda watched her ex-lover squirm in agony and said, "Thy got it wrong, John. Yes, I hexed thy body but I also hexed thy rotten Soul," she said and smiled.

It was a smile of pure and utter revenge and it chilled both Amys to the bone.

John opened his mouth and a terrible, agonized scream burst out as his flesh began to ripple and rot and the outer skin slid off his body, like water off a duck's back.

Everyone in the room watched in horror as

this now skinless man continued to scream and squirm in excruciating agony until, finally, they saw his stolen organs detach themselves and fall away.

With one final and terrible shudder, Dr. John Lambe's Soul was abruptly rejected from the monstrosity of a body, and the remains of his misappropriated body parts exploded violently with the power of the hex and splattered all nearby with warm, hideous gore. The remains of the corpse collapsed into a sinking, wet puddle of dripping body parts and vital fluids.

The original Amy stood shaking and her Erda took her by the arm out of the place, saying she was taking her home.

Spirit Amy and her Erda stood looking at the gory scene and the body of Emily, both frowning but not saying a word.

Their faces betrayed how confused they were by these happenings. It was so different from what they remembered had happened. Originally, Detective Andy had taken Amy and Bryer to the hospital.

It was the same detective who didn't want

to know all the paranormal details and who'd closed his mind to what he had witnessed for the sake of his sanity and his career.

A sharp intake of air made Amy and Erda both jump as Emily coughed and slowly sat up looking dazed.

Amy and Erda looked at her and then at each other.

"John, oh, John... what have they done to your glorious body?" Emily cried over his remains despite the fact he had just tried to kill her. "I shall find more of your line, resurrect your soul again and then you must give me what I deserve: eternal youth at last." Emily placed her hand in the pool of bloody organs and smeared the blood on her face and her hands as if washing in the fountain of youth.

"Dear god..." Amy said and watched as the mad woman who was covered in blood left the basement through the hidden doorway and escaped into the night.

Chapter Eighteen

Present Day

Detective Andy sat behind the wheel in his car, watching and waiting.

Mitch sat next to him looking at his phone. "It says the shop closes at 5:30pm."

"Well, it 6:05pm now and the light is still on, and we haven't seen her come back from her last appointment. So maybe they forgot and left the light on or perhaps she is coming back to work late," Andy said as he reached into the cooler for a cold drink.

The mid June heat and humidity had lasted all day and it looked like it would be the same overnight.

"What, in a Realtor's office, could keep you working late? I remember my last move, they don't hurry on anything once you're hooked."

Andy shrugged and sighed deeply, he hated waiting around for criminals but he hated the heat of summer even more and especially hated it at night, which always meant he got no sleep because of it.

"Fucking humidity, one of these days I'll move out to Vancouver or somewhere where it's cooler."

"Can't see that happening, Boss. You love this job too much."

"What gave you that fucking idea?" Andy looked at him with an astonished and serious look on his face, the can of pop stalled on its journey to his mouth.

"I don't know, you seem happy here in this job. Well, perhaps happy is not the right word, probably a bit too strong a word for it but I can't imagine you leaving it anytime soon."

"Happy? Fuck no. Hate all this horror, but someone needs to do it. Anyway, can't afford to move."

"You need a rich wife," Mitch said and laughed.

"Oh yeah, another wife... I need one of those like a hole in my head."

A car pulled up and parked across the street outside the Realtor's office and drew the attention of both men who watched as the woman climbed out of the car, locked it and stepped onto the pavement.

"That's her," Mitch said. "Are you sure about this, Boss? I mean look at her, she looks like my grandmother."

"Yes. I would have discounted that phoned in tip if you hadn't already put her on that list, and her travel records show her to be in several of the murder locations around the same time."

They watched as the elegant lady in her sixties went into the office that said Emily Carpenter Realtor above the door. She closed and locked the door behind her and walked towards the back, shutting off the office lights as she went.

The men sat in the car and watched for a while. there was no one around on the streets. It was that time of day when most people had gone home or were having dinner, so the road was empty of cars and people.

"What's that?" Mitch said and pointed out of the windshield at the Realtor office.

A strange flickering could be seen through one of the windows behind all the images of properties for sale.

"Is she using a candle?" Mitch said and leaned forward squinting.

"Maybe or... it could be a fire, albeit a little one," Andy said, frowning at the view. "And therefore giving us reasonable grounds to enter," Andy said, smiled, lifted his eyebrows and nodded to Mitch.

The two men were out of the car and across the road in seconds. Mitch kicked the door a couple of times until the frame and lock tore itself apart and they both entered.

"O.P.P.! We saw flames! Are you here, Ms. Carpenter?" Mitch called out. "Definitely saw the flicker of a flame," he said to Andy, "What's that smell? Is that incense? What the hell is she doing?"

Andy shrugged. "How the fuck should I know what old ladies do at night?"

There was no reply to their shout nor any sounds of a fire. The office looked absolutely normal, except, of course, for the broken door.

Weapons in hand and pointing down the corridor, Detective Andy and Mitch made their way to the back of the offices and saw that Emily's office, obvious by the sign on the open door, was empty. Both of the men turned their heads sharply to the left towards the small kitchen area where a loud thud had suddenly come from. They walked as quietly as possible towards the kitchen but also found it empty. Another muffled thump sounded as if someone was in a cupboard. Looking around and seeing no cupboard big enough for the old lady to hide in, they spotted the door to the cellar.

Mitch tried the door but it was locked.

"Go around the back of the building and see if there is another entrance, there should be one as per fire regs and I'll try to get through this one," Andy said.

Mitch nodded and went back through the offices and outside to look for another doorway in or some kind of access.

Holstering his gun, Andy threw his weight

against the door. It did absolutely nothing. He tried again, only harder this time and again nothing happened.

"Fuck. Work smarter not harder." He reminded himself and looked closely at the door handle and realised that although the door was sturdy, the lock wasn't, and all he needed was some leverage.

In the fully stocked, if small, kitchen Andy raided the cupboards and drawers for anything useful. Eventually he found a small cupboard with odd tools in it. The type of tools most offices have, such as screwdrivers, a small hammer and a few picture hooks. Taking the sturdiest looking screwdriver and the rather lightweight hammer, Andy returned to the basement door, inserted the screwdriver between the frame and the door, and hammered it in. He then levered it hard against the frame and with a sudden sound of splitting wood, the door swung open, freed from its locking mechanism.

A flickering light could just be seen down the darkened steps of the basement, and extracting his gun again from his holster, Andy took a deep breath and called out: "O.P.P. Don't move." Moving carefully but quickly, he went down the steps and into the candlelit space of the basement, holding his gun out before him.

Andy stood stock-still on the bottom step of the stairs and stared at the unholy scene before him.

The old woman was wearing large black headphones with her back to him and was bent over a table. Around her, on the table, were several jars holding what looked like body parts. On the table, spread out before her, like material ready to be sewn into a garment, lay pieces of flesh that she was currently fully occupied in sewing together by hand. With every stitch she made, the flesh seemed to infuse with life and the colour changed from mottled blue-grey to a healthy pink colour.

The colour drained from Andy's face. "Ho...ly Fuck," Andy's voice croaked out, his throat having dried with horror. He gulped in the heavily-scented air. His brain was still working on some level, despite the shock, as he suddenly remembered the smell: it was some kind of Patchouli incense like a lot of the goth kids wore as perfume.

She would need it to mask the smell, he thought to himself, suddenly understanding the stink. It took a moment for his cop brain to kick in fully, and he swiftly moved down the last step and headed towards the table. With a deep breath that almost made him cough, he reached out with his free hand, still pointing the gun at her with his other, and grabbed the earphones, yanking them from her head.

Emily jumped, let out a small squeal as she whirled round to see who was invading her room and disturbing her work.

Andy jumped back and placed both hands on his weapon to steady his aim.

The muffled sound of Mozart's Requiem could be heard from the headphones, which made the scene even more surreal.

"Put your hands up," Andy said in his stern voice. "Do it now."

"What the..." Emily said with a look of pure amazement on her face that rapidly changed to annoyance and then fury. Her cheeks flushed and her eyes sparkled with her rising temper.

"How dare you force your way into my property! I shall call the police!"

"I am the police, and I announced myself but you couldn't hear me. You were... otherwise engaged... obviously," Andy said, his eyes flicking to the table and back several times as he tried really hard not to stare at the jars of organs in liquid or the handmade human suit on the table. He shuddered involuntarily.

"Get on your knees and put your hands on your head."

"I will do no such thing!" she said indignantly, as if she had been told to drink Guinness rather than sherry, instead of standing around in a plastic apron with surgical gloves on and her hands covered in a dark visceral liquid of some kind.

Andy blinked, he had not expected such a reply. "Do it now!"

Emily took a step closer to Andy. "You don't want me to do that, do you? You look like a nice man, you wouldn't hurt a nice old lady, now would you?"

"Stay where you are and put your hands on

your head," Andy said and could now hear banging from the back of the basement. It was muffled and seemed far away, and he hoped it was Mitch trying to break down the back door and not the old woman's accomplice.

He stared intently at the old woman who looked at him and smiled nodding to herself as if she was having a conversation in her head. In a second she was upon him with a scalpel in her hand. He saw it flash in the candlelight as she launched herself at him aiming for his throat. He struggled against her, amazed by her unusual strength and speed. It was as if she was a well built, strong man. His mind panicked suddenly and realised he may have underestimated the woman. The blade sliced through his cotton shirt and ripped into the flesh on his left arm before he could grab her hand and stop her. He didn't hesitate and he fired his weapon point blank at her chest.

The old woman crumpled onto the concrete floor instantly, lying bleeding and scarcely breathing as Andy stared at her for a second.

He then kicked the blade far from her and heard the other door break. He hoped it was his partner who would be in the room with him any second and he would be grateful for it. The woman... and indeed everything about this case had seriously fucking unnerved him.

Emily reached out with one hand towards the table, feebly trying to touch the atrocity that lay on it. "I will see you soon, John, I promise," she said, exhaled deeply and died.

A shelving rack moved on one wall and Andy turned sharply and said, "O.P.P. Come out with your hands on your head."

Mitch's head appeared out of the side of the shelves, "Don't shoot, Boss. It's just me."

"Thank fuck," Andy said and lowered his weapon.

"What the hell happened here?" Mitch said as he surveyed the room and its horrific contents.

Andy looked back toward the table and watched the healthy looking-flesh of the man-suit fade in colour and return to the blue-grey of dead flesh.

"What the actual fuck?" He blinked, swallowed hard and looked away from the rotting flesh and down at the remains of the crazed serial killer who had horrifically killed so many members of the same family tree over many years. His mind couldn't take in what he saw.

At the end, Emily Carpenter was just a little old lady laying on the floor, her apron askew revealing a pale cream dress covered in small pink roses like an unholy garden in the middle of chaos.

"Fuck, fuck, fuckety fuck," Andy said, leaned against the wall and closed his eyes.

Chapter Nineteen

Present Day

The Scribe lit several candles around the small room. Once pleased with the amount of illumination they then had achieved they walked across the rug to the book cabinet and carefully withdrew the aged, wooden bound book from the shelf and placed it on the nearby desk. The steady hands unwrapped the book from its protective layer of non-acidic material, unlocked the large clasp, opened the heavy wooden boards of the cover and slowly turned each of the ancient pages. Then, paused to read the entries for a while before continuing past them and onto the few remaining blank pages. Past them the Scribe leafed until they reached the back of the book and the long list of names written there. Each of the book's owners had sealed their fate, and that of everyone around them, by signing their names in their own blood, therefore creating a blood-linked pact between the power of the book and each of the Scribes.

The first entry was clearly dated 1665, which was a surprise to the Scribe. They had not expected to be able to read it so clearly from so long ago. They placed a finger over the first name and smiled to them self, that first name was the creator of the book and who must have wielded such powerful magic to do so. They were also the first one to discover its horrifying secrets and used them to their own advantage, causing death and mayhem throughout the ages. The Scribe's finger ran down the many entries of names and dates until they rested on the last name and its date. The last Scribe was recorded as one Reginald Mortimer, who had signed his name in 1966, but now the book had a new scribe and it was at last time to add their own name to the list.

The Scribe knew the bonding ritual as they had already memorized it. They also knew that they needed the proper oak gall ink and a quill of suitable quality. Preparations had been carefully made, and, with a swift slice of a penknife, blood was drawn from the thumb and dripped into a pot that already contained the ink.

Without any hesitation or fear of the consequences, the name of the Scribe was written in a mixture of their own blood and the oak gall ink upon the page and the year next to it, just as all the other Scribes had done. The Scribe held their breath, they were not sure what they expected to happen, but expect something they did. Nothing happened for several moments as they watched the blood-ink soak into the page's rough fibers. As the Scribe sat and watched the blood-ink drying, the other names on the page seemed to flicker in the light as if they rippled with fire... or perhaps it was just the flickering candlelight, the Scribe thought rationally.

The hairs on the back of the Scribe's neck began to stand on end and a shiver went down their neck, followed by a sudden trickle of cold sweat. The room was warm from the heat of the day, but the body of the Scribe felt a cold chill wrap around it as if it had been encased by the centuries-old book and absorbed into it by the blood on the page. The big brass catch, which fastened the two wooden covers together protecting its contents, began to feel like they had locked the Scribe's Soul into the book itself, and maybe they had.

Taking a deep, shaky breath, the Scribe reached out and closed the book suddenly. Not from fear for their Soul but because they had heard a sound outside and they were not willing to risk anyone stumbling upon their ritual nor the precious book. Deciding that the regular book cabinet was not safe enough for the book, now that they knew it was truly the book they had hoped it would be, the Scribe moved across the room, book in hand, and pressed their outstretched arm against a panel in the wood-clad wall. A small door swung open to reveal a high-tech safe. Entering the code, the Scribe opened the metal door and placed the book safely inside next to a passport, a collection of 17th Century coins and a large buff folder full of papers.

Closing the safe door and then the wooden

panel, the Scribe turned and listened hard for any more noises. It was too risky to continue with the work that had to be done in the book, especially when the Scribe was not sure if they were alone or not. The Scribe also needed time to preserve the book properly as it was beginning to decay, and they decided to move it to a safer and more secluded location as soon as they possibly could.

"We will continue this tomorrow, book," the Scribe said and left the room with a rapidly beating heart and a mind full of possibilities.

****

Inside the safe, the book waited in the darkness as it had always done.

It waited for its instructions.

It waited to release woe upon the Scribe's enemies.

It waited to serve.

To work its magic.

To create chaos.

To once more feed the dark, trapped Souls inside it.

Chapter Twenty

Saturday 21st June, Present Day,
Canada

"Thee looks comely," Erda said from the end of the bed where she sat watching Amy try on outfit after outfit.

"Thanks," Amy said and turned one way then another in the full length mirror, "I've never been to a Solstice Party before, not sure if that means it's a summer BBQ in the garden or a semi-formal dinner."

"Did thee ask thy friend?"

"No, I just kind of said yes on the spur of the moment," Amy stripped off the blouse and shorts and put on a pale yellow dress that had ivy and little flowers around the neck and the edge of the short sleeves. The material was cool against her skin and it flowed softly around her legs when she moved.

"Ah, that be lovely," Erda said with an appreciative smile.

"I got it a while ago but haven't worn it yet. I guess it works for both an informal BBQ and a smarter dinner. Feels nice and cool too, and that's a bonus in the crazy hot weather Canada has in summer." Amy turned around a couple of times, satisfied with the outfit. She scooped up her shoulder-length brown hair into a ponytail and then twisted it up into a bun and pinned it there, pulling a few tendrils back down on either side of her face to soften the style a little and she nodded to herself satisfied.

"Aye, 'tis warm here... I feel it upon my skin when I am in body," Erda said, but her voice seemed distant and distracted. "Did thee read thy broadsheet?"

"Broadsheet, what's that?" Amy turned towards her with a look of confusion on her face.

"Thy one that comes with thy letters."

"Oh, you mean the newspaper. No, not looked at it today, why?"

"I think thee should."

"Oh, well, ok then," Amy said and frowned, not sure why Erda would want her to read the newspaper. Leaving her bedroom, she walked along the hall and into the kitchen where the newspaper sat unfolded on top of the pile of opened mail. Erda had obviously looked at it as it had been under the mail and still folded in half when Amy had collected it from the mailbox earlier and thrown the pile casually on the table without really looking at any of them. She had been preoccupied about the party at the time.

Looking down at the front page, four words stood out in bold heavy type:

LOCAL SERIAL KILLER CAUGHT

Amy's stomach dropped and a deep dread spread through her like ripples on a pond. Her pulse quickened as she snatched up the paper and heavily sat down on one of the kitchen chairs.

"Oh my god," Amy said as she read the

details of how Emily Carpenter had been identified as the serial killer and that she had been killed by police while resisting arrest.

"Wow," Is all Amy could say as she read the gory details which had somehow been leaked to the press, about the hellish scene in the woman's basement and what the police had found her in the middle of doing when they tried to arrest her. Amy shuddered, remembering the original version of that night and what was on that table with the clarity of the traumatized.

"Aye," Erda said as she rested a comforting and now corporeal hand on Amy's shoulder.

"But this is not how it happened. How can I, *we*, remember something from the past and yet it just has happened? And it's different to what we saw and know? What the hell is happening?"

Erda walked around the table and sat down opposite Amy. "I hath furrowed my mind to find ye answers, all which comes forth is ye past hath been changed in enough ways to change ye present."

"But I thought... when we travelled to the past before and tried to change things, it didn't work. We couldn't change anything," Amy said and remembered the death of her parents and how she had gone back and tried to change their fate and save them, but it hadn't worked.

"'Tis naught can be changed by visiting ye past, nay this is a'nother thing, a'nother way. A person hast changed their fate and that has changed others so that all ye things we know hath changed ye way they happen."

"You mean someone has deliberately changed something, somehow, and that has had an effect on other things?"

"Aye."

"So... would that mean many other things have been changed too, if they were somehow connected to it?"

"Aye. 'Twould have to be powerful though to change thus. I hath to think upon it for a'while. Thee should go to thy party and enjoy thyself while I attend my thoughts."

"How can I go and enjoy myself when we know someone is changing the world around us? And who knows what for, what are they changing it to? Amy frowned, not liking any of this conversation; not one little bit. The thought and the possibilities were so huge, it was just all too frightening.

"Thee can do naught 'til 'tis known ye who and ye why of it. Let thy party be thy distraction 'til then."

"Hmm... I don't like it at all. My god, they could do anything to anyone. Wait... so how come we are not affected by it? I mean, nothing has changed with us, has it? Would we even know if it had?" Amy said, rubbed her hands together and shook her head to try to clear it.

"Mayhap, 'twas done while we were on thy tour, mayhap nothing hath affected us yet. Nay, we 'twould knowest if we hath changed. 'Twould be like a thorn in thy mind, 'twould feel wrong and strange, yet familiar 'cus of thy Soul's knowledge."

"Wait... you mean like Déjà Vu?" Amy said as her eyebrows rose in sudden understanding.

"Nay understand thy words."

"Erm... a feeling of something being so familiar, almost like it has happened before?"

"Aye, that be it," Erda said and nodded.

"That kinda makes sense," Amy said as she let her mind wander with the idea.

"Get thee gone and I shalt worry on it for thee." Erda gave Amy an encouraging smile and patted her hand.

"Ok, ok... I'm going. Don't wait up!" Amy said and grabbed the bottle of wine she had bought especially for the party. She also collected her phone and keys and headed for the front door.

"I nay sleep, thee knows this," Erda said, taking Amy's words literally as she appeared by the front door just when Amy was reaching for the handle.

"I know that, it's just a saying to not let people worry if you are away a long time."

"Oh. I wilt nay worry for thee but if thee needs me just call and I wilt hear thee no matter where thee stands."

"Yeah, that's weird, isn't it? Kinda comforting too, though. How does it actually work?" Amy said as she opened the front door and a wall of heat hit her. The difference between the AC cooled cottage and the warmth of late afternoon was the difference between fire and ice.

"'Tis ye blood connection. Thee are blood kin and 'tis like a beacon to a familial Spirit as I."

"Oh, right then. That's kind of freaky but good," Amy said, feeling a little reassured by the knowledge. "See you later, bye." Amy said and grabbed her sun hat from the coat hooks, put it on and closed the door and left the lovely cool air behind her. She walked down the garden path toward her truck, feeling the heat beat down on her as if it was the noontime sun and not 4:30 in the afternoon.

Will I ever get used to the seemingly endless heat of summer? she wondered. In England, the hottest part of the day is at lunchtime and by bed time it is usually cool enough to easily sleep, but not here. Once again, Amy thanked the gods for her AC.

****

Maggie's house was situated off one of the roads near Morton Creek and away from the lake where Amy's cottage sat, but it was right on the edge of the river that ran past the town and towards the lake. The maple tree lined road twisted and turned around the two small hills on the outskirts of town. The houses that snaked past were small but looked neat and well cared for.

Seeing several cars parked ahead, Amy pulled up behind the last one and climbed out. She picked up the bottle of white wine from the seat and locked the truck. Walking down past all the cars, Amy had a chance to look at the lovely houses of Maggie's neighbours and also check the house numbers as she went along. "1326..." she said to herself as she walked a little further and could hear the chatter of several people and presumed it was the very party she was heading to. "1328, next one." Amy looked ahead at the upcoming house, finding herself rather excited and intrigued as to what Maggie's house was like.

1330 Weaving Road East was a small but elegant two story house with white painted boards and pale blue window frames and door. The front door stood open at the end of a cobblestoned pathway, past the garden, which was divided in two by the path. On each side of the path, the garden was full of plants, flowers and several bees hopping from one flower head to the next. The entire place was surrounded by a small wooden fence which was stained a dark, deep warm wood colour with a beautiful wrought iron gate that came up to Amy's waist.

Amy smiled to herself as she looked at the front of Maggie's home. It delighted her in so many ways and she happily opened the gate. Noticing the gates had iron blades of grass and flowers molded in it, she closed it behind her, "Oh, you are lovely," she said to the gate and made a mental note to ask Maggie who had made it.

Turning back towards the house, Amy followed the path and stepped through the open front door. She found herself inside a small, bright hallway with three doors leading off it and a dark wooden staircase leading up the second floor. The hallway had a pale cream wallpaper with small summer flowers on it. It wasn't busy, just a nice, peaceful pattern for one's eyes. At various places on the walls there were framed images of plants, flowers and herbs similar to the Victorian botanical prints one could find at the Victoria and Albert Museum in London. On the wall opposite the stairs there was a half-round table with a huge vase of fresh flowers on it next to a picture of three dark-haired children; one boy and two girls, all smiling at the camera, and each had a single tooth missing. Their likeness was so acute they had to be very closely related and probably even siblings.

Amy could hear people laughing and followed the noise down the hall past the doorway leading to what looked like a very cosy sitting room full of soft sofas, cushions, books and an old fashioned fireplace with a mantelpiece over it. The door ahead of her was wide open and she could see the kitchen units and cooker in there and hear people talking. The last of the three doors that lead away from the lovely hall was closed.

Amy continued past the closed door and into the kitchen where three people she didn't recognize were in the process of making what looked like Sangria in a big bowl. One middle-aged woman with 'salt and pepper' hair was chopping fruit, a young woman with bright ginger hair and a very pale and freckled face was pulling cartons of orange juice out of the fridge and the last person, a man of about fifty with sunglasses perched on his head, was opening bottles of lemonade and wine and pouring them into the large glass bowl.

"Hello," Amy said and she looked around at all three of them with a smile on her face.

"Hello, my dear, welcome… if you're looking for Maggie she is in the garden," the middle-aged lady said.

"Yes, thanks. I'm Amy by the way."

"Hi, I'm Dimina," the woman said and nodded her head towards the young woman who had just taken a strawberry from the fridge and put it in her mouth, "That's Ginger and this is Stuart," she said, indicating the man standing next to her.

Ginger waved with a free hand, smiled as she chewed, and nodded hello.

Stuart put down the bottle he was emptying into the bowl and thrust out his hand to Amy, "Nice to meet you," he said in a very noticeably English accent.

"Nice to meet you too! You're English too?"

"Yes, originally. I now live here. Well, obviously not here but in Glendale. I'm the English Professor at the university there," he said and smiled shyly at her.

"Oh, how lovely. It's amazing how many Brits I've been bumping into recently," Amy said with a grin, remembering the lovely lady from the book signing.

"You're the first I've seen in a while. Perhaps we can reminisce sometime when you get a free moment?" he said hopefully with a slight blush.

"Oh, yes, that would be lovely," Amy said, not sure if she had just been asked out on a date or not. "You said Maggie is in the garden? I'd better go and say hello to her then, thanks."

Amy smiled at the three of them and walked out through the kitchen's back door and into the bright sunshine. Looking around at all the people, she finally spotted Maggie, who was talking to the man that was cooking on the BBQ, halfway down the beautiful garden. As she headed towards her friend, Amy looked around her at the people all dressed in summer dresses or shorts.

They were of all different ages and ethnicities and were standing around small, decorated tables in small groups, talking easily to each other as if they had all known each other for a long time. The atmosphere was relaxed and friendly and Amy felt comfortable at once.

The garden itself was full of roses, honeysuckle and climbing clematis, which all grew entwined with each other along the trellis walls on each side of the garden. There was a large area of well-tended grass in the centre of the garden and the side beds, below the climbing plants were full of flowers and herbs all growing together.

They were obviously companion planted to encourage good growth and were a huge attractor of butterflies, ladybirds and bees. *My father would have loved this place*, Amy thought as she walked around enjoying it. The garden seemed so utterly alive with so many forms of life that breathing in the same air with them was a refreshing balm to Amy's soul and she fell in love with her friend's home immediately.

Chapter Twenty One

Erda sat in her chair by the now empty fireplace. Her room, in the attic of Amy's cottage, was warm despite the AC that hummed away downstairs. The heat or cold could never affect her as a Spirit but when she was corporeal she could actually feel it upon her flesh and she enjoyed the simple pleasantness of both sensations. She was always amazed by the small things, the things that living folks took for granted to the point of not even noticing them anymore. She was amazed by the things she missed since being dead and even after four hundred years of being dead, some things still begged her to be enjoyed.

She wasn't enjoying herself at present though. She had been sitting thinking about how someone would be able to change time and its events for the last hour, and, although she knew, but had not told Amy, that one could actually change the past by visiting it and altering circumstance to one's preferred outcome. She also knew that God, time, fate or whatever one called it would contrive circumstances back on track in a way that was meant to be. It was as if one grew a vine up a tree, removing a limb from the tree would not stop the vine, no, it just found a different way to get to the top and the sunlight. It was the same thing with changing the past. Important events such as death always came to pass even if the path there was a different one than expected or even planned. However, these changes felt magickal and that had a whole separate slew of consequences and laws.

Erda mused on such thoughts for the next few hours and racked her memories for spells, hexes, potions, folklore and people who could create a way to change things so much that entire lives were altered and events on a large scale were twisted one way or another. No matter how she tried, she could not find the way forward... how could she remove an obstacle if she could not see it nor know who had put it in their path?

"I need assistance from an'other," she said, finally admitting to herself she could not solve this problem alone.

It was time to use some information she had gained by looking at the interesting people down through history who had at various times helped her ancestors and descendants.

Erda suddenly knew exactly who she needed to see and when.

Closing her eyes she focused on the place and time, and travelled there in but a blink of an eye.

JUNE, 1580, TECHLENBURG, GERMANY

Erda stood before the house her Grandmother had described to her when she was young, so many years ago. It was odd to know that her Grandmother would not meet this man, whom she had come to see, for another seven years and not until he was unwell, just before his death.

Erda had chosen this time as she knew his

library and knowledge were at its peak and she needed all the knowledge he had to solve her problem. Making herself corporeal she looked up and down the street to make sure she hadn't been spotted appearing out of thin air. The street was empty, thanks to the fading light, and most people were now retired for the evening from their labours of the day. Erda looked up at the timber-framed house across the road in front of her with its whitewashed panels filled with wattle and daub. The windows had small, diamond-shaped panes of glass edged in lead which peered out to the night, glowing with candlelight as if they were eyes watching the streets of Techlenburg.

The old house belonged to Johann Weyer, a doctor and scholar of the old arts who, in just a few short years, would influence her own grandmother as she and her family had passed through the area.

Approaching the imposing, solid-looking wooden door, Erda took a deep breath. If Johann could not help her she was not sure what to do next. She knocked and waited, hoping he was home.

The door opened and the candlelight spilt out onto the pathway, illuminating Erda's face.

"Guten Abend?" the young female servant said.

Erda knew Johann was a learned man and spoke several languages, but she had no idea about his staff. She frowned, annoyed that she had not thought of the language barrier until now.

"I came to seeth Dr. Weyer," she said in slow, deliberate words.

The servant looked at Erda blankly until she said the doctor's name again and then nodded with a smile and opened the door widely, making motions with her hand for Erda to enter the house.

The entrance hall was panelled with dark wood on the walls and even darker boards on the floor. It gave a gloomy atmosphere to the room that the lit candles could not fully dispel.

The servant pointed to the floor indicating that Erda should stay in the hall while she went off to presumably tell her master he had a visitor.

Within moments Erda could hear footsteps returning in her direction. These were not those of the young servant girl though, these were shuffling footsteps of the old but determined.

The balding, grey-haired man stood before her with a cane, but otherwise he looked healthy but of a good age. His close-cropped beard was the same grey colour as the remaining hair on his head and gave no indication of the colour it had once been in his youth.

"Wie kann ich Ihnen helfen?" the man said.

Erda shook her head, not understanding his words.

"Johann Weyer?" she said.

"Ja?" He nodded and looked at her expectantly. Erda frowned. "I hath come for ye help," she said, looking worried.

"Ahh..." the old man said, "Cometh within," he said in perfect English, turned and slowly walked to the end of the hall and quietly entered into another room.

Stunned and relieved, Erda followed him into his keeping room where there were two chairs by an empty fireplace and next to one chair was a small table with a book, a small silver bell and a half full glass of deep red liquid on it. The room was lined with bookselves that overflowed, all manner of scrolls were stuffed into the small spaces between the hugely valuable books and many curiosities such as skulls and feathers also adorned the shelves. Erda saw these things in the dim light, from the two candles in the pewter candlesticks on the mantel over the fire, she wanted desperately to go over and examine everything in the room, but first she knew he had to get this man to speak with her about his dangerous knowledge, without him feeling his life was in danger.

Johann held out a hand for her to sit in the other chair as he went to sit in his own next to a small table.

"Thank thee," she said, sitting down and watched him slowly lowering himself to his chair.

"What is thy name, child?" he said in a kind, grandfatherly way.

"Forgive me, sir. My name is Erda Miller and I hath come a long way to speak with thee."

"How may I help thee, Erda Miller?" he said with a bright and intelligent twinkle in his eyes, his curiosity piqued by the arrival of the

English woman in his home.

"Thou art known for thy wisdom and thy library, I cometh for advice of a... unusual nature," Erda said, struggling to find the right words.

"Doest thou need of ye physicks or of an'other more delicate matter?" he said carefully.

There was nothing for it, Erda just had to come out with it and if he called her witch and sent for the watch, then she would go back to Amy's time in the blink of an eye. "Thou hast knowledge of a great many things and I needeth thee to help me with finding how ye can change events and people's lives by ye transmuting of forces around us."

"Thee wants to talk of Magicks?" The old man eyebrows rose swiftly and his forehead crinkled with the movement of skin.

"Aye, 'tis right," Erda said and looked him straight in the eye, "I nay mean thee harm and I wilt go at once if thee thinks otherwise and bids me to."

"Ahh... I hath lived long enough, child, to knowest whence comes danger and 'tis naught of thy doing," he said and picked up the little bell from the table. He shook it once and placed it back down. Within seconds the servant who had opened the door was at the old man's side. He spoke to her in German for a few moments and she left the room. Johann held one finger in the air to indicate to Erda to wait before she spoke again and not another word was spoken between them for several minutes.

Erda would always respect a person's wishes in their house and she followed his request and waited patiently.

The servant soon returned with an extra glass, a dark-coloured bottle and a plate of small pastry parcels. The young woman served Erda some of the wine and offered her the pastries.

"They art delicious, sweet pastry filled with apples, almond paste and sugar. They art called Epffelbolster, it doth simply mean apple pillows." He smiled and his face crinkled in such a delightfully friendly way that Erda smiled too and helped herself to the sugary treat. She could feel herself beginning to relax in his kindly presence.

The servant placed the plate on the small table next to Johann and left the room, closing the door behind her. Erda watched her go, wondering how much she knew of her master's secret life.

The old man watched Erda as she watched the servant leave. "'Tis safe to talk in this tongue, the girl and my other servants only speak German."

Erda looked and felt relieved and she relaxed a little more and bit into the pastry. The shocking but wonderful sweetness of it filled her mouth and her taste buds tingled with delight.

The old man nodded knowingly, and, after considering her for several minutes more, he simply said, "Tell me."

Erda told him everything she knew or thought she knew of the changes that had been happening but she didn't tell him what she was or that she was from so many years in the future.

He sat contemplating all she had said with one hand on his chin, absentmindedly tweaking the short hairs of his beard. Eventually he spoke again, his voice seriously concerned, "'Twould be a strong spell to change ye direction of lives upon years." He slowly climbed out of his chair and shuffled over to the far book shelves. He rummaged through several of the piles there and eventually returned with a small tattered notebook clutched in his wrinkled hand and sat back down in his chair with a deep sigh.

Erda sipped her wine, tasting the delicious flavour of the sweet fortified wine known as Malmsey, which she remembered had been her ex-lover's, John Lambe's, favourite drink. She pushed all thoughts of the evil, cold-hearted man who had burnt her alive from her thoughts. She refused him entrance to her mind and her afterlife, for the thousandth time.

"In six score and five years I hath seen many a'places, 'twas Paris, where I learned English, I came upon a friend of ye divine arts, who I shalt not name for fear of exposure upon his person. 'Twas him who told me of an incantation, if done upon right wouldst give thy practitioner ye power to control ye fate of another. I wrote in my pocket book of ye notion as 'twas so intriguing to mine ears."

He opened the book carefully as there were many loose pages and went through it finding the page he was after. "Here... yes, here it lay. 'Tis known a family of ye Roma from Seville area knew such great Magicks, my friend hath spoken to one of their line but could nay get information except they called such a thing ye 'Lamentar Ninguno', upon translation 'tis 'Regret None'."

"Regret None? I've nay heard of such a thing," Erda said. "Spanish Gypsies thee says?"

He nodded and closed the book, "'Tis all I know of such. Perhaps thee can find a Roma to speak with on such matters?"

"Perhaps," Erda said, finished her glass of wine and rose from her chair eager to return to Amy and tell her what she had found out. "I thank thee for thy time and wise counsel. I wouldst love to visit thee again to talk of Magicks and ye like," Erda said, truly interested in his mind, his library and strange collection.

"Workers in ye divine arts art most welcome in my humble home. Come when thy wilt for I am free to discuss ye works of nature." He smiled broadly and his eyes lit at the thought of future conversations with someone so vital and interested in his work.

Chapter Twenty Two

Summer Solstice Party,
Present Day, Canada

Maggie's smile spread across her face in a genuinely pleased expression at seeing her friend walking towards her. She excused herself from the man she'd been talking to and stepped forward a few paces to meet Amy.

"Hey, I'm so glad you came, Amy," she said and hugged her friend.

"Thank you for inviting me. You have a lovely home and this garden is amazing."

"Thanks, I'm glad you like it. It's taken me a few years to modernize the house and restore it, but I'm very happy with it."

"Well, it's lovely. You made a good job of it. I presume the river is beyond the trees at the bottom there," Amy nodded to the end of the garden where several fruit trees stood blocking the view of beyond. Many of them had glass jars hanging from the branches with candles in them and a few wind chimes. Two sturdy-looking apple trees had a white hammock tied between them.

"Yes. Past the trees is my vegetable garden and more herbs and then there's a small sandy area next to the water."

"Wow, you have your own beach too? Very nice."

"Well, I'm not sure it's big enough to be called a beach, I can just get two chairs on the sandy part. The rest of the area is large rocks but I do rather like sitting down there with a glass of wine and watch the sunset."

"Oh, talking of wine, I know you like red as I do, but I brought you this to try. It's Wolf Blass Chardonnay, one of the few whites I really like."

"Thank you," Maggie said, taking the bottle from Amy, "let's open it now and then I'll introduce you to some people and give you a tour."

"Oh, I would love that... the tour and the wine," Amy said and laughed. She followed Maggie back into the kitchen, which was now empty, and watched her open the wine and pour out two large glasses.

Taking a taste of her wine, Maggie looked up at Amy, surprised, "Oh, that is good, it's almost buttery."

"I know, right?" Amy said, raised her glass to her lips, drank and enjoyed the wonderful taste of it as it slipped down her throat and left an amazing aftertaste. "So how long have you had this place?" she said as she gestured around them with the hand that held the glass of wine.

Maggie, who was leaning against the kitchen counter said, "I bought it ten years ago when I moved here from Toronto and started the book shop. Come on, I'll show you around."

Delighted, Amy followed her, and, as they went from room to room on the ground floor, she fell in love with the place more and more and decided she liked Maggie's style. They visited every room except the one on the ground floor which still had its door closed, just as it had when Amy arrived.

On the second floor, there were two lovely, sunny bedrooms. One was obviously Maggie's and the other a spare for guests. Maggie's room looked out over the back garden and down to the water. It was filled with books, flowers and sunlight.

"I love your room, and what a great view," Amy said as she knelt on the window seat and looked out of the open window to the party guests below and the trees, vegetable garden and small riverfront further away from the house.

"Thanks, it is one of my favourites too and the other reason I bought this house. The main one was the garden and this place was a bonus."

Out on the landing there was a separate bathroom between the two bedrooms. At the end of the hall there was a small, iron spiral staircase leading upward.

"You have an attic too?" Amy said.

"Yes, that's my library and herb room," Maggie smiled, "C'mon, I'll show you."

The staircase was only big enough for one person to go up at time but it was beautifully built and in the same pattern as the garden gate.

"This iron work is gorgeous," Amy said as she traced her fingers along the leaves and flowers of the design.

"Thanks, the guy is local and so damned talented."

The attic was warm but not overly so, and Amy could hear the low hum of an AC unit somewhere nearby. The entire attic was divided into two rooms with a half-wall separating them. One room was filled with a desk, a couple of comfy chairs and lots of books, and what a curious collection it looked to be. From across the room where Amy stood, she could see there were many new, brightly coloured books mixed in with much older leather bound ones. In the middle of the many book cases was a specialist bookcase that had glass doors that sealed out any harmful air and pollutants, presumably to protect the contents from the damp air of the river. Inside the sealed book case were several ancient-looking books.

"Wow, that's nice," Amy said, stepping

closer to the sealed cabinet.

"Yeah, I inherited some old and rather rare books from my father and they are prone to crumbling, so I keep them in a temperature and moisture-controlled cabinet."

Amy was impressed. It seemed that Maggie knew a lot more about books than just selling them. She looked around the rest of the attic and across the other side of the half wall. There were counters filled with dark-coloured bottles and containers full of dried herbs. It also had many bundles of herbs hanging from the ceiling rafters to dry.

"Oh, this is lovely. I didn't realise you were into herbs. I have a friend who would love this place. She loves herbs too." Amy immediately thought of Erda and how she would indeed have loved to see this attic which was so much like hers, and rifle through the books and herbs. Sadly, she knew they could never meet. Erda after all was a Spirit and if Amy told people she lived, learned from and travelled through time with a Spirit they would lock her up and throw away the key.

"Oh, who is your friend? I'd love to meet

them," Maggie's eyes sparkled with interest. "Yeah, plants and books are two of my greatest loves. It was my mother's passion, you know. Dad had his books but mom loved her garden. She made all her own shampoos and lotions. They were a strange mixture, the two of them. She was definitely a hippie, and he was a bit of a bookworm," Maggie smiled to herself at the memory of her parents, who had been such opposites and yet so happy in their marriage.

"Sounds like you got the best of both of them. Is your mum still with us?" Amy decided it was best for all concerned to move away from the subject of Erda and how she would love the attic.

"No, she died of cancer several years ago and my father passed two years ago. He died of a heart attack. Probably from sitting all the time and reading books, that's all I ever saw him do. He wasn't an outdoor-type person, unlike mom."

"I'm sorry, both of my parents are gone too," Amy said as that familiar heartache sat heavily in her chest again.

"Well, we'll just have to keep each other out of trouble then, won't we?" Maggie said with a grin. "Let's go down and get some food."

As they came back down the stairs Amy asked, "Does this place have a basement too? I've come to realise basements are very popular here. More so than in England."

"Actually yes, but it's an unfinished one and has the furnace, the washer and dryer and the usual storage stuff down there."

"Right. Well, that's useful anyway. I sometimes wish my place had one and I've often wondered why it doesn't."

"Perhaps you should have one put in. Might cost a bit though, with the foundation and everything, but they are great for laundry and storage." Maggie said as she passed the closed door on the way back to the kitchen.

"What's in there? Is it a downstairs loo?" Amy said as she came level with the unknown room.

"Ahh... no it's not a washroom," Maggie said and looked indecisive for several moments.

"Sorry, didn't mean to pry," Amy said, thinking she had overstepped their friendship, judging by the reaction on Maggie's face.

"No, you didn't, not at all. It's just... well, I don't show this room to many people. It's rather personal."

Amy frowned and began to walk toward Maggie and the entrance to the kitchen, "No worries, let's find some food."

"Ok, but when the party quietens down later, I'll show you then," Maggie said looking a bit more relaxed.

"Right-oh."

Maggie took Amy around the forty or so people, introducing her, and by the time the evening began to get dark, Amy's mind was full of names and faces. She wasn't absolutely sure she could get them all in the right combination, but she didn't worry too much about it. The party was wonderfully relaxing and fun, the food was delicious and a good mix of finger food and BBQ delights. The drinks were free-flowing and the company and conversation were great.

As night came upon them, many candles in the hanging glass jars were lit around the garden, on the trellis fencing and in the fruit trees. The garden now glowed in a most comforting and magickal way.

Amy hadn't realised until after the house tour that there was also a modest fire pit in the centre of the garden as it had a cover over it and a table placed on top, but now it was opened up, lit, and chairs were gathered around it. Although some of the party-goers were beginning to leave bit by bit, several people were now comfortably sitting around the fire and relaxing with drinks in their hands, chatting easily to one another.

Amy watched the conversations of the remaining people. She loved people-watching and how they interacted with each other: their tones of voice and hand expressions, the way their eyes flicked at each other or just looked at the person who was talking. Even the way they sat in their chairs fascinated her, and all these details were logged away in her author's mind to be brought out at a later date when she was writing once more.

The three people Amy had met in the kitchen when she first arrived were still at the party and were sitting around the now glorious fire. The night air had brought with it an usual chill for a summer's evening, and people shuffled their chairs closer to the fire to keep warm. The people who were sitting, she counted fifteen in total, were familiar faces and Amy tried to match all their names but to no avail and she gave up, certain she would catch their names sooner or later.

At a lull in the conversation, Ginger, the young woman from the kitchen, stood and raised her glass in the air. "Happy Summer Solstice!" she said, smiled and took a drink from her glass.

Everyone chorused "Happy Summer Solstice!" back to her.

Amy saw one person, who was presently without a name in her brain, rise and said "Hail, Sunna!" Amy wasn't sure what that meant and was surprised when everyone else called out "Hail!" really rather loudly and then cheered.

Amy looked puzzled and leaned over to Maggie who was sitting next to her, "What did you all just say? The Hail Sooma bit I mean."

"Hail, Sunna. Sunna is a Germanic Goddess and the personification of the Sun in old high German and she is often celebrated during our Summer Solstice party."

"Oh," Amy said. She didn't know what answer she had expected but it wasn't that and she felt surprised and rather curious to know more.

"I'm going to get some blankets and shawls, the wind off the river is getting really chilly tonight, would you help me, Amy?" Maggie said and was heading off toward the house before Amy could reply.

Amy followed her quickly. She had to admit her bare arms were getting goosebumps and her thin summer dress, though lovely and cool during the day, really wasn't warm enough tonight.

Inside, she found Maggie grabbing two shawls off the coat hooks by the door. "Here, put them on the kitchen table while I go upstairs to fetch some blankets." Maggie said, handed Amy the shawls and walked up the steps looking preoccupied.

Amy folded the two shawls, placing them on the table to wait for Maggie. One shawl was black and made from chenille and was very soft, the other was made of woven wool in many bright autumn colours.

"Right, that should be enough," Maggie said as she put down a pile of folded blankets of assorted colours on the old wooden kitchen table.

"Follow me," she said, turned and walked out of the kitchen and into the hall.

Amy followed behind thinking she would have to borrow a shawl or a blanket. *Why did I not think of bringing something of my own?* She wondered and almost walked into Maggie as she suddenly stopped moving.

"Time to show you this, I think," Maggie said and opened the closed door in the hallways, flicked on the light and stepped back so Amy could go into the room.

A feeling of breathless anticipation gripped Amy as she slowly stepped over the threshold and into the unknown room. She immediately had a full view of the room and its four walls and a window with a blind pulled down. There was no furniture except a stone table with candles, a small statue, fresh flowers and a large drinking horn on a stand.

"This is my winter ritual room. For the rest of the seasons I do our rituals in the garden or down by the river," Maggie said from behind Amy.

"Oh, erm. Right, you're... um... a..."

"Pagan, Amy. I'm a Pagan or Heathen if you prefer but I don't particularly like labels, I'm just me."

"Right," Amy said and looked back at the altar. She admitted to herself she was a little surprised but somehow not as much as she thought she would be. It kind of felt right when she thought about Maggie as if she had already thought it about her in her unconscious mind.

"Don't believe the bad press we get, we don't eat children or worship Satan." Maggie looked at her friend and tried to work out how she was taking the news. Not everyone took it well and Amy was important to her life both personally and professionally, and she decided to trust her instincts and tell her.

"I, well, ok then. You said 'our' rituals?" Amy turned to face Maggie with a look of honest interest on her face. "You have... others around?"

Maggie relaxed a little, "Yes, some of the people here are in my kindred... erm... group. Actually, most of them are around the fire right now. You met them all tonight, Ginger, Adam, Dimina, Julie, Rebecca, Stuart and Dan. We always have a circle before the party as the Summer Solstice is special to us."

"Oh," Amy said suddenly feeling left out of the excitement for some strange reason but glad that her friend had been brave enough to share this with her.

"Thank you for trusting me with this."

"You're welcome, but it's not like we are a secret group. Most folks know about us around here. Some even come to me for herbal remedies and teas, but I do like to keep this door closed when I have company as...well, it's my private space."

"Understandable. You remember that person I mentioned to you in the attic, who would love your stillroom? Well, she would definitely want me to introduce you to her now," Amy said and tried to imagine Maggie and Erda meeting and talking shop about Witch work and then wondered if she should have brought it up again. Amy realised, as she thought about her two friends, exactly what her new friend was. "You're a

Witch." Amy blurted out and desperately wanted to bite her own tongue off.

"Some would call me that but, like I said, I don't like labels," she said with a smile.

****

By 1am, Amy was constantly yawning and the night sky had clouded over, the rumbles of a distant thunderstorm could be heard as the last of the guests helped Maggie clean up. They doused the fire with water and brought in all the glassware and debris from the party. Ginger went around the garden blowing out the last few surviving candles and everyone thanked Maggie, said their goodbyes and soon departed to their cars or walked home.

Thankfully, not having had alcohol for the last couple of hours, Amy could drive home. She said goodbye to Maggie with a promise to meet in two days time for lunch, which had made Maggie very happy, and then Amy climbed wearily into her truck. She pulled away from the curb and executed a u-turn in the empty street and headed home. Before she'd even gotten off Maggie's road the summer storm burst with loud cracks of thunder overhead and the rain beat down noisily on her truck. It was so fierce that Amy had to drive slowly with the windshield wipers on the highest setting. She considered turning back but knew she was only a twenty minute drive from home and she plowed on through the darkness doggedly.

She travelled as slowly as she could along the highway, peering through her windshield while sheet after sheet of almost horizontal rain distorted her view of the road. She was happy when she spotted the turnoff toward the lake and her home. Taking the correct lane she headed off the main highway and onto the back roads.

The water accumulating on the road was getting dangerous and she wondered if she should pull over and wait the storm out. She told herself she would soon be home and continued on, but carefully.

A sudden flash of headlights dazzled her and she swerved to get out of the way of the speeding car heading toward her. Amy's truck aquaplaned dangerously across the road, shot off it and straight into the ditch on the opposite side.

The truck hit the corner of a large rock, rolled onto its side and slid along the wet ditch until it came to an abrupt stop.

Amy was instantly and completely knocked unconscious.

Chapter Twenty Three

Moments later Amy came to and opened her eyes. She blinked a few times and realised she was laying on her side door and looking out of the cracked windshield over the top of the steering wheel and deflated airbag, which had probably just saved her life. She sat and stared as the raindrops fell on the glass in the wrong direction and she took a deep, grateful breath. Letting the air slowly out of her lungs she spotted the lights of another vehicle as it pulled up to the side of the road just above where her truck lay in the ditch.

Amy made a mental check of all her body parts ensuring she could feel all of them and, thankfully, there was no pain and apart from her left wrist, which ached a little and her chest that felt rather sore from the seat belt, she was amazingly free of injury.

"Are you okay? Shall I call an ambulance?" A voice shouted above the noise of the rain from outside of the truck.

Amy couldn't see the person's face but said, "No. No, I'm fine. Can you help me to get out?" She said as she unbuckled her seat belt and tried to get past the steering wheel.

The passenger door opened and let the rain in, the cool drops of water fell on Amy's skin making her suddenly feel very alive. A faint shadow fell over the open doorway, illuminated a little by the car lights in the background and Amy saw an outstretched hand in the partial light. She climbed up on her seat, and, putting one foot on the headrest and the other on the dashboard, she levered herself upward, clasped the offered hand and felt it pull her up towards the sky. She pushed up with her legs and climbed out of the doorway and sat on the edge of it.

"You?! Are you bloody nuts driving like that?" She said and glared at the owner of the hand.

"I didn't see you until the last minute, and by then it was entirely too late," Cabot said as he climbed down off the truck and offered her his hand.

Ignoring it completely, Amy shuffled over to the front of the truck and climbed down herself. When she safely got her feet on the ground, her legs felt weak and wobbly and she sat down suddenly in the mud and stones as if someone had just disconnected her knees.

"Are you sure you don't need to be checked out? Perhaps I should call 911," he said, pulling his cell out of his jeans pocket.

"I'm ok, just a bit shaky," Amy said as she pushed back her wet hair and felt the refreshing rain on her face. She closed her eyes for a moment, raised her face and let the cool water splash on her skin.

Cabot eyed her curiously as if she were some kind of unknown creature. He wondered and almost panicked for a moment, *what if she was about to pass out and die?*

Amy opened her eyes and noticed him

watching her.

"Stop looking at me like that, I'm not gonna die. Just a bit wobbly, is all."

He looked shocked that she had said the very thing he was thinking.

"The least you can do is call for someone to get my truck out of this ditch, seeing as you put me there," Amy said feeling somewhat grumpy at the fact that neither he nor his car seemed affected at all.

"Of course, but first let's get you out of the rain," he said, and held a hand out to help her up.

Disregarding the offered hand again, Amy climbed to her feet slowly, and although she was still a bit wobbly in the legs, she managed to stand for a few moments before she began to climb up the ditch. Slipping and sliding in the rain, she didn't make much headway until she suddenly felt a hand on her bottom pushing her upward.

"Hey!" she said, but kept moving.

"You won't come to the mountain for help, so the mountain has come to you. Just deal with it and get up to the top," he said and pushed.

At the top she stood feeling wet, muddy and a little indignant.

"Thanks," she said begrudgingly.

"Good God, woman. I didn't ask you to marry me, it was just a push. Next time I'll ask if I can touch you, okay?"

"So I should think," she said and had to force her mind from thinking about the 'next time' and what he would be touching.

"Here, get in my car and get warm. I'll call for a tow truck."

Amy looked over at the car whose headlights were shooting beams that skimmed over the ditch and highlighted the trees and rocks on the other bank. The car was a fabulous looking sports car with a pale-coloured soft top. The lines of the car were so beautiful and it looked almost old-fashioned, like something from the 30's or 40's. It was a dark colour, maybe a dark green or blue. She was kind of impressed at his intriguing taste. She walked to the passenger's side, opened the door and slid into the low seat of cream leather, secretly pleased she was getting mud all over it and the cream carpet.

Cabot got in on the driver's side, closed the door seemingly not noticing the mess Amy was making and tapped a number on his cell.

Amy only half-listened to his conversation as she put her head back and closed her eyes for a moment. She just wanted to put everything on pause, just for a few minutes. Finally she opened her eyes and sighed deeply.

Cabot, who had now ended the call, looked at her.

"Yes, I'm fine... before you ask. Just sad about the truck, my father restored it and it was his pride and joy," she said pre-empting his question.

"Well, he can now repair it and make it as good as new again," Cabot said.

"He is no longer with us," Amy said and watched the pattern the rain was making on the windshield, pleased to see that this time it was going in the right direction.

"I'm sorry, I didn't know." He cleared his throat and brushed back his hair as it had fallen forward and was making water drip on his face.

"I'm sure we can find someone to restore

it, though. The tow truck guy will be here in a couple of hours. Apparently there is a big accident up on the highway between here and Glendale because of the storm and everyone is out there," he said, changing the subject.

"Crap," Amy said and noticed she had started to shiver.

Cabot flicked on the heater on the walnut dashboard and started the engine.

"We need to get you some place warm and comfortable."

He pulled the car away from the ditch and turned it onto the quiet, wet road.

"Where are we going?" Amy said, a little alarmed. "We can't just leave my truck there."

"I've already put warning signs on the road and an emergency light. If you are worried about the police, don't be. I know the local guy. I'll get him to come to us. My place is only a couple of minutes away. We can dry you off there and give you something hot to drink."

"My place is only ten minutes away, I would rather you take me there," Amy said.

"So you can be alone with no vehicle and

you just having had an accident. I don't think so," he said, brooking no argument.

Amy was stumped at that. She could hardly tell him she wouldn't actually be alone and that Erda the ghost would be there to look after her. She sat silently in the car, determined to stick it out until the tow truck guy came and then she could be done with him and go home.

Just as the car lights faded in the distance, Erda appeared by the truck. Her face contorted with worry as she called out and searched the entire area for Amy. For some reason her timing and locating regarding Amy was off this evening and that disturbed Erda more than she was ready to admit.

****

Amy sat in the chair next to the huge fireplace as it roared and crackled next to her.

She had rubbed her hair with the big fluffy towel which Cabot had offered her when they arrived at his place, and now she sat wrapped in it over her clothes. At long last she had relaxed enough to stop her teeth from chattering and the goosebumps had now gone too.

"Here, I think these will fit you," Cabot said as he held out a t-shirt and a pair of jogging pants. "There's a shower in the third room off the corridor on the left," he nodded in the direction, "please feel free to get cleaned up, and I'll get a hot drink for you."

Amy looked up at him. He had also rubbed his dripping hair with a towel that was now around his neck and the ends rested on his chest where his own t-shirt was plastered to his well-defined chest. She quickly averted her eyes and looked at the clothing he offered. Standing, she took the clothing and, not looking him in the eyes, knowing full well that she was blushing furiously, she murmured 'thank you' and quickly walked away toward the bathroom. She felt strange using a shower of someone she really didn't know, but her body ached so much and she was covered in dried-on mud that the very thought of the hot water sent shivers of delight down her spine.

The bathroom turned out to be the size of her own bedroom and was really luxurious. The house itself looked rather old and very large and Amy wondered, as she climbed into the two-headed shower space the size of her entire bathroom, if it was the type of house that British folks used to call the 'big house' in the old days.

Having showered and dressed in the borrowed clothes, Amy folded her filthy dress and tucked her underwear within the folds of fabric. She washed the mud off her sandals in the sink but they were too wet to slip them back on, so bare foot it would have to be. Running her fingers through her shoulder-length hair, she made herself as presentable as possible and turned to go back and sit next to the lovely warm fire again.

As Amy walked down the oak floored corridor back to the main room she could hear voices. There was definitely another man in the house and she wondered vaguely if Cabot had staff in such a big house.

"Ah, there you are. Do you feel a bit better for the shower?" Cabot asked as she stepped into the room.

"Yes, thank you. It was most kind," Amy said to him and her eyes flicked to the other man who was standing by the fire. He was a middle-aged man with a slight paunch and dressed in a suit that looked to Amy as if it was made of good old-fashioned tweed.

"This is Dr. Michael Cleves, a personal friend of the family. He kindly consented to pop over and take a look at you, just in case."

Amy's gaze whirled back to Cabot and her eyebrows rose in surprise, "I said I was alright... and it is the middle of the night."

"Actually, it's early morning, and you never can be too careful, my dear," the doctor said and stepped forward with his hand out to shake hers.

Amy took his hand in hers for a moment, "Thank you for coming out on such a horrid night, or indeed morning. It's most kind of you."

"Nonsense my dear, a friend of Cabot's is a friend of mine. Now take a seat and I'll just check you over, if that's alright with you?"

"Of course, thank you," Amy said and sat in one of the deep red coloured leather chairs by the fireplace.

As Dr. Cleves took her blood pressure,

checked her pupils and felt her head for tender spots, Amy's eyes wandered around the room. She noticed that Cabot had left them alone, and honestly, she was pleased he had, as he made her feel just a little uncomfortable. Not necessarily in a bad way, but made her feel very aware of herself and her body as if she was being watched all the time like the prey of some feral creature. Her eyes flicked to the antlers attached to the wall above the huge fireplace and she forced them to move on and look past them.

The rest of the room contained three more of the red leather chairs. There was another one by the fire and then two others: one on each side of a small gaming table that had a chess game set up on it. The walls were half-panelled with what looked like old and richly polished oak, while the upper part of the wall was covered with a Victorian-looking flock wallpaper in dark green, it was the type that had a raised pattern with a velvet feel. There were several swords and pieces of armour displayed on the walls, as well as paintings of men, women and assorted children. Presumably they were family portraits.

Cabot returned with a tray of three large cups and a large, steaming jug.

"Can you stay for a hot chocolate, Michael?" Cabot said as he placed the tray on an occasional table which sat under a painting of two small boys standing next to an enormous dog which was almost as tall as them.

"No, but thank you, Cabot," the Doctor said as he finished listening to Amy's breathing and then put his stethoscope back in his small leather bag by his feet. "I am on call for a midwife who is expecting a difficult birth with one of her ladies and I was thinking of checking in on them before heading home," he said and closed his bag. "Well, my dear you are correct. You escaped the accident mostly unscathed. A few minor contusions here and there but nothing serious, and you don't have a concussion. All the same, if you start feeling dizzy or nauseous, please do get yourself checked again, alright?"

"Of course. Thank you, Doctor."

"My pleasure, my dear. Now I must take my leave. Don't worry about seeing me out, Cabot, I know my way. Good night to you both."

"Thank you, Michael," Cabot called out as the man nodded and waved goodbye. He turned back and looked at Amy, "Chocolate?"

"Yes, please. That would be lovely."

Cabot nodded and poured out two large mugs and passed one to Amy before sitting down in the chair opposite her, cradling the warm mug in his immaculately manicured hands.

"Thank you," Amy said and also held the mug in both of her hands, letting the warmth of the liquid seep through and into her fingers.

A deep silence fell between them and Amy felt like an intruder inside someone else's life. She wished dearly that the tow truck man would ring to say he had arrived at the truck. Apparently, the plan was for him to call, hook up her truck and take it away to his garage and she would call him in the morning to say what she wanted done with it. Once it was done and Cabot could be convinced that she was okay to leave, then he would happily drive her home and she was to expect the local police to call on her the following morning for a statement, as they were having a very busy night apparently.

Amy sipped her drink and was surprised at the thickness and rich flavour of it. This wasn't your ordinary 'just add milk' type of hot chocolate.

"Oh, this is divine," she said.

"Happy you like it. It's a family recipe, and I do believe it originates from Spain. Many years ago, one of our servants had a special way to make it that my family loved, and we have made it ever since. The secret is in the quality of chocolate you use and then when it's ready you add a shot of dark rum to it for that extra kick."

"Whatever was done, it's lovely and so thick. Definitely the best I've ever had," she said and smiled at him over the top of her giant mug. "Did a servant make it tonight? Do you still even have servants?" Amy knew she was being nosey but didn't care and the thought of servants in this day and age seemed strange and somewhat elitist to her.

"Yes, we still have several members of staff who work for us but they go home after dinner is finished. We don't have any live-in staff anymore."

"Right," Amy said, not sure of how to reply to that news.

"And I made the chocolate."

"Oh," she looked surprised at that and then wondered why she was. She supposed she hadn't thought of him being the type to be able to make something as gloriously tasty as this.

Another silence opened up and loomed between them like a great crevice.

Amy sipped her chocolate and tried not to constantly look at this handsome man lounging in the chair before her.

"Would you like to see the house?" he said out of the blue.

"Actually, I would love to," Amy said, glad there would be a distraction.

"Good. Relax and enjoy your drink and then I'll show you around, and, if you are ready, I will drive you home after that."

"Ok, thank you," Amy said and snuggled back into her chair drinking her chocolate enthusiastically.

Later, as they walked around the large house, looking into bedrooms, ensuites and the most amazing kitchen Amy had ever seen, Cabot told her some of the history of the building. It had been built in the 1880s by the settlers of the nearby town of Morton Creek for their mayor and founder, William Cecil MacArthur, and it was passed down his line and then onto the Tanner line by marriage at the turn of the 20th century.

"Wait, you said MacArthur?" Amy said thoughtfully as she slowed her steps. She turned to him and stopped walking out of the large sitting room, which was attached to a Victorian conservatory to the back of the house.

"Yes, William Cecil MacArthur, have you heard of him? He was rather well-known around here and a bit of a local hero."

"Is he, or rather was he, related to Cyrus and Kathleen MacArthur who run the store in town?"

Cabot stopped walking too, "Yes, I believe they're cousins of the original family. Second or third cousins or something; definitely related anyway. Why, do you know them?"

"Actually, yes. They were very good friends of my parents and I grew up knowing them as my 'aunt' and 'uncle'."

"Well, well, isn't it a small world."

"So it seems. They mentioned that their family had a big house back in the day. I never imagined I would be standing in it though."

"It never ceases to amaze me how everything and everyone is connected in one way or another," he said and continued with the tour.

The next room off the main hallway had a set of double doors that were presently closed.

"This is my favourite room and I saved it for last. It's my study," he said, stepping forward to open both of the doors at once and flicking on the light.

The room suddenly appeared from the gloom of the night, and Amy gasped as she stepped forward into it. Directly in front of her was a huge fireplace encased in marble, a large family portrait above it. But that wasn't what made her gasp... the ceiling of the room was much higher than the rest of the house, and three of the four walls were covered with book shelves that ran up to the twelve or thirteen foot high moulded ceiling which was painted white and pale blue. The shelves themselves were made from a beautiful wood with a deep reddish tint to it, maybe mahogany, and they were absolutely packed with books. There was even a small, wheeled ladder against the bookshelves on the left to enable someone to get up to the highest books.

On the floor of the room was a huge ancient-looking rug on top of the highly polished oak boarded floor. A massive and very elegant desk sat at an angle to the huge fireplace and there were several display cases with books and ancient scrolls in them. There were even small objects of art encased within some of them.

"Wow," Amy said as she turned around the room, enjoying the awe-inspiring view. "I can see why you like it so much. What a wonderful place."

"I think so. I try to be in here as often as I can. I just love the feel of this room and knowing that I'm surrounded by the works of some of the best minds humanity has to offer."

Amy looked at him again as he stared up at the thousands of books with a look of pure awe on his face. The antiques she had expected, him being from a wealthy family and in the auctioneer business. She knew he liked books. After all, he had won the bidding for the collections when she first met him, but this place was a surprise. He truly loved the books. She could see it on his face: they weren't just another acquisition of a bored rich man. It made her like him just for that reason alone.

Amy wandered over to the huge fireplace and ran her fingers along the smooth, cold surface of the white marble, peering at the grey streaks in it. As she came to the end of the mantel piece she noticed a wooden door at the side of the fireplace. "Where does this go? Is it a secret passage?" she said and laughed.

Cabot laughed at her childish enthusiasm, "Sadly, no. That's the conservation room. It's for the rarer part of the collection and where I do repairs on the most fragile of the books. The room has within it temperature and light controlled cabinets to protect the vulnerable tomes."

"Nice. I know one or two people that would love to have a look around this place," she said gesturing to the entire study and thinking of Erda and Maggie.

"I'm sure they would, but I let very few people in here," he said and stepped closer to Amy, so close that if he reached out he could easily touch her face with his hand.

"Oh?" she said. She swallowed hard and discovered her breathing had become more rapid in response to his closeness. "Why's that?" Her voice came out almost as a whisper.

"Because I'm very careful whom I let into my life. Very careful indeed," he said as his green eyes bore into her soul.

"I...."

"May I touch you?" he said. His voice seemed suddenly deeper.

Amy didn't trust herself to use words and simply nodded as he stepped into that last foot's length that separated them and, placing his hand gently on her neck below her ear, tilted her head slightly as he brought his down and laid his lips upon hers.

At first, the kiss was gentle and tentative but when she responded to it, it exploded in a rush of passion that forced them both to gasp for air and quickly led them both to lose control.

Before either of them could think again, bare flesh was touching bare flesh as he lifted her and sat her on the edge of his desk, both of them stripping away layers of clothing as if their very lives depended on it and discarding them hurriedly to a pile on the ground.

The sensation of needy hands and hot lips with wet tongues on each other's flesh made them pant heavily and the last barrier of clothing urgently vanished. He lifted her back off his desk, spun her around and pressed his body against hers. He kissed her neck and back with little nibbles making her groan with lust. He could feel himself pressing against her, aching with need. He moved his hands around onto her breasts, cupping them, feeling the sensual weight of them, and he could feel her nipples were erect with his thumb tips.

Amy felt his chest on her back; that delicious warm flesh pressed against her naked skin. His warm hands were leaving a hot trail behind where he had touched. She could feel herself wanting him, aching with urgent need.

As if by an unconscious decision, they both descended to the floor and the beautiful rug that lay seemingly waiting for them.

Cabot took his cue from Amy as both of their needs were great and entered her in one hard and fast moment. He heard her gasp and groan deeply. Holding her by both hips he started to move, slowly at first but then his movements quickly became faster.

She cried out with pleasure, wanting him too much for words.

"You feel so good." he moaned.

He could feel her pushing against him, wanting all of him.

All of a sudden, Amy rolled him over and was on top, moving to her own wild rhythm. The light in the room highlighted the sweat on them both as they flexed against each other.

Amy could feel that delicious build inside and just let go, losing all sense of time or place. She no longer had a perception of the room nor the rug beneath them as she got ever nearer to bone-melting bliss.

He was groaning with every thrust, louder and deeper, over and over again. He couldn't stand the build up any longer and let go of all control too.

A low guttural groan came from her throat and he gripped her tightly by the hips as she squeezed him with her inner muscles. They came together at last and were carried away on a tide of passion and the age-old movement and rhythm that silenced all words. The wild form of lovemaking brought both of them to a climax so quickly that neither were prepared for the sensation of ecstasy as it rushed through their bodies making their muscles twitch and their minds float away.

Breathlessly, she lay down against him, sweat glistening on their bodies.

Carefully, he moved over to hold her in his arms. She lifted her hand and brushed her hair out of her eyes and laid her head on his chest. She smiled a deeply satisfied smile. They kissed slowly and sexily, her passion growing again. Just kissing him turned her on and made her feel horny. She looked at him smiling that wicked smile of power that every woman knows and watched him as he laid there panting and sweating.

"Wow," He exclaimed loudly as he peered

at her with blurry eyes.

As their breathing became easier, and the sweat was starting to cool on the skin, neither one knowing what to say to the other. It has been so unexpected that now they lay together shocked by it all.

As Amy's mind slowly regained control from the instinctual needs of her body, she vaguely wondered why almost dying in a car crash made her so damned horny. She had wanted him so much she could scarcely believe it herself, that is if she hadn't been right there enjoying every moment of him.

Right at that moment, Erda appeared by the desk and said, "Thanks be to God ye art yet alive!"

Chapter Twenty Four

The Next Day

Sitting at her kitchen table sipping tea, Amy tried not to think of the previous night's events, but her mind would just not leave it alone. Not only was she now without transport, she was somewhat embarrassed by the sudden intimacy with Cabot. She barely knew him, and the fact that Erda appeared when she did, well, if that wasn't the most embarrassing thing ever! Having your 14th great-grandmother find you on the floor of a stranger's house, naked and in post-coital bliss.

Of course, Erda had only been worried about her, but still, appearing like that made Amy make a small shriek in surprise, which she had to pretend was a bout of cramp in her calf just to cover it up. Thankfully Erda vanished again once she knew Amy was alright and she saw the intimate situation Amy was in.

True to his word, Cabot had taken her home when she had asked, and was a perfect gentleman thereafter. He neither said nor asked about their shared and frantic moment, leaving it to her to speak of if she wished.

Amy rubbed her hands over her face and shook her head slightly in disbelief at how a lovely day with a summer party could turn so quickly and become something so very unexpected and particularly satisfying.

Supporting her head on her hands, with her arms on the table, she closed her eyes, realising just how little sleep she'd actually had last night—this morning. She had fallen into a physically and emotionally exhausted sleep when she'd got home but had awoken only three hours later as her alarm went off. As usual, it rang at 8:30am and she was unable to get back to sleep as her mind raced and tumbled over all the events of the previous day.

"Art thee well?" Erda said as she appeared in the kitchen.

Amy wasn't sure if she had walked quietly down her staircase or just appeared, either way it made Amy jump. "Yes, fine."

Erda sat down opposite Amy, "Apologies for disturbing ye last night, I felt ye were in deathly trouble deep in my bones. I found thy truck empty and thee had just left with... with..."

"Cabot. His name is Cabot," Amy said just a little too sharply and then guiltily eyed Erda.

"Cabot, aye. I checked back here to see if thee hath come home but 'twas nay here. I did a blood spell to find ye. Cabot and his house be well warded and I couldst nay see thee without ye spell."

"Yes, we both know where you found me... wait, he and his house are warded?"

"Aye, I was a'feared for thee and wanted to be sure thee were safe," Erda said, the worry in her voice was plain to hear.

"I was," Amy said and drank deeply from her cup of tea. She felt mad at Erda because she was embarrassed, and felt guilty with herself for being mad at Erda. She was, after all, only worried for her safely.

"Sorry, I'm feeling a bit out of sorts today and a bit snappy. Thanks for checking up on me," Amy said with a genuine smile of gratitude.

"Thee be welcome," Erda said and smiled in return.

"I wonder why Cabot and his house are warded though. That seems odd. How does he even know of such things, and why would he need it?"

"I nay knowest."

They both sat for several minutes in contemplative silence and then both spoke at once.

"I saw some things you would..." Amy said.

"I found the help..." Erda said.

They both stopped speaking and laughed.

"You first," Amy said.

"Thank ye. I went a'visiting a man who my Alma sayeth was full of knowledge so he couldst answer any question ye had."

"Oh?" Amy's eyebrows raised as she said the word.

"'Twas Johann Weyer. He be a Dutch physician and man of ye Cunning Arts. My Alma said he spoke against punishing ye Witches in ye dark times when 'twere burning all ye healing folk. He called such as Magicians, careful never to use ye word Witch."

"Brave man," Amy said, knowing how dangerous it was at that time in history, when speaking out against the Witch hunts meant you could be accused of being one too and burnt or hung alongside them with no other evidence needed.

"Aye. A goodly man. My Alma only knowest him for a short while when she was a young'en but he left a great impression upon her." Erda wondered to herself if her grandmother, the one she called Alma, had been sweet on Johann.

"Did he give you any help?" Amy finished her tea and placed her favourite, hand-thrown mug back down on the table.

"Aye." Erda's mind returned to the telling of her events the previous night. "He gave me such thoughts as to question those of ye Gypsies who came from Spain. He thought they wouldst help.

Upon his advice, I did journey to one of your ancestors who married into a Gypsy family and they led me to ye family of Gitano, 'tis what they call them in ye land of Spain, who..."

"Yes, yes. Just tell me what you found out," Amy said a little sharply.

Erda stared at Amy and had completely stopped speaking.

"Sorry. Carry on," Amy said and rose to make herself some toast and more tea. *Today is definitely a copious amount of tea day*, she thought as she listened to Erda's long-winded explanation.

"Aye, well, it took several questions and much time, but they told me one branch of ye family who hath boasted to their cousins they could change events, such as ye know of. They hath travelled to ye new world to begin a family of their own. I hath a date we canst travel to and a name."

Amy spun round bread in hand, "A name? Wow, that's great. Maybe if we visit them we can find out what is happening." She grinned and stuffed the bread into the toaster. "Maybe we can even change things back to how they should be, because it's all getting rather confusing."

Pressing down the lever of the toaster, Amy saw in her mind's eye the face of Bryer, the man she had fallen in love with last year, who had suddenly vanished from Morton Creek to be with his much hated ex-wife. *What if that was a consequence of events changing?* A small spark of hope burst in her chest and was quickly doused by the sudden image of Cabot in her mind and what they had done the night before. A thought occurred to her, *had she actually really cheated on Bryer if their relationship had never existed?* Amy's brain began to ache.

"If thee is nay busy this day we couldst travel to visit this person... this Jabez Mort."

The name pulled Amy from her thoughts, "That's the person's name? What kind of name is that? Doesn't sound very Spanish nor a gypsy name to me."

"Perhaps 'tis a name he chose and nay was born with. Some folks dislike gypsies nay matter what country they came from."

"Yeah, it may be a false name."

Amy busied herself with her breakfast and

when it was ready she sat back down at the table. "We can travel, as you put it, after breakfast. I have nothing planned today apart from having to phone the mechanic."

An hour later, with breakfast finished and the call made to the mechanic telling him to do whatever was necessary to repair her father's truck, and another call made to set up a rental car to be delivered to her the next day, Amy was at last free to investigate the Spanish gypsy.

In the bedroom, Amy's phone rang just as they were about to start the Spirit travelling. She peered at the screen, it was an unknown number and she suddenly hoped it was Cabot. "Hello?"

"Amy? It's David... David MacArthur," the solemn voice said.

Amy's heart sank, not that she was unhappy to hear from Aunt Kath and Uncle Cy's son David, but her thoughts had been on Cabot.

"Hey, so I'm free on Friday if you want to come over," Amy said, thinking they still hadn't had the chance to catch up properly.

"I think that will have to wait. I'm sorry to tell you but dad... dad passed away in the night."

Amy's brain stopped and for a moment it refused to work. "I... oh, I'm so sorry, David."

"We knew it was coming, but still..."

"Oh, god, I'm sorry," Amy just didn't know what to say.

"Thanks."

"How's your mum doing? Ok, stupid question. Do you need anything, can I do anything for either of you?"

"No, thanks. The doctor gave mum a sedative. Just wanted to let you know."

"Ok, right, thanks."

"I'll call you when I know more."

"Right, ok. Please do call if you need help with... everything, or if you just need to talk, ok?"

"Ok. Thanks, Amy," David said and hung up.

"Shit," Amy said as she sat down on her bed. Her heart was broken and ached so much. A deep pain spread through her chest as tears fell down her cheeks and she cried in stunned silence.

Amy explained the situation to Erda, and although Erda offered to do the Spirit travelling another day, Amy needed the distraction and they agreed to do it later that afternoon. The last thing she wanted to do was dwell on the loss of her dearly beloved uncle and her father's greatest friend, it hurt too much and reminded her of the loss of her own parents.

Determined to resolve the problem of changing events and secretly hoping that her uncle Cy was one of those unnaturally changed things, she lay down on her bed and let her tears fall until they could fall no more.

****

Later that afternoon, Amy breathed in the scent of the Partitive Unguent once again and she realised she had begun to enjoy the smell of it. It was a pleasant smell of gardens and cut grass, of sweet herbs and green growing things and it lifted her heart each time she breathed in. It had made her warm and relaxed and she soon drifted as if into a kind of sleep.

A moment later, Amy opened her eyes and saw in front of her a huge warehouse with the light of oil-lamps escaping from every small window in the house next to it and even from between the wooden boards of the warehouse's walls.

"When are we?" she said to Erda.

"'Tis September 20th, in ye yeare of our lord God 1690," Erda stated simply.

"And where are we?" Amy said as she looked at Erda.

"'Tis ye new world, a place called Boston."

Amy eyebrows shot up, "Boston? As in Boston, Massachusetts? Cool! Never been here... in any time," she laughed and chuckled to herself. There was just something so deliciously fun about being able to travel to any place and time, and deep down inside her, her inner child wanted to explore everything, everywhere and in every time.

"Come, we must find Jabez Mort," Erda said and began walking toward the large building.

"How do we know he will be here?" Amy said and walked quickly to catch up with Erda.

"'Tis said that in five days he and his partner, Benjamin Harris, wilt be printing the first newspaper in ye colonies," Erda said as she reached the door of the warehouse and made herself corporeal in the blink of an eye.

Amy stared at Erda in surprise, "You want to be seen?"

"Aye, needs must he tell me what he doth know. A Spirit doing such would scare the words from him."

"Good point. What about me?"

"Thee hast nay learned to be corporeal yet, thee can stay Spirit only," Erda said matter of factly and opened the door.

The warehouse was a busy hive of industry and very hot; the air within was incredibly humid. Several dark-skinned slaves, with sweat glistening on their faces, were shredding old clothing and adding it to big, boil pots on several fires placed down the middle of the warehouse.

Erda walked determinedly through the throng of workers toward the back of the building to where she hoped to find the owner. She saw an office with a large slave standing by it blocking her way.

"No. No go 'ere, M'am," the slave said with heavily accented English.

"I must speaketh with thy master."

"No. M'am." The slave folded his arms

and puffed out his chest. It was an impressive chest.

Erda wasn't in the least bit perturbed by the slave. "Tell thy master if he wants to survive ye week he shalt see me."

The slave looked at the young woman in surprise and turned, opened the door and entered the room, closing the door behind him.

"I guess he understands more than he speaks," Amy said to Erda knowing full well no one else could hear her while she was a Spirit.

"Aye."

They both waited without speaking and within moments the door opened again and the slave gestured for Erda to enter. When she did he went out and closed the door quietly behind him.

Erda lingered at the door for a moment.

Amy looked around the room for a moment. It was filled with tables full of jars, with liquids and dried plants in them. There were three books on a wooden shelf behind the desk, and on a table in the middle of the room was a pile of newly made stuff that looked like thick paper.

The man within the room who was now

standing behind the desk leaning on it with his fisted hands was glaring at Erda. His dark eyes cloudy with anger and black hair curled wildly about his head.

"What dost thou mean by this, interrupting a man at his work and threatening his life?" Jabez Mort demanded.

"I do not threaten thee, I come to ye for answers and in exchange I shalt save thy life," Erda said as she moved forward and sat on the stool situated in front of Jabez's desk.

Amy looked at Erda, stunned by her words. This was all news to her as indeed it was to Jabez, evidently, by the way he deflated and suddenly sat in his chair in shock.

"I shalt spare thee ye how and why of all I knowest," Erda said glancing at Amy and remembering their earlier conversation, "Tell me of thy knowledge of Lamentar Ninguno."

Jabez' eyes opened wide in surprise and swivelled to the point where Erda had just looked at Amy, and, finding nothing there of interest he turned his gaze back toward her.

"Regret None? How doth thee know of

it?" Jabez said with a wary look upon his face.

"I know thy family hath knowledge of it and I want thee to tell me if thee hath used it."

"I hath heard of such. Though thy name used is old. Whence last I heard of, it was thirty years a'fore, 'twas by ye name of Hangman's Regret. Why shouldst I tell thee of what I knowest of such matters?" he said and leaned back in his chair with a faint smile on his somewhat devious looking face. He was obviously presuming he had the upper hand in the conversation.

"Hangman's Regret? Well, that's a scary name," Amy said as she sat on the edge of the desk and carefully watched the dark-skinned man, who had obviously come from Spanish stock. She realised she had disliked him instantly and as if her instincts were coiling away from him, she got off his desk and stepped closer to Erda.

"In five days thou art releasing a newspaper with thy partner Benjamin Harris but thee will not live to see ye end of said day. Thee wilt be murdered and I hath ye knowledge of by whom and how it comes to pass... so thee can escape it."

Jabez's mouth fell open and his face drained of all colour. For a few moments the man was so stunned he could not utter a word. Eventually regaining some of his composure and colouring, he blinked and sat forward. "How dost thee knowest this?"

"Tis only I do which concerns thee."

"I... well... we..." Jabez swallowed hard, folded his shaking hands on the desk in front of him. He breathed in and out slowly for a moment and then tried again. "None knowest of what we plan for ye 25th. None except myself and Benjamin Harris."

And all your slaves, Amy thought amazed at the man's arrogance and dismissal of his workers because they were merely unimportant slaves.

"Believe thy life is in danger and thee hath knowledge I need, so I propose a trade for each."

Jabez looked skeptical.

"How do you know all this?" Amy said to Erda.

Erda replied to both Amy and Jabez at once, "I hath spoken to thy family in times to come and they told me of thy death and thy plans for this occasion. Thy newspaper wilt be seized by ye men of ye Governor Simon Bradstreet and there wilt be a trial against Benjamin Harris for publishing thy paper. Thee wilt nay see the end of ye day as thy man from Seville, whom thee cheated out of his son's tuition hath knowledge of how thee fled to ye New World upon his monies. He wilt come upon thee on thy day of celebration amidst ye crowds and cut thee down in ye street."

If Jabez had gone pale before it was nothing compared to the colour he went now. It began with puce and defused into a sickly cream colour, and now, his once olive toned skin was a decided shade of green. The man's eyes bulged and his mouth opened and closed several times like a fish out of water.

"I suggest thee tells me of thy knowledge of ye spell and then leaves this place for unknown shores before thy pursuer catches thee," Erda said as she sat back in the chair and watched the man's mind process the news and the horror of having to give up all he knew and owned to run for his life.

After a few moments, the olive skin on his face returned to a normal colour and a calculated look appeared in his eyes.

"Now thee hath told me of thy knowledge why should I tell thee of mine?"

Erda watched him and, as if making a decision, she nodded slowly to herself and rose from her chair. She stared at him and as her body rose into the air and became Spirit, she moved forward so that her body was in the middle of his desk and semi-transparent.

"Whoa!" Amy said and staggered backward in surprise.

Horror-struck Jabez gripped his chair with both hands and leaning as far away from the apparition as he could get, so far in fact that his chair toppled over backward. He was still sitting in it, laying on his back on the ground, as the Spirit of Erda hovered over him. She looked down at him closely, barely two inches from his face.

A strangled cry escaped from Jabez's throat as he closed his eyes and tried to shy away from the spectral face.

"We should lock that big guy out!" Amy said, sounding panicked.

"I hath already locked ye door upon our

arrival," Erda said to Amy over her shoulder.

Amy rushed over to the door and quickly checked the key in the lock just as the big man outside was trying to gain entry.

Jabez heard the loud knocking on the door, presumed the demented Spirit had even more powers than first thought and a shiver of fear ran down his spine.

"Tell me about thy spell or thee shalt die this very day."

"I... we..." he began and opened his eyes only to close them quickly when he saw she was still there. "A young man by the name of Benjy Thomas found me out and asked for help. His mother had been hanged as a Witch and he wanted revenge." He gulped and continued: "He brought ye bark wood from her hanging tree and ye root of it with some locks of her hair and a bone from her grave. We made Amate from it," His voice shook with fear as the words rushed forth from his mouth.

"What be Amate?" Erda demanded.

"'Tis... 'tis ye Aztec's shaman's paper... a process makes it from wood and creates a magickal paper. My... my... family learned the way of it many years ago when we... we... invaded Mexico in 1520...I believeth... we hath passed it down through generations... we use it for... for ye magickal purposes."

"Where is thy magic paper?" Erda said.

"We... we... made it into a book and made wooden boards... for protection of ye delicate pages. I... I... made ye Hangman's Regret spell upon those pages so he... he.. could write upon it his revenge and it would happen thus."

Erda looked at Amy and Amy looked at Erda.

"So it's not a person we are after, but a book?" Amy said, astonished.

"Aye, 'tis a very special book," Erda replied to Amy.

"Who art thee talking with? Is there more of ye demons here?" Jabez's voice raised an octave with fear.

"There is a room full of thy demons to devour thy soul and they wilt only leave thee be if thou tells of where thy book is," Erda said in a level and very threatening voice.

Amy was impressed, Erda really knew how to scare someone. She laughed to herself at how crazy her life had become since meeting Erda.

"No! No, please I wilt tell thee!" Jabez begged. "He took ye accursed book with him and he... he.. got his revenge and changed many things to become very wealthy without a'care for ye consequences."

"Like what, pray tell?' Erda said.

"He... if thee changes thy fate, thee changes an'other's fate too. As a stone thrown upon a pond, ye stone vanishes but ye ripples continue. 'Tis ye danger of such magicks and why 'tis not done lightly."

"Where be thy book?"

"I do knowest not, he died of ye pox in the yeare of our lord god 1678. I nay knowest of thy book since."

Erda moved away from the man, stood up and looked down at him as he quailed on the floor.

The man frantically crawled out of the fallen chair and backed up against the wall.

"Leave me, demon," he said, his hands covering his eyes so he could no longer look upon her and her evil.

"Ye magic used on thy book is powerful. Can it be tracked?"

Jabez nodded quickly. "With a Seerer's blood. If thee canst find one of great power."

"Come, we hath all we need." Erda took Amy's hand in hers and they both vanished from Jabez's office and left the man whimpering against the wall with his slave still banging on the stout oak door.

Chapter Twenty Five

Present Day

"So what now?" Amy said to Erda as she climbed off her bed. Travelling with Erda was not tiring but every time she woke up back in her own body she had a raging thirst. "I need a cuppa," she said and headed towards the kitchen.

Erda followed quietly behind and Amy could almost hear the thought processes of Erda's mind ticking like an old grandfather clock.

Or should that be a grandmother clock? She wondered. A moment of amusement fluttered inside her mind and her mouth twitched and lifted in a half smile. The amusement died down quickly, though, as she remembered the reality of the world she had returned to, a world without uncle Cy. Sighing deeply, she pushed all thoughts of his death from her mind and tried to concentrate on what they now knew. If they could find the book and somehow reverse the damage it had caused, perhaps they could save uncle Cy. She didn't even want to contemplate all the possible things that could go wrong or what she would do if it didn't save him. No, thinking like that was not an option.

Amy rubbed her hands over her face, trying to push away all the thoughts that clouded her mind. She put the kettle on for tea and waited patiently for Erda to speak. She had gotten to know the woman well enough by now and could tell when she was still processing and ordering her thoughts.

"Hmm... Benjy got wood of ye tree his mother died upon and with Jabez made a book of magickal wood paper, which was already soaked in many deaths 'afore from the Hangman's tree. 'Tis now spelled and channels ye deaths into ye power of change upon events and lives," Erda said as she sat down at the kitchen table. She was not looking at Amy. She stared in front of her as she thought upon the recent news and was ordering her thoughts out loud.

"Yes, that's what I understood from your... conversation with Jabez."

Erda turned to watch Amy put two tea bags in the bright yellow teapot.

"You know, you were a bit scary there for a while," Amy said and turned round to look at her friend.

"Aye, well, needs must," Erda said and shrugged.

"Didn't realise you were so good at haunting someone. Have you done it before?"

"Oh, Aye. On occasion."

"Interesting... I look forward to hearing all those tales," Amy said.

Amy grabbed the squealing kettle, turned off the Aga hot plate and poured the hot water into the teapot. She placed the kettle back on the stove, but on another cooking plate which was cold.

"When needs must, I suppose?" she said as she closed the small lid of the teapot.

"Aye."

"Sooo... what's next? How do we find the book?"

"We shalt track ye magic of ye book. Magicks that strong and powerful doth leave a trace like a snail does upon thy window." Erda nodded to the window behind Amy.

Amy followed the direction of Erda's gaze and saw that there was indeed a slim trail across the glass of the kitchen window. It appeared as if the snail had found its way onto the glass and then turned around in a big loop. It had then gone across the pane and disappeared somewhere. It then occurred to her that she had a snail in her conservatory as that was where the window now looked into instead of outside. She made a mental note to go and find it before it chewed too many of her indoor plants. Her mind then came back to the conversation at hand and she turned back to Erda.

"How does one track the trail of such magic, though?"

"By magicks, of course."

That sounded reasonable enough and somewhat obvious to Amy and she nodded her head as she poured out a cup of tea out for herself. Bringing it to the table she sat down next to Erda.

"Do you know how to do it?"

"Aye. My Alma taught me when I was but a child. All magicks hath a trail like ye snail, but ye stronger it is, ye brighter ye trail is. Just as all magicks has a price, thee can nay take without giving too: 'tis a balance."

"Oh, and what price will there be for such magic?"

"Nay, can tell but 'tis never what thee expects."

They sat quietly for a while, both lost in their own thoughts.

"'Tis ye waxing crescent moon on the morrow. I shalt do ye magicks then," Erda said and nodded as if agreeing with herself.

"Right, then," Amy watched Erda for a moment. She wasn't sure why the phase of the moon was important, but if that was when she thought it was best, then so be it. Sipping her tea, Amy glanced up at the clock on the wall "Damn, I forgot with everything happening today," Amy jumped up, poured some of her hot tea down the sink and topped the mug up with cold water and swiftly drank it down. She placed her now empty mug in the sink.

"What vexes thee?" Erda said, looking startled.

"Maggie is coming over for dinner today and I'd forgotten all about it. She'll be here in about thirty minutes. I'm off for a shower," Amy said and rushed from the room.

By the time Maggie's car pulled into Amy's gravel driveway, Amy had created a bowl of salad and was grilling two succulent salmon steaks. She had already made a large jug of iced tea, which was sitting in the fridge and was the perfect antidote for a hot summer's evening. Erda had returned to her attic and was doing whatever it was she did when not around Amy. Amy had ceased to wonder about Erda's movements long since.

Maggie knocked on the door right on time and walked in calling for Amy.

Amy rushed to greet her guest who had looked a little nervous for a moment and then warmed up to her and they stepped into a friendly hug. It was the first time they had seen each other since the Solstice party and the revelations of that night.

Perhaps she is nervous now that I know she is Pagan, Amy wondered but didn't ask and was determined to show her friend that she was quite comfortable with it all. Perhaps one day she could tell her that she wasn't her only Witch friend.

One day.

Maybe.

Maggie helped Amy carry out the drinks and the food to the table in the garden. It was down near the lake and under a small grove of luscious maple trees. The table was wonderfully shaded by the trees and so they were able to sit at it in the early evening and be protected from the still bright and hot sun. Amy had learned as a small child, when she came to the cottage for the summer holidays with her family, that the Canadian sun was much stronger and hotter than the British one. At least that was how her mother had put it, as if there were two different suns. Amy had always thought her mother was right; it did seem like a much bigger and stronger sun in comparison and she quickly learned she would get sunstroke if not in a hat or in the shade most of the time.

This was one of Amy's favourite spots on her land, with the slight breeze that came off the lake, the table enjoyed a slightly cooler temperature and the soft rustle of the overhead leaves were enchanting and soothing.

"Ah, this is lovely. I could do with being here like this every day," Maggie said as she served herself some salad.

"Yes, I love sitting out here and I often bring my laptop down and sit here to write."

"Good spot for it too, but if it was me I think I would just be tempted to stare out over the lake and let my mind wander in the quietness of this beautiful place."

Amy poured them both some iced tea, ensuring they both got slices of lemon in it. "Oh, I do that too and I've been known to just close my eyes for a few moments and suddenly wake up when the sun sets and the chill comes in the air from the lake."

Maggie laughed, "Yeah. I'd do that too down by my part of the river." She paused for a moment and then said, "Hey, I was sorry to hear about Cy's passing. How are you doing?"

"Yeah, it's so sad but I'm okay. Such a shame, he was a lovely guy. I understand aunt Kath had to be sedated. I'll go and check on her tomorrow," Amy said and sighed deeply.

"If there is anything I can do for her or you, you will let me know, right?"

"Yeah, thanks."

They sat in silence for a while, watching the sun move inexorably towards the western horizon. At last, the conversation returned and they ate and drank while chatting about everyday things and the future of the book store, until eventually they came to the subject of Amy's next book.

"So what's your next one about? Am I allowed to know?" Maggie said as she sat back in her chair, having devoured her dinner, and was now sipping her iced tea with enthusiasm.

"Well, I'm still working on it, but I'm getting the story formed in my mind. Usually, I write a bit and then do something else while my mind works on the next part of the story and then, when it's full again, I sit back down and type it all out. As for the actual storyline, well... I'm doing another book in the same series as Witch Bottle," Amy grinned at Maggie, "I've actually managed to get about twenty five chapters of the draft written, which I'm so happy about. This one seems to flow so easily, it's like I'm reciting it from a movie in my head and putting it down on paper. Love that feeling, it's so satisfying. I'm looking forward to seeing where this one leads me," Amy said with a knowing smile.

"I know you won't tell me about it yet, but I can't wait to find out what's happening in that awesome brain of yours," Maggie said and laughed, then looked thoughtful for a moment. "I find your witch Erda so interesting. What a great character."

The talk of witches had them both thinking back to the conversation at Maggie's party where Maggie had admitted her beliefs to Amy.

They both sat quietly for a moment.

"I'm glad you told me and trusted me with something so personal," Amy said and took a sip of her own drink and kept looking out at the lake.

"Me too. I'm glad I didn't scare you away," Maggie said with a nervous half-laugh.

Amy turned to her friend, "Wouldn't happen. Anyway, you are not the first nor the second or even third Witch I've met," she said with a mischievous smile.

"Oh, do tell." Maggie said and leaned forward putting her arms on the table.

"One day, I will," Amy said and promised to herself that one day she would tell Maggie everything.

Maggie smiled, "Okay, I shall look forward to it. Hey, I noticed your truck wasn't in the driveway, are you having something done to it? Or did you finally decide to sell it to a collector?"

"Oh... that is a long story," Amy said and blushed remembering how the night of the party ended.

"Now, you have to tell me," Maggie said, seeing the raised colour of Amy's cheeks.

"Don't you have to get back to work or something?" Amy said and laughed nervously, secretly wishing to escape the conversation and hoping Maggie had a late night stock check or something.

"Nope, Rob and Laura are closing up for me tonight, so spill. What happened to your truck and why haven't you already called me and told me about it?" Maggie said with a look on her face like a child that just found a new toy.

Damn it, Amy thought and blushed some more.

Her words rushed out in an almost crazed tumble as she told Maggie about the crash, about it not really being Cabot's fault because of the rain, and about his lovely house and then after a slight pause of looking at Maggie's shocked face, she told her the entirety of what happened next.

When she had finished explaining everything she looked at her friend right in the eye and saw what could only be described as a look of utter incredulity on Maggie's pretty face and then a fleeting look of anger.

"Oh fuck," Maggie said.

It's was all she would say on the matter.

For now.

Chapter Twenty Six

The new crescent moon shone brightly and glowed in the sky like someone had turned on a spotlight directly on it.

The stars could clearly be seen as Amy looked up and tried to make out various constellations. Sitting under the maple trees once again, this time in the dead of night, Amy found the night air just a little chilly and the breeze off the lake made goosebumps ripple up her arms. She grabbed the hoodie from the back of her chair and put it on, all the while watching Erda as she set out candles, a large world map book from Amy's bookshelf, several bowls, sprigs of different herbs and various kitchen implements including a pestle and mortar. There was also a half-finished bottle of wine that she had been saving. All these items made Amy wonder if Erda was about to do a spell or bake a cake and drink the wine with her under the glorious moon.

Erda saw Amy eyeing the various tools as she placed them on the table from the cloth bag, which was currently sitting on the nearest chair.

"When doing thy magicks, thee dost nay need all ye fancy things thy Witchcraft shops sell these days, thy just needs simple kitchen knives, spoons and bowls. 'Tis nay ye tools which make ye a Witch."

"I suppose so. Anyway... when have you gone into witchy shops?"

"Thy knowest I hath been around for hundreds of years. Dost thy think I spent my time a'sleep?" Erda raised an eyebrow.

"No, just never imaged you going into New Age shops."

"Tis nay ye new age I care for but ye old age and ways. Some of thy places still remember those ways."

"Glad to hear it."

"Aye, but today's Cunning Folk art nay

properly trained for ye mess with things of old thee knowest nay about and hath naught control over what ye do," Erda said, the aggravation plain on her face.

"That might be true, but tell me, what are you doing now and how will this work?" Amy said, rose from her chair and came to stand by Erda, looking down at the collection of items on the wooden table.

"I wilt cast to find ye book with ye power of ye waxing moon. These herbs which wilt open ye trail of magicks and show us on ye yonder map where ye book rests."

"Right," Amy said, having no clue how that would all work but willing to be open minded because Erda always seems to know what she was doing. She watched Erda finish setting out everything she needed, then stepped back and stood quietly for a moment.

"'Tis right to clear thy mind of thy thoughts and think only upon thy need."

Amy closed her eyes for a moment too and just thought about finding the book, then opened her eyes and watched Erda begin working the spell.

"Put thy herbs of mugwort and wormwood within thy pestle and grind them 'til mixed, add thy juice to thy wine and drink."

Erda offered the cup of herbed wine to Amy.

"Me?" she said, looking stunned. She took the cup and looked in it. There were two, maybe three mouthfuls of the dark liquid.

"Aye, thy is alive and thy hath eyes 'twill see."

"Oh," Amy said and felt a twinge of fear in her stomach.

"'Tis well, I wouldst nay hurt thee," Erda said and gave Amy an encouraging nod.

"I know, just never had these herbs before, and I know they can be powerful and mind altering, even dangerous in the wrong amounts. Erm... do you want me to drink all of it?"

Erda nodded and watched as Amy bravely drank the mixture down in one go.

"Yuk, that was like drinking wine with a broken tea bag in it," Amy said and tried to get the small pieces of herbs off her tongue.

Erda took the cup and placed it back on the table and picked up the sharp kitchen knife.

"Thy thumb."

"My blood too? You should have told me all this first," Amy said, a little annoyed, but duly held out her thumb as Erda made a quick cut and added two drops of Amy's blood to another cup.

"Wouldst thee nay hath helped?"

Amy thought for a moment, "Of course I'd still help, but it's nice to know what will happen beforehand. It's nice to prepare yourself for such things. Oh, I'm feeling a bit lightheaded."

"'Tis ye herbs, there's nay enough to have much effect, thee only needs to open thy mind. Watch ye map book and tell me what thy sees."

Amy sat down a little hesitantly next to the map book and watched Erda as she took the second cup, poured a dark liquid into it from a small stoppered bottle and mumbled words that didn't sound like English over the cup.

Erda then picked up a small-tipped paintbrush, dipped it into the cup and painted onto the cover jacket of the map book a very strange and detailed drawing that reminded Amy of the pictures she used to draw on her Etcha-Sketch years ago. The drawing on the book cover consisted of intricate scrolls and curls, lines and dots.

"What's that?" Amy said as she tried to peer at it closely while Erda continued painting.

"'Tis a Stave, like a Sigil, but it hath much more strength. Thee wilt be able to see, if thy wishes, throughout ye world, backwards and forwards. Thee should concentrate on it and think only of ye magicks book we seeketh." Erda said and stepped away from the drawing and placed the cup and paintbrush on the table. She then held out her hand inviting Amy to come closer and look into the Stave.

Standing up, Amy looked down over the beautifully intricate Stave drawing and did as she was told. Seconds ticked by and they quickly turned into minutes but nothing happened except a weird floaty feeling in her mind.

"I don't see anything," Amy said and began to feel rather self-conscious, "and I feel kinda funny now."

"Trace ye pattern with thine eyes and

think on ye book only."

Amy did as instructed and followed the lines of the image as if it was one of those labyrinth puzzles where you had to find the route that led out, only she couldn't find one. The picture coiled back in on itself and wherever the end was it was attached to the beginning and it had become a perpetual puzzle picture. Amy squinted her eyes as the colour of the ink went from a strange earthy brown/red colour to a deeper, darker shade. "It's changing... the colour of the ink is changing!" she said excitedly.

"Hush, concentrate thine eyes."

Amy watched and concentrated. Before her eyes the ink went to a royal purple colour and seemed to sink into the book through each and every one of its pages like a brand burning through layers of flesh.

"Oh my god," Amy said, stunned by the sight.

"Hush, Amy. Let it do thy magic," Erda said in barely a whisper. As she watched Amy's face and the changing emotions she was going through, she deeply wished she could see what her descendant was seeing right at that moment.

Amy watched as the design melted its way down to the very wood on the table. She could see the grains of the wooden surface right down through the hollowed out pages of the book. Suddenly the ink vanished and Amy blinked at the book before her and all was back to normal. There was no design on it nor any other pattern, and she could no longer see the table through it. All there was before her was the slightly tattered dust jacket of her old map book sitting on the garden table.

"It's gone," Amy said as she felt a strange sadness and looked at Erda. "The pattern has gone now, but I could see down through the pages to the table."

"Aye, 'tis right."

"Well, that didn't tell us much, did it?" Amy said and sat back down in her chair, grabbed the remains of the bottle of wine and drank a gulp straight from the bottle, not caring if it made her more floaty or not.

"It giveth us more than thee thinks," Erda said and reached out for the book. Lifting it off the table, she sat down next to Amy with it on her lap.

Amy glanced at the table, expecting to see the pattern outlined on it like a brand but there was nothing, no sign of what she had seen. She took another gulp of wine and looked at Erda. "What now?"

"Now, dearest Amy, we find ye book," Erda said and opened the book at the first page. She flicked through until she came to the first map, which was of the entire world.

Amy looked at the page before them and on it was a round dot on North America in the colour of the royal purple ink.

"Whoa... that's crazy," she said and squinted closely at it.

"It be on thy continent, find thy page for the Americas," Erda said and passed the open book to Amy.

Amy peered closely as the mark which was on the east side of America, maybe in New England. A flutter of excitement raced around in her stomach as she turned the pages and saw the mark was on the larger map of America. She was right, it was just above the name of a town.

"Boston. The mark is next to Boston. Is that where the book is then? It stayed in Boston all these years?" Amy looked up excitedly at Erda.

"Nay, 'tis where 'twas made we must now followeth ye book's journey until ye marks end and 'twill be where ye book lays now."

Amy turned the book's pages carefully as she watched the dot jump around New England.

Then it went to England, where it changed places twice and then came back across the ocean to New York and then up into Canada. "Oh my god, the book is here. Here in Canada! No way!"

"Find thee thy page for Canada," Erda said, the excitement also plain in her voice.

Amy's stomach churned as she turned page after page until she found the right one. She had reached the detailed map of Canada and there the dot sat on the province of Ontario.

Her province.

The Province where they were both sitting, right at that very moment.

Amy and Erda looked at each other in shock as Amy turned the page, looking for a detailed map for Ontario.

The page lay on her lap before them both with the dot squatting like a fat evil toad upon their very town of Morton Creek, alongside four other smaller dots.

"Ho...ly Shit," Amy said as they both gaped at the map in utter disbelief and horror.

Stunned silence prevailed for several minutes.

"What are these other dots?" Amy said.

"'Tis other magicks around us. 'Tis nay important now. Only ye big dot for ye book concerns us presently," Erda said and peered closely at the map. "Dost thee have a town map?" Erda eventually asked. "Ye shalt need to do thy ritual again."

Chapter Twenty Seven

December 1678, Plymouth,
Massachusetts

Benjamin Thomas Hibbens, as he now called himself, lay in his warm bed, surrounded by his family, as he struggled against the high fever and pain of the pox. He was in his last few hours and he knew it. He had asked for his family to leave him for a little time while he communed with his maker, and, once they had left the room, he had his loyal and ever discreet servant Samuel fetch the book.

Propped against pillows, drenched in fever sweat, Benjy opened for the final time the magickal and extremely powerful book to reread his entries and gloat at what he had done. His damp, shaking hand moved over the ink and the soft pages of the book he had created so many years ago with Jabez Mort. Another spasm of pain wracked his weakened and ravished body, and he could feel his fever returning. Closing the book upon his lap, he closed his bloodshot eyes for the last time, he hoped. As he lay in his fevered state he recalled the first entry he had made and what he had accomplished over the last seventeen years with the power of the book.

****

It had taken Benjy a few days after the book was made to have the courage to use it, and, as he sat in his mother's cottage by the river, he inscribed the first words with ink mixed with his own blood on the night of November 6th, 1665.

"I charge thee, book of mine," Benjy said aloud as his hand scrawled the words messily over the page. He had never had the time nor practice to perfect his handwriting skills, but thanks to his mother Ann, he could read and crudely write the letters and that was enough for this magic. "To henceforth do my bidding, as I set my will upon thee thou shalt set it in stone and time," he said with the most commanding tone of voice he could muster.

His hand paused over the page as he contemplated all the possibilities, and, at last, he returned the quill to the paper and made a list. "Firstly, thou shalt make me rich, respected hereabouts," he had spoken aloud again, as if in conversation with the magic directly. As the ink dried, a great whirling wind surrounded Benjy, full of smoke, flames and ash, so that he could no longer see the room around him. He gripped the book, fearing for its safety, and when the wind abruptly stopped, Benjy was sitting in the same position at the old, rough-hewn table in the centre of the cottage. However, there were several leather money pockets on the table that had not been there before.

Benjy jumped off the bench and grabbed at one of the pockets. He emptied the contents onto the table and laughed loudly as the Spanish gold tumbled noisily onto the wood. He emptied another and found the same. In manic excitement, he emptied all the bags onto the table and found within them gold and silver pieces. It was beyond his understanding, almost. He had never seen so much money in his life and he sat down heavily upon the bench, in shock. His eyes sparkled with the glow of the coins. His mouth hung open and his heart raced, and eventually his brain caught up with the spectacle before him and he began to plot his life and revenge. First he would bring his mother back with the power of the book, and then they would get her revenge on those who accused her of witchcraft and testified against her. They would kill everyone who had dealings with her trial, including the hangman and, of course, the magistrates who had condemned her.

He had vowed to put things right, and at long last he was about to do just that. A deeply excited thrill ran the entirety of his body, energizing him to his very soul.

He took up his quill and once again wrote his desire in the book, which was to have his mother by his side again that very moment, but nothing happened. No wind, no whirl of flames and no ash spun around him. There was no reaction from the book at all. Over and over he tried but for naught, until he grew tired and cursed the book, throwing it across the room in a fit of rage. Finally, he collapsed exhausted on the bed and fell into a fitful sleep.

"Benjamin, my sweet boy. Do awaken now."

The woman's voice said close to his ear. So close in fact he could feel her breath upon his flesh.

"Mother?" Benjy shot straight up on the bed and looked into the face of his beloved mother, who looked just as she had during those times he was allowed upstairs and in her presence.

"Yes, my boy, it is I," Ann said and stroked the ruffled hair from his face gently.

Benjy's face lit up with happiness. "It worked, mother, it worked!" he said and pulled her into his aching arms.

Ann pulled away from him after a brief moment.

"It did not, Benjy. I be nay whole and of blood and bone. I be in ye book, made of ye book just as 'tis made of me. I canst nay leave it except by Spirit and be with thee as ye wish. So I be here with ye in thy dreams, my sweet boy."

"Oh mother... I'm sorry, I tried... I tried so hard."

"I knowest, but thou hast brought us thus far and so we shalt proceed with thy plans. I hath a list of names ye must remember upon awakening for ye must avenge me, Benjy," Ann said gravely. "I wilt help thee."

Her voice rang in Benjy's head like a hammer tempering steel at a blacksmiths. Each name rang out and engraved itself on his mind. Once the list was indelibly forged upon him, Benjy awoke with a start. He had a sense of such determination that he knew no matter how long it took, he would kill each and everyone on the list and give his beloved mother her revenge. His heart soared with happiness that she was still with him, even if in his dreams only and his soul now knew its purpose.

After breaking his fast with porridge and warm beer, Benjy sat before the book once again and wrote 'Benjamin Thomas Hibbens, Scribe of this Book 1665'. He then listed all the names his mother had given him, and next to each of them he wrote the most painful, gruesome and hideous death he could imagine for them all, and waited for the whirling wind to take his directions and make them real.

****

Joshua Scottow, a middle aged, portly man of distinguished looks, examined himself in the mirror before him as he watched his servant dress him with the disinterest of one used to such sights.

"Fetch my gloves," he said, not even bothering to look at the slave he spoke to and stood admiring his reflection, turning this way and that, enjoying his newly tailored overcoat.

"Joshua..."

Joshua spun on his heel and looked around him, startled as he knew he was alone.

"Joshua, I'm over here."

He turned again but this time back to the mirror and gasped, his hand going in horror to cover his mouth.

"Joshua, there you are my love."

"Ann? Ann art thou there? How canst this be? Thou art dead," he said and whimpered in fear, staggering backward.

"'Tis truth. I hath died upon ye hangman's rope and thee did naught to stop them my lover." Ann's ghostly face peered at him forlornly from the mirror.

"'Tis nay truth, I gaveth my deposition in favour of thee over and over but they wouldst nay listen."

"Perhaps thee did but thou recanted thy deposition, did thee not?" Ann said as her face grew larger in the mirror.

"I... well, thee hath to understand... to ally myself with thee... afterward, 'twas...dangerous, my love."

"'Tis more dangerous for thee now, my lover."

Ann moved forward and loomed out of the mirror as if the glass was soft and pliable, stretching her image out to reach him as her sharp hand of glass rammed into his throat, tearing flesh, muscle and bone as she grabbed him, vocal cords included, and ripped them easily apart from his body.

As his body fell to the ground, forever torn asunder, Ann's apparition fell too and exploded into a thousand pieces of looking glass upon the floorboards and glistened in the ever-growing puddle of blood.

****

Benjy's mind cleared briefly from the fever which was eating his mind and he smiled to himself as he remembered the last name from the list and the killing of his mother's lover who had betrayed her even after death. "I hath enjoyed our revenge mother," he said to himself.

"As have I, my sweet boy. But 'tis time for thee to be with me eternally now."

"I knowest mother, and I'm glad of it at last."

With one last breath, Benjy's fevered, pox-ridden body died and his soul passed into the book to remain alongside his mother's for all eternity.

He was the first of all the Scribes to do so.

He certainly wouldn't be the last.

Chapter Twenty Eight

Present Day

Amy sat in her rental car, staring out of the window, unable to believe that the book was here.

In Morton Creek.

At this address.

With this person.

Erda sat in the car's passenger seat and she kept turning her head between the house and Amy, worrying how deeply this development would affect her friend.

They were parked on the road that the second map and ritual had indicated, although a few houses further up, however, they could clearly see the actual house ahead of them. They were waiting in the early hours of the morning for the owner to leave so they could break in and steal the book. That was their best idea and it was as far as their plan had got since the shocking revelation of its actual location at midnight the previous night.

At last, the owner of the house exited, climbed into their car and drove off for a day of business.

At least that's what they both hoped.

Looking at each other, Amy and Erda silently climbed out of the car and walked down the road toward the house. They made their way around the back and looked for an easy access point. They found a secluded window and Erda evaporated only to appear inside the house, she unlocked the window, pushed the sliding sash upward and put a hand out to help Amy climb in.

"You're really rather handy, aren't you? We could be cat burglars and steal such amazing things from museums and private collections... we could make a fortune with your talents," Amy said. It was a nervous conversation to fill the void that the deep dread in Amy's soul had created. It didn't work.

"'Tis nay right stealing," Erda said as she helped Amy through the window and closed it quickly behind them.

"Erm... yeah. I was joking. Anyway, if I was caught it would be pretty damn hard to explain the invisible person opening doors and windows on the security footage, wouldn't it?" Amy said as she straightened up and looked around her. She knew she was distracting her mind with nonsense to avoid the feelings of guilt that she was now having because she was breaking into the house of a person she knew. How had her life come to this? To have to do such a thing?

"Where doth thou think ye book t'would be?" Erda said, looking around herself at the room they were in the middle of.

"I can guess. There is a special place where the valuable books are kept, follow me." Amy headed out of the room with the determination of one who knew the way.

Amy froze mid-step as she heard the front door open and close. "Shit, someone's here," she whispered to Erda.

Erda immediately disappeared and

reappeared beside Amy, "'Tis thy lover."

"What?" Amy looked startled and was tempted to say which one but denied the urge. Life certainly got complicated when one's personal history got changed by magic. Amy felt like a fool but had to say it, "Who?"

Erda's eyebrow raised, "Dost thee not remember how I saw thee naked with him after thy tuppin'?"

"Ah, right...yes of course. Shhhh... he might hear us," she said as she remembered that particular naked moment and it sent a ripple of embarrassment and excitement along her spine, but it was quickly quashed by a sudden noise in the hallway close to the room they had hidden in.

The door of the room slowly opened and the man stepped in. "What the fuck are you doing here? And who the fuck is that?" Cabot said to Amy and gestured toward Erda.

"I'd like to know what the fuck you are all doing here?" Maggie said from behind Cabot as she stood in the doorway.

Cabot spun round on his heel at the sound of Maggie's voice.

Amy stood with her mouth open, her brain racing through the moment as if the world was in slow motion. How had they all arrived here now, at this same moment? What did they all truly know? How could Cabot see Erda? How could she explain her presence in the room?

A stiff, awkward silence full of secrets and questions filled the spaces of what seemed a never ending stream of seconds. Then they all spoke at once as if a dam had burst and their words were the water rushing down to crush upon that special place known as friendship.

"Stop!" Maggie shouted above the noise and waited until there was silence. "This is my house, please explain what the hell you are all doing in it, and, why are you all here uninvited?" Anger had rightly boiled up in Maggie's veins and her heart thundered in her chest. She looked from Amy to Cabot and back again. "Amy, you get the benefit of the doubt being my friend, so you can explain all this to me first."

Amy sat down hard on the bed in the spare room of Maggie's house. The room where they had hidden and the very same one that now seemed so small and packed with so much energy it felt like a powder keg. She knew she had to tread very carefully before the situation exploded more than it had and she lost a dear friendship with Maggie and Cabot as a temporary lover.

"It all started when I returned from my book tour. Everything had changed, you see. Stuff I knew had happened, hadn't, and Emily was still alive. Bryer had gone and Cy and Kathleen..."

"Take a breath, Amy," Maggie said, looking concerned that her friend was pale and rambling.

"Right, well. I, we, I mean I..."

"Stop right there, Amy, you need to know right now that I can see Erda and have been able to since you introduced us at the Hallowe'en party last year and I know she is Spirit. I was just waiting for you to confide in me."

"You can? But how?" Amy said in disbelief.

"I can see her too, since that night she... arrived in my library...when, well, you remember," Cabot said.

"I do. Oh god, can anyone else see her?"

"Rest thyself lass, on occasion I canst be

seen and heard by those with ye gift. 'Tis a rare thing, but it doth 'appen," Erda said, seeming completely undisturbed by the revelations. Even, perhaps, a little pleased by them.

"So many questions. But we are off track. Tell me what brings you to my house, Amy," Maggie said, obviously trying to control the conversation so she could get some much-needed answers.

"We worked out the only... magic..." Amy looked from Maggie to Cabot and back again. "There's just one type of magic we found that could cause these changes and so we investigated and have been following the historical clues about a book, the Hangman's Regret book, made by Benjamin Hibbens in 1665, and we finally tracked it here to your house," Amy said, feeling a sense of relief about being open at last, but worried she would lose her friend because of this madness. Of course, there was also the fact that she had just broken into her house. Amy nibbled her lip nervously. This definitely wasn't the plan for today.

"And you?" Maggie turned to Cabot, her

voice sounding colder and harsher.

"I am also looking for the book said to contain the Lamentar Ninguno or Regret None spell. I believed Amy knew of its location, so I've been following her."

"You have? You've been spying on me?"

"Well, yes. As soon as I saw you had more help than I could ever get," he glanced at Erda directly, "then I figured, let you do the work and I would be saved all the time and effort," he said and looked pleased with himself as if he thought he was being clever.

"Such a goddamn man," Maggie said exasperated.

"'Tis important we find ye book and set a'right again," Erda said returning everyone to the point of the moment.

"I do have the book. It came to me accidentally in an old collection at an auction some time ago. At the time I stored it carefully, not realising what it was exactly, until a professor friend and I were having dinner and we spoke of magickal books and that got me thinking. Later that night, I returned to the book and sat and read its contents cover to cover, and I could not believe what I had in my possession. Not only was it an original book from 1665 but it was also an extant original source book of witchcraft in Massachusetts almost thirty years before the Salem witch trials, which made it very rare and valuable. Then, however, the importance of it truly sunk in and I realised just how dangerous it would be in the wrong hands and I knew I would be in danger just by owning it," Maggie said and sat down on the bed next to Amy. "I did the ritual and signed my name in the book as the Scribe as it will protect the Scribe from harm as long as I wish it no ill will. I thought I was being smart as it means no one can take it from me nor can I be harmed while we are linked."

"That's the flaw in your plan, right there," Cabot said as he leaned against the windowsill in the small flowered room.

"Oh, why? You know something I don't?" Maggie said, finding it hard to hide her dislike for the man.

"Actually, as surprising as you may find it, I do."

"Stop postulating and spit it out then," Maggie said.

"You see, the Scribe's soul is trapped in the book with all the other Scribes from over the many years of its existence. There is no way to separate them, the soul of each and every Scribe has been killed by the book when they have finished changing the things they want and no longer have use for it or they have died owning it, either way the book gets the souls. It then goes and looks for another Scribe and because the book can't be destroyed, you are trapped within it forever. So, yeah, not the best decision you've ever made, Maggie," Cabot said looking smug.

"Fuck you," Maggie said, hurling the angry words at him across the room.

"Shit!" Amy said. "Wait, how do you know all this, Cabot?"

"Yeah, what makes you so damned knowledgeable?" Maggie said with a frown.

"My great grandfather was one of those Scribes, and died by the book's evil ways. But not before he told everything to my grandfather, and my family have been searching for the book ever since it vanished at his death."

"Holy shit. Your Great Grandfather? He was a Scribe?"

"Explains a lot about your family," Maggie said.

"Fuck you back," Cabot said childishly.

"I just mean the wealth, not the reason you're all assholes," Maggie said and smirked.

"'Tis time to see thy book, Mistress Maggie," Erda said and stepped into the middle of the room like an umpire.

"Alright, come up to the attic. That's where I keep it in a controlled environment," Maggie said and led the way out of the spare bedroom and up the staircase to the attic.

Everyone followed silently. The three of them who had not seen it wondered what the book would actually be like. Their expectation hung in the air like a fog over a field on a quiet morning with no breeze to move it away.

In the attic, Maggie extracted a wrapped parcel from the environmentally controlled cabinet and placed it on the table nearby. She unwrapped the book from the archival protective material and revealed the wooden board book.

"That's it. That's the cause of so much pain and heartache over the years. I tried to write in it my wishes, to correct several things, but I think I just made things worse. It's all about the actual wording, not the intent. It's a tricky little thing: very literal."

"Well, at least you tried. But I don't like you now being forever linked to it. What were you thinking?" Amy said and placed her hand on her friend's arm to give comfort.

"I just wanted to stop the changes that had been made through it, the lives that it had altered unfairly and put everything back as it should be... to restore the balance."

"Thy be honourable in thy intentions but thee risks much."

"So this is what all the fuss is about," Cabot said as he stepped confidently closer to the table.

Erda instantly disappeared from her position next to Amy and reappeared directly between Cabot and the table. "Step thee away or deal with me," she said as she seemed to grow and tower over him.

Maggie gasped and looked at Amy.

Amy discreetly nodded to Maggie as if to say: don't worry it's okay.

Cabot, however, looked horrified and took a step back, looking wildly around himself for an escape route. By the time he looked back at Erda, she had returned to her normal size but was watching him intently.

"You misunderstand my intentions. That book has been the bane of my family for generations. I want it destroyed and my great grandfather set free, if that is at all possible."

"So what do we do with it?" Amy asked, as she peered at the ancient, wooden cover boards.

"Needs must, we doth destroy it."

"How? Can we burn it? But if we do, what will happen to Maggie?" Fear built quickly inside Amy at the thought of her friend's life being in danger.

"Let's do a small test," Cabot said and pulled a lighter out of his pocket and flicked it on.

Erda watched him closely for a moment and seemed to come to a decision about him, nodded and moved out of his way.

Cabot stepped up to the table and held the flame next to one of the wooden cover corners which was so old and dry, it would easily catch fire. As they all watched in amazement, the flames curved themselves away from the book, as if a wind was pushing it in the opposite direction.

"Well, that's not going to work," he said, and closed the lighter, putting it back in his jeans pocket.

"Did you really think it would?" Amy said.

"Maggie, didst thou feel any heat upon thee?"

"I, well, no. Is that good or bad?"

"I nay knowest. If as thee say Master Cabot that ye book is indestructible, we must cometh at ye puzzle a backward way."

"What are you thinking, Erda?" Amy said.

"We shall speaketh to those that knowest ye most," Erda turned to Maggie, "I doth need salt and candles, if thy pleases."

"Certainly." Maggie crossed the room to the area of her magickal studies and quickly returned with both items.

"Can I help?" Amy asked.

"Aye, place ye book upon thy floor boards and move away ye yonder table. Then thee all come stand by me."

Amy, Cabot and Maggie moved the table to the side of the room, leaving a large open space in the centre and Maggie carefully placed the book on the floor.

For the next several minutes they all watched Erda create a double circle, several feet away from the book and all around the four of them. One ring was drawn smaller and inside the other with the salt, and between the two circles she used the salt to draw protective symbols and placed four candles in with them.

"Nay matter ye outcome, ensure thee all remain within my protection warding, dost thee comprehend?"

"Yes," Amy said a little breathlessly from the building fear that was creeping down her spine.

"You got it," Maggie said and stood close to Amy.

Cabot said nothing but checked the 360

degrees around him to ensure he was completely in the inner circle. "Wait, I recognised some of these symbols, they are what Dr. Dee used when raising angels, though some would say demons."

"Who's Dr. Dee?" Amy asked.

"Dr. John Dee was from your home country, England. He was a mathematician, astronomer, astrologer, occult philosopher, and adviser to Queen Elizabeth I.

He devoted much of his life to the study of alchemy, divination, and Hermetic philosophy. He also had one of the largest libraries in England until it was destroyed and he wrote 'De Heptarchia Mystica', which is where a few of these symbols come from. Some of those others I've never seen before," Maggie said intrigued.

"'Tis for raising ye souls of trapped Spirits," Erda said, and then began speaking in a low voice.

The words she was speaking tumbled out over each other in an unusual and foreign language.

Nobody spoke nor moved except for Erda for what seemed like hours.

It looked like she was drawing the words in the air too.

Suddenly, she stopped speaking and gesticulating with her hands and she stood silently for a few moments.

"Nothing is happening," Cabot said in a disbelieving tone, although a hushed one.

"Hush thee," Erda whispered.

For several more minutes they waited.

Finally, when they almost couldn't stand the quiet any longer, the air shimmered in front of them and the room darkened as the spot in front of them brightened and a strangely dressed middle-aged woman appeared before them.

"Dost thou remember thy name, lost one?" Erda said in a gentle tone as if she was speaking to a child.

The woman looked bewildered and her eyes searched each of the faces now looking at her, for signs of recognition. She frowned and said, "Aye, my name be Goody Hibbens, Ann Hibbens."

Chapter Twenty Nine

"Good meet, Goody Hibbens," Erda said, "Dost thee knowest where thou art?"

"I... indeed nay, I dost not," Ann looked around her and seemed frightened by her surroundings and the people staring at her.

Erda tried hard to explain to Ann, in a language she could understand, what had happened. Why she was here and that we hoped that she, as the first soul trapped in the book, would know of a way to destroy and release her soul.

"Nay, I knowest of none such. 'Tis a binding spell used against me, 'tis beyond my abilities. Thou must find thee who cast it and make them uncast such a masterful spell. Ye needs ye one who first giveth it life but sure thy one is long since gone and I nay knowest who that be," Ann said knowing full well that even if they knew it was Benjy, he would never uncast the spell, no matter how they try to persuade him.

"That would be thy son," Erda said, already understanding that Ann was not to be trusted.

Ann pretended to look horrified.

"Of which dost thou speaketh, for my sons were last in England with their father." Ann's attractive face crumpled in a fake frown of confusion.

"'Tis your other son, Benjamin."

"Benjy? Benjy did this?" Ann said as she closely watched the faces of those looking at her from their protective circles and her mind calculated. "Thy shouldst bring forth my son and we may work ye uncasting," she said, knowing he would outwit them all once freed.

Erda nodded and began speaking the strange quiet language again, making the same gestures and symbols in the air with her hands. The air in front of them once again shimmered and there, next to his mother, stood Benjamin Hibbens.

"Benjy!" Ann exclaimed and wrapped her arms around him in sheer pleasure.

"Mother!" Benjy said and gave in to his mother's attentions.

It was a touching scene, if you discounted the murder and mayhem that had been caused by this man and his love for his mother.

"At last, I canst hold thee again," Ann said.

Benjamin soon released his mother and stood holding his hand in hers. "What dost thee want?" he said directly to Erda in a demanding tone.

Erda evaluated the man before her for a moment and then said, "Thy book must be destroyed and ye changes thee hath set forth must be righted. Uncast thy spell and release ye souls."

"Nay, 'tis nay for thee to say. We all do ye will of ye Scribe," Benjamin said and suddenly the room shimmered around him. "And thou art nay Scribe, be gone and leave us be. Let thee Scribe come forward and banish thee."

From within the protective circle, the three humans and the Spirit watched as every Scribes' soul came out of the book and stood before them filling the room with their ghostly presence.

"Holy shit," Amy whispered to herself.

"Oh, crap," Maggie said and held Amy's hand tightly.

"Fuck me," Cabot said as he searched the faces of the Spirits trying to distinguish his great grandfather's features from amongst them, but he could not. None had any of the facial similarities of his family.

Only Erda was silent for several minutes, and then she looked at Maggie.

Maggie looked back at Erda and a great sinking feeling started in her chest and rushed toward her stomach, almost making her retch in fear.

"'Tis time for thee to do as thee must and write thy wishes in thy book, Scribe," Erda looked pointedly at Maggie.

Maggie nodded, making a move toward the edge of the protective circle.

Amy grabbed her arm, "Wait! You can't go

out there, you will not be protected by Erda's magic."

"You don't understand," Maggie said as she turned to her friend, "I am the Scribe, they will protect me as will the book, at least for now."

"And when they decide not to anymore, what then? What protection will you have then?" Amy said, her voice wavered as the fear welled within her throat.

Maggie gave Amy a half-smile and hugged her, then turned and determinedly walked out of the circle.

Once outside of Erda's protection, Maggie walked slowly but purposefully past and on some occasions through the many Spirits that surrounded the book until she reached it. Picking it up from the floor, she took it to the nearest counter and grabbed the gall and blood ink mixture and her quill. She began to say the secret words of command over the book as she always did before opening it, "I charge thee, book of mine," she said, "to henceforth do my bidding, as I set my will upon thee thou shalt set it in stone and time." She lifted the heavy wooden cover and turned the ancient pages until she came upon her own writing. Dipping the quill in the ink mixture she began to write upon the old paper, carefully placing word after word all the while feeling the presence of the other Scribes' Spirits close to her, almost like a humid day feels oppressive on the skin, only colder.

Suddenly the atmosphere changed and Benjamin, still holding his mother's hand, stepped forward. "What doest thou?" he said, looking sharply at Maggie.

"I'm simply writing my wishes down just as you did, when you were the Scribe, as is my right," Maggie said.

"Stop her, Benjy. She wilt bring forth ruin to all," Ann said, her face clouded with hatred.

"I command thee to cease, Scribe," Benjamin said and took another menacing step forward and became a solid form, much like Erda. He reached out and grabbed Maggie by the hair, jerked her head backwards and dragged her away from the book.

The quill fell from Maggie's hand onto the floor, making a splash of the blooded ink on the bare floorboards, where it sank into the dry, hungry wood.

As Amy watched transfixed, once again all the movements seemed to slow down and she just saw out of the corner of her eye as Cabot flew out of the protective circle and tore Maggie out of Benjamin's grip and pushed her back toward the book.

"Finish it," Cabot shouted and threw himself at Benjamin, taking them both to the ground where they rolled around punching each other.

Ann, on seeing the danger to her son, immediately became corporeal and jumped onto Cabot's exposed back as he pummelled Benjamin.

Maggie quickly picked up the quill and returned to the book as the other Scribes began to become solid and move menacingly towards her.

Erda looked toward Maggie and then toward Cabot.

"Do something, Erda!" Amy cried.

The spirits were now trying to separate Maggie from the book.

Ann had her arm around Cabot's throat

trying to choke him.

Erda disappeared and instantly appeared by Maggie's side and she held the book firmly in place for Maggie to finish writing.

A sickening crack was heard from the far side of the room and all eyes turned towards it.

Cabot lay unmoving on the floorboards with his head at an unnatural angle and Benjamin and Ann stood over him with an identical look of glee on their faces.

"Noooo!" Amy screamed and began to move to the edge of the circle.

"Stop!" Erda shouted so loudly it stunned Amy into non-action. "Nay leave my protection, Amy."

"But... I need... oh God, Cabot." Tears came to Amy's eyes.

"'Tis nay the time. Do as thy must when safety is upon us," Erda said as she struggled to maintain hold of the book because the Scribes were all pulling at her and Maggie to wrench them free from it and, unfortunately, were beginning to get the upper hand.

Finally, the Scribes combined their

corporeal strength and tore Maggie away from the book, and Erda, just as the last stroke of the quill hit the paper and Maggie was thrown across the floor carelessly.

"Maggie!" Amy screamed and fell to her knees, tears freely falling down her face. She desperately wanted to help but could do nothing for anyone in the room. A frustrating feeling of uselessness overwhelmed her as angry tears streamed down her face.

Erda, who had valiantly held onto the book, said to Benjamin and Ann, "Thou art bound by the Scribe letters." She placed the book back on the floor and stepped back from it.

It was then, in that very moment, when the air changed, a subtle shift of force and energies that everyone in the room knew what happened next would determine history, the present and the future.

Benjamin looked stunned and puzzled as he began to recite the spell of creation, the Lamentar Ninguno that he had cast upon the original items during the making of the book, over three hundred and fifty years ago. After each line of the spell he added the words "I uncast thee". His mother grabbed him by the shoulders and shook him violently.

"Benjy, stop thy workings. Nay, go forth for thee wilt destroy all. Benjy, BENJY!" she screamed at him and pleaded with him, but there was nothing she nor he could do but obey the written words of the Scribe.

Erda quickly helped Maggie up and got her back inside the safety of the protective circle.

Maggie collapsed on the floor and sat within Amy's protective arms.

A huge wind burst into life sending a gust around the room lifting items off shelves and blowing them around in a violent whirlwind.

Maggie and Amy clung to each other as their hair flew up and around their faces.

Erda stood inside the circle and shouted above the howling winds, wardings of protection over the women at her feet.

Ann screamed at Benjamin to stop and eventually she grabbed shards from a broken glass shelf and tried to stab him with it but now his corporeal body was protected by the book because he was doing it and the Scribes bidding. She could not harm him nor stop him.

Benjamin finished speaking the spell of making and uncasting.

The book rose up from the ground and opened itself in midair, each of the pages tore themselves from their binding and gravitated away from the book. They floated next to it until all the pages formed a ball around it, like seeds on a dandelion, completely oblivious to the raging winds swirling around it.

With a rush and a howl, the terrible wind was sucked into the floating page ball, past the pages and right into the very shell of the book, and, for a second, all was utterly silent and still. The only movement in the room were the pages still floating gently around the book.

A page in the ball burst into flame as if ignited by sudden and impossible indoor lightning and then another and another until it was a fireball surrounding the shell of the book.

Both Amy and Maggie jumped as the pages became a wild ball of flame and the room became unbearably hot and smoky. Still, Erda stood concentrating hard on protecting them.

Amy looked down at the boards where she was sitting and noticed that the salt protection lines and symbols had vanished, presumably from the strange howling wind that had whipped around them like an angry beast. Amy knew that the only thing protecting them from the fire and the Scribe Spirits that seemed oblivious to the flames and heat was Erda who stood alone with her magic against all.

Across the room, the flames died out to leave ash floating in the air in their place, and, just like the howling wind, the ash began to be sucked into the shell of the book. Amy was reminded of the way water is sucked down a plug hole; she was fascinated by the ash disappearing to who knows where.

However, the book didn't stop there and it then began to suck back into it the souls of the Scribes: their ghostly figures were lifted from the ground and drawn to it. As if knowing they would never return, the ghosts struggled against it and flailed their arms and legs, but to no avail. One after the other they vanished within, until just the corporeal forms of Benjamin and Ann were left.

Benjamin, who had control of himself once more, grabbed his mother's hand and ran for the staircase in the hope of escape.

The book now turned itself towards Benjamin and Ann, and, as if with invisible hands, they began to be dragged backwards towards it, kicking and screaming the whole time. Try as they might, they were not strong enough to fight it and they too were sucked within, cursing and fighting all the way. Once they were completely within the book and gone from sight, the wooden shell of the book crumpled in on itself until there was nothing but a dot floating where the book had been and then with a small 'pop' the dot vanished.

Maggie and Amy looked at each other.

"Was that it? I was expecting something more...." Maggie said.

A rumble could suddenly be felt in the floor boards and became louder and louder.

Maggie and Amy looked at each other again.

"I think you spoke too soon," Amy shouted over the ever-growing noise.

Erda hadn't moved an inch and still she continued to repeat over and over again her protective wardings. She had now returned to her corporeal state and appeared to be sweating with the effort.

The rumble became so loud it was as if a thunderstorm was actually in the room with them.

Then at the point where the book had vanished, a small white spot appeared and expanded quickly and so brightly that Amy and Maggie had to shield their eyes from the glare. The light exploded with enormous power, pushing everything, including the furniture to the side walls. Even Amy, Maggie and Erda were slammed against the walls as the explosion ripped a huge hole through time, right there in the air in front of them in Maggie's attic.

With a bright flash, the gaping hole revealed many different days, nights and locations. As they watched each and every one flash by, occasionally the flashing images would stop in one place and time and the immense energy of the book threw the soul of a Scribe into the hole. They fell through the air until they were sitting or standing in the original spot where they had signed the book and became a Scribe. Only this time there was no book and they would look around themselves, puzzled, and try to remember what they were about to do. They no longer had a memory of those events and shrugged and continued on with their normal lives, oblivious to their misdeeds and the cascading effect of them. All traces of their intended evil wiped away. One by one this happened to each and every Scribe as they were taken back into their own time and their lives before the book.

Finally, Benjamin and his mother were returned to theirs. His mother was back in her grave and he was now sitting in a tavern, but couldn't remember who he was waiting for. Soon he rose from his seat and walked out to return to spending his stepbrother's money. Once that was gone, perhaps he would go to yet another town looking for work in a stable again. It was, after all, all he had known.

As Amy, Erda and Maggie watched, history was returned to how it should have been without the powers of the book changing it through the

Scribes. Each of them fascinated and awed by the workings of the spell and its incredible power to change the world.

The gaping hole in time, rimmed with the piercing white light closed shut with a sudden bang, which echoed around the attic as if someone had just slammed the door on time itself and nothing remained of the light, the book, nor the Scribes.

Except one: Maggie was whole and safe, if a little crumpled in a heap next to Amy.

"Oh my god," Amy said as she sat blinking and put her fingers to her ringing ears. "Is it over?" she said rather loudly.

"Aye, 'tis. Time hath righted itself and ye evil book is destroyed," Erda said as she climbed to her feet and helped Amy and Maggie to stand up.

"I owe you my life. My fate would have been that of those other Scribes if you had not protected me. Thank you, Erda," Maggie said and drew Erda into an embrace.

"Thy is most welcome, Mistress Maggie," Erda said, touched by Maggie's gratitude.

"Not sure I will ever get used to being called that but I do like it. It's a pleasure to meet you properly, Erda Miller," Maggie said with a huge smile.

"Thy pleasure be also mine," Erda said.

"Yes, thank you, Erda for protecting us. I don't know what we would have done if you weren't here," Amy said.

Erda nodded and said, "'Twill be my pleasure to be here always."

Amy knew in her heart that Erda's words were true and it made her feel loved and cared for.

"Gods, my ears are ringing," Maggie said.

"Yeah, mine too," Amy said. "What the hell did you write in the book for it to do all that?" Amy asked as she looked appreciatively at her friend.

"I simply told the book that I wished for Benjamin to uncast his spell that had formed it and return all to the way it should be without any of the Scribes' words."

"Clever, because we would never have been able to make him do it."

"Exactly, it was Erda who gave me the

idea," Maggie said.

"So does this mean everything, all the changes those Scribes made after all these years have been reversed and everything is now back to how it should be, and we're back on track again, as it were?" Amy said and couldn't help thinking about Uncle Cy. *Was he now alive? And Bryer, was he back in his shop and divorced again?*

"I canst nay tell from in here. We must go abroad and look for ye signs and changes," Erda said as she righted an old wooden chair and sat in it.

"Are you alright?" Amy asked as she came and stood next to her.

"Aye, 'tis but naught. A sapping of mine energy 'tis all."

"You might be alright but I'm not so sure about my attic," Maggie said half-jokingly, and wearily laughed as she looked around at the chaos of her attic room. The furniture, books, plants and everything else had been flung about by the wind with wild abandon.

"Wait, where's Cabot's body? Did it get sucked in too?"

"What? Oh, I dunno, I didn't see him get sucked in though... anyway, why would he? He wasn't a Scribe," Amy said and frowned, "He was... dead, right?" Amy said, horrified she was actually asking that question.

"Oh yeah, definitely. I heard his neck break," Maggie said. "Poor Cabot, never liked his arrogant ass but that was no way to go."

"Aye, his soul left his body, I saw it," Erda said.

"You saw it?" Amy's eyebrow rose. "So where's his body?" She said as she looked around her but Cabot's body was nowhere to be seen.

Chapter Thirty

The Next Day

Amy was delighted to find her father's truck was outside her cottage the next morning and in immaculate condition. She and Erda concluded that seeing as Cabot's great grandfather was a Scribe, and had now all he did was undone, the only answer was that the accident never happened. But if it didn't happen then she never had sex with Cabot, but she could still remember it vividly, too vividly for comfort. Amy's head began to ache again. She decided to not think on such things any longer and go into town to check if the other changes had been reversed. She hoped with all her heart they had.

She drove down the main street of Morton Creek, and slowly drove past Uncle Cy's and Aunt Kath's store on the left. With a happy jolt of her heart she could see them both, one inside the store and the other outside, speaking with customers, but there was absolutely no sign of David, their son.

"Oh, thank God," Amy felt a huge wave of relief wash over her. They had done it, they had managed to save Uncle Cy. She pulled over by the side of the road and watched him in his overalls talking to a lady who seemed interested in buying a new broom. The simple joy of knowing he was still in this world filled her up so much that tears rolled down her cheeks as she smiled at the view before her. Now, knowing this happiness the other things she needed to check on felt utterly small and insignificant in comparison.

Unable to bear the happiness any longer, she parked her truck, jumped out and almost ran to the store, trying to breathe deeply and calm herself all the way. By the time she reached the store, Uncle Cy had gone inside with the customer and she watched him and his wife serving their friends and neighbours as they had always done, with a smile and a kind word.

She had her family back. Joy welled in Amy's heart as she entered the store and the little bell over the door announced her arrival.

"Hello, Amy, we weren't expecting to see you today," Aunt Kath said as she said goodbye to her customer and came round the counter to hug Amy.

"Yeah, erm... I was passing and just wanted to say hello." Amy grinned and hugged her back, watching Uncle Cy over Aunt Kath's shoulder as he also finished with his customer.

"Hey, Amy. How's your day going?" he said, and his brown, wrinkled, old face lit up in a huge smile and he also gave her a hug.

"Hi, Uncle Cy," Amy said as she enjoyed the hug from his strong and healthy arms, and she was glad of it as a huge lump of emotion had swelled up in her throat.

"You alright, lass?" he said as he let go and saw the raw emotion on Amy's face.

"Oh, yes. I'm fine, in fact... I'm very fine. It really is the best of days today, isn't it?" Amy said, overflowing with gratitude.

"Every day is," Uncle Cy said and was called away by another customer who had just entered the store.

"Let's have you over for supper again this week, Amy," Aunt Kath said as she watched Amy carefully and wondered what was happening in the young woman's life at that moment.

"Definitely, this week, next week... every week," Amy said.

"Sounds good to me, sweetheart," Aunt Kath said with a huge smile. "Catch you later then," Aunt Kath said as she saw Amy begin to head to the door.

"Yes, definitely," Amy said as she felt an urgent need to get out of there, before she started crying in happiness again as that would be very difficult to explain.

At last, Amy forced herself to drive away from the general store and the utter contentment she had found there.

She continued onward towards Emily Carpenter's Realtor office, which, thankfully, was now empty, with a closed sign hanging on the door and the windows dirty. It looked like nobody had used the place for over a year.

"Just as it bloody well should be." Amy could feel the stress leave her body. She was so relieved that part of history was utterly over with.

She continued along the road, past the White Oak pub towards the bookstore.

Breathing in deeply as her stomach fluttered, Amy glanced at the bookstore ahead and then her eyes slowly slid toward the building next to it. This would be the moment, the moment that she knew for sure that all the things were back to normal. Back to how she remembered it. Would it be a building that was under construction, to be converted to the expanded bookstore, or would it be Bryer's photography shop again? Would everything actually have been put right. She swallowed hard and tried to calm her breathing again.

As she drew nearer, she saw the window display in Bryer's store, it was exactly the same as she'd remembered it from before this nightmare happened. "He's back... everything is the same from before it all got messed up with that bloody book." She let out a long breath that she hadn't realised she'd been holding and pulled the car over to the curb in front of the bookstore. She sat and stared at Bryer's windows and a sudden calmness washed over her in the knowledge that they had set things right at last.

Looking toward the Blinded Eye bookstore, the last thing that she had to check was how it all stood with Maggie and their friendship and partnership in the store. Would they still be partners? Hadn't that happened after the changes started? Amy chewed her lip, *a person could go mad thinking about all this*, she thought.

Climbing out of the car into the fresh morning air, Amy paused for a moment, unsure of who to visit first: Maggie or Bryer? The thought of Bryer made her stomach drop and filled her with excitement but she was still a little afraid. What if his ex-wife was with him or would that have changed again, too? She had no clue if everything had been restored or just reworked. Deciding to cross that bridge later and maybe after a stiff drink over lunch, she decided to check in on Maggie first.

The doorbell tinkled as Amy entered the store and she saw her friend dealing with a customer over by the travel section. Maggie looked up as Amy entered and she nodded at her. Amy nodded back and headed to the back of the store where the small cafe sat. The whole store was as it had been before the expansion and it made Amy wonder if Maggie had written about creating the expansion in the book when she first owned it.

Hmm... I must ask her about that sometime, she thought and ordered a green tea. Then, sitting in the big leather chair by the empty fireplace that had now been filled with summer flowers, Amy relaxed and waited for her friend to come over.

A few minutes later, Maggie strolled over to Amy after she'd sold the book to the customer and smiled, "Hey."

"Hey, how's business?" Amy said, wondering how much of the events of yesterday Maggie wanted to talk about.

"Great, I just have to phone through an order and then we can go to lunch," Maggie said.

"Okay."

"Come through to my office; there is

something I want to talk to you about," Maggie said and turned toward the door between two bookshelves.

Amy suddenly felt rather nervous, as if being summoned by a head teacher or something. Pushing the nervous feeling down, she picked up her cup of tea and followed Maggie into the back office.

Maggie was already on the phone when Amy arrived and she gestured to Amy to sit in one of the two chairs in front of her desk.

Amy sat and sipped her tea, wondering what was coming, while she listened to Maggie placing an order for more muffins and butter tarts.

Maggie ended the phone call and smiled at Amy.

"So I've just heard this morning that Robertson, the guy who owns the landscape gardening business next door is retiring and he has offered me the lease of the place. And... well, I wondered if you would like to become a partner in this place again and we could expand into his store instead of Bryer's like we did before... before history changed. What do you think?" Maggie blurted out rather quickly, as if she had been nervous of the conversation. She looked at Amy and tried to wait patiently for her reply, hoping she would like the idea again but her twitching fingers betrayed her nervousness at waiting for the reply.

"Depends," Amy said with a smile.

"Oh? On what?"

"Do you forgive me for breaking into your house with Erda?"

"Water under the bridge. All forgotten and forgiven, seeing as you saved me an eternity inside that evil book."

"I didn't...that was Erda."

"You two are a package deal, even I know that."

"Yeah, we are and thanks, I was worried it would ruin our friendship."

"Not a chance. You can't get rid of me that easily."

"So, next door? The other side? Yeah, I'd love to," Amy couldn't help but grin widely in utter delight.

"I know it's a bit different from before but

I still just love the thought of it," Maggie said, the hope shining on her face like a ray of sunshine escaping from darkened clouds. "That's awesome! Oh, great. I'll get contracts drawn up and plans made for the store, if you want to add anything you just let me know. Oh, this is going to be so much fun again," Maggie couldn't contain her joy much longer and leapt out of her chair and was round the table with her arms out for a congratulatory hug before Amy could blink.

Amy jumped up and returned the hug. Her mind was reeling at how the events had evolved to create this opportunity for them both once again as if fate would not be denied.

"Let's go and get lunch and celebrate with a bottle of wine," Maggie said as she let go of Amy and grabbed her bag.

"What an excellent idea."

Leaving the bookstore in the hands of her two employees, Maggie led the way down the street toward the White Oak, rapidly talking about all the ideas she had for this extension over what they had done before as the building next door was configured differently. Amy listened to her friend and loved how excited she obviously was about it all.

Indeed, Amy was excited too. It had saddened her to think it might have been lost if their friendship hadn't survived the book. It was a second chance and she was very glad of it.

A U-Haul truck pulled up opposite the pub just as Maggie and Amy were about to enter and it caught Amy's eye.

"Looks like someone's moving in," she said as she held the door of the pub open for Maggie to enter and looked back over her shoulder.

"Oh, yeah. Jo, at the Deli, said that a new store is coming. The folks that bought the lease also bought the old MacArthur house out near the lake. Apparently they are renovating it too. That house originally belonged to the founder of the town and it's about time someone restored it to its former glory."

Amy only half-heard what Maggie was saying as she was rooted to the spot, looking at the man who had just climbed out of the truck.

Amy couldn't believe her eyes and she

blinked. "Who's moved in?" she said, her voice sounded stunned, even to Amy.

"The Turners, I think. I could be wrong, though. Not sure what Jo said the surname was now, Anyway her name is Natalie and she didn't know the husband's name, as she didn't meet him. Apparently they are in the antiques business. It will be nice to have some new folks in town, and maybe we can pick something up from their store for the new expansion."

"Yeah," Amy said, as if her mind was far away. She watched as the man opened the back of the truck. There was something familiar about him, about his movements: kind of lithe, like a large cat. Suddenly, as if feeling her eyes on him, the man looked across the road directly at her and smiled. A fission of remembrance of their passion rippled down Amy's spine.

A look of recognition passed between them.

It was Cabot.

Amy's brain stalled and she stood with her mouth open, blinking. Why was she so surprised he was alive. Hadn't Cy also come back? What really unnerved her was that Cabot had definitely recognised her. The only way he could do that was if he remembered everything that happened when the book had changed things. Changed his family's past and future via his great grandfather being a Scribe and history being put right. That meant he remembered the accident, the sex, and getting killed in Maggie's attic.

"How the hell?" Amy said out loud. As he looked away and climbed into the van.

Maggie turned round, "You okay, Amy? You look like you've seen a ghost."

"Yeah, I think I have," Amy said and at long last managed to pull her eyes away from the spot where Cabot had been standing looking at her from across the street. "I need a whisky."

"Best idea I've heard today and you can tell me what just happened to you over it," Maggie said and closed the door behind them.

Epilogue

1st October, Present Day.

The phone rang for the fourth time as Amy rushed half-dressed into the living room to answer it. "Hello?" she said, a little out of breath.

"Amy, Darling! It's Felicity, your agent, of course!" The woman's imperious voice said loudly.

Amy held the phone a little away from her ear: "Hello, Felicity. Yes, I know who you are." Amy grinned to herself. Felicity was the only person she knew who could make darling sound like it had an 'h' in it and who had to announce her own presence wherever she went, as if she was a narrator in her own life. "You've only just caught me, I'm on my way out and I'm running late.

What can I do for you?"

"Well, darling, I've just finished reading your manuscript for the next book and I utterly love it darling, it's so complicated, but so utterly and positively scrumptious!"

"I'm so glad you like it, but can I call you tomorrow? I'm desperately running late and really must leave now."

"Oh, yes, yes, of course, my darling. Just wanted you to know you have a green light, as it were, for it. Witch Tree I mean, of course. Not that you're writing more than one book, obviously. Or are you, my clever little darling?"

"You never know," Amy said and laughed as that very afternoon she had been plotting out a book completely different from anything she had written so far and had lost herself in the details. It was the reason why she was now running late.

"Oh, how thrilling! Do tell me everything, darling. No, yes, tell me all but not now... phone me, darling. Ciao!"

Amy looked at her phone as she heard the call disconnect and smiled to herself at the whirlwind ball of energy that was Felicity. Without further ado she rushed back to her bedroom to finish getting ready.

"It would not do to be late for the grand opening of the newly-expanded book store, especially when I'm the co-owner, now would it?" she said to herself with a huge satisfied grin on her face.

****

The place was packed. It seemed as if the entire town of Morton Creek and indeed the neighbouring towns had come out for the grand opening. Amy and Maggie greeted everyone as they entered. The cafe, which had also been extended in the new design, was currently serving free refreshments. The store was decorated with autumn colours and early, although discreet, Hallowe'en decorations.

Maggie took Amy by the hand and made her way to the centre of the store, where the reading area was located with comfy chairs and where folks could take their purchases from the café. She let go of Amy's hand and stepped forward a little. "Everyone, if I could have your attention, please?"

The crowd grew quiet and turned to face Maggie expectantly.

"Thank you," she paused and smiled. "Thank you all for coming out today and welcome to the new and improved Blinded Eye book store and café." A huge smile spread across her face as the audience clapped. Maggie held up her hand to ask for quiet and the clapping soon evaporated.

"Of course, none of this would have been possible without my business partner and the new co-owner of the Blinded Eye, our very own writer in residence, Amy Grey!" Maggie turned towards Amy and began the applause herself and it was quickly echoed by the crowd.

Amy smiled at everyone around her. "Thank you, thank you."

Maggie spoke again, "Okay, remember to buy your raffle tickets folks. The first prize is to get your name in one of Amy's upcoming books, and a personally signed copy of any of Amy's books. Also, two free tickets to the Hallowe'en Fancy Dress Ball at City Hall. The second prize is a meal for two at Martel's Italian Restaurant on Clover Street and the third prize is a $50 dollar voucher for any purchase here at The Blinded Eye including in the café. All the proceeds from the raffle will go to the "Sponsor a Child" campaign which helps children in poor and war-torn countries get access to all they need including a good education. Nancy Holden is in charge of sorting all the raffle takings, and, if you feel the urge to simply donate to her for the cause, she is over by the travel section and will be happy to help you. So please have a good look around, enjoy some free refreshments and buy as many raffle tickets as you can for this great cause. Thank you." Maggie smiled and the crowd clapped enthusiastically.

Amy approached Maggie.

"Well said."

"Thanks. Have you been working on the crowd as these are all potential readers you know," Maggie said with a cheeky look on her face.

"I think these folks know what they want, but I'll work on a few."

"Hello, Maggie. Congratulations on the

expansion," A voice said from behind the women and they both spun round ready to greet their guest. A hard look flickered over Maggie's face though it quickly vanished, but not before Amy and the man saw it. Amy's reaction was quite different. She was a little stunned to be face to face with Cabot and his wife Natalie.

Amy, Erda and Maggie had many long conversations over Cabot's death, and although they understood he was alive again due to events being put back to how they should be, no one could understand how nor why he could remember everything, if it all hadn't happened to him now. A strange distrust of him had developed between the three women and Erda had advised caution around him until they knew more. He also knew about Erda and that made him even more dangerous.

"Cabot, Natalie, it's good of you to come," Maggie said with a smile plastered on her face, professional as ever.

"Amy," Cabot simply said and nodded in her direction.

Amy was at a loss for words as the last time she had seen him, apart from by the U-Haul truck, he had laid dead against the wall of Maggie's attic with his neck broken by Benjamin and Ann Hibbens. Being so close to him now after all that and knowing she'd had passionate sex with him only a few days ago, before they found the book and the Scribe, all these details overloaded Amy's brain. She just stared at him, unable to put a sentence together.

Cabot spotted her lack of a working brain and stepped into the breach.

"Let me introduce you to my wife, Natalie. Natalie, this is the author Amy Grey and co-owner of this bookstore."

"Nice to meet you. I'd shake your hand but as you can see I'm holding on to all the important things," Natalie said with an disingenuous smile as her arm was linked through her husband's and in one had she had a glass of wine and in the other two books.

"Not to worry, I understand," Amy said, understanding utterly the meaning of Natalie's words.

Stay away from my husband, Yes, Amy understood the meaning perfectly and it made

Amy wonder if Natalie knew about the sex. Otherwise why would this woman see her as a threat? History had changed everything hadn't it? Unless it hadn't and she'd had sex with a married man. Amy was beginning to get a headache again thinking about everything.

Just as Cabot and Natalie began moving away, and Natalie started chatting with a portly man from the local bank, Cabot brushed past Amy and said quietly to her, "I would love you to come and see the new house and the library. I'm sure we could have as much fun as we did last time."

Amy looked at him, horror-stricken. He did remember... everything.

Oh shit! Her brain said loudly. Before Amy could reply or remind him he had a wife, he was gone in the crowd, leaving Amy angry, confused and full of the need to break something. Pulling herself together, she stepped outside of the store to get some much needed cool night air.

"Hey, you ok? Saw you sneak out," Maggie said as she suddenly appeared beside Amy.

"Yeah, just wanted a moment to get some fresh air."

"No worries. It is really busy in there. It is nice that so many people came out to support us and the store."

"Yeah, there are a lot of good folks in town."

"I just wanted to ask, while we have a moment alone, if you would like to come to the Witch Ball with me as my guest?"

"Sure, would love too. Not sure what costume I'm going to do this year though. What are you going as?"

"Oh no, not the one at City Hall, that we went to last year. The one I'm talking about is a real Witch Ball, my Kindred are in charge of the Samhain celebration this year and many folks from other Kindreds, Covens and Circles will be travelling into town to celebrate."

"A real Witches' Ball? Am I allowed? Isn't it a secret thing?" Amy said looking shocked and somewhat amazed she would be asked.

"This is not Hollywood. We don't sneak around doing black magic and have secret handshakes. Well, not often anyway," Maggie said and burst out laughing.

"Right, of course." Amy blushed a little.

"Seriously, I'd love you to come and it would be great research for your books."

"I'd love to, just to enjoy it with you, the bonus of research is secondary."

"It's sorted then, we'll talk about the details later. We'd better get back to our guests," Maggie said and began walking back to the door, "You coming?"

"Yeah, in a minute."

"Ok, see you inside."

"Yup."

Maggie went back in the store leaving Amy alone on the street with only the streetlights for company. She looked up at the stars, grateful that Morton Creek was a small enough town that it had very little light pollution and one could still see the stars at night.

"Hello beautiful."

Amy spun round at the sound of the familiar voice. Bryer stood a few paces away from her in the half-light that hovered between two streetlights. His lovely nut-brown hair shone in the light, making her want to play in it with her fingers. She'd always had a thing for men with longer hair, his slightly wavy hair just met the top of his shoulders. She tried to ignore her racing pulse, as she took in the rest of him and she gave him a bold, and appreciative, once-over with her eyes. *God it's good to see him,* she thought, her breath coming faster at the sight of him.

He wore a dark green shirt over jeans with his usual cowboy boots sticking out from under them. Sometimes, in life, you find people you are inexplicably and sexually attracted to, and that was exactly how she always felt about Bryer Burnett since the first day they had met last year. She tried really hard not to stare too much as he walked the few steps between them.

"Hello handsome."

"I missed you, it seems like months since I last saw you." he said with a strange quizzical look on his face.

"No, it wasn't that long ago, but it does feel like longer I admit." Amy wasn't going to tell him everything that had happened, nor that in that other life he was still with his wife. No, she was going to put it out of her mind and just enjoy the moment. She walked towards him, gently put her hands on his face, took one look in his gorgeous eyes, then rose up on tiptoe. "Kiss me."

"Yes, ma'am," he said and whole heartedly did just that.

Amy kissed him back with enthusiasm that made them breathless, and she continued to kiss him before anything could change again.

Acknowledgements

My deepest thanks go out to Julie Desrosiers, Senior Druid of the Thornhaven ADF Grove, for her invaluable advice on several herbs and their trance inducing qualities as used in this book.

Source

1   The 'Nine Herbs Charm', by person unknown, is recorded in the 10th-century AD in the Lacnunga LXXIX-LXXXII manuscript. (Translator is also unknown)

~ Adapted slightly by J.E. Marriott to fit the 17th century vocabulary and story.

The next installment of 'Witch Books':

Witch Ball

Amy and Erda are invited to a real Witches Ball, by their friend Maggie, to celebrate Samhain. However, it's not just a party but an entire weekend festival where they meet many Covens, Circles and Kindreds from all over.

They discover one of them has an incredible talent for scrying, and, once that inner door is opened, visions of the future plague them night and day but can they control the visions? Or will they lose their mind?

Is their fate set in stone?

Can insanity and death be beaten?

All these questions, and many more, will be answered in 'Witch Ball', Book 3 of The Amy Grey Novels.

Witch Ball

Foretold is Forewarned.

About the Author

J.E. Marriott is an internationally acclaimed author of paranormal mysteries, supernatural thrillers and magically enchanted tales.

In 2008, she permanently moved from her home in Lincolnshire, in the UK, across the pond' to Brockville, Canada, where she has permanently, made her home with her husband and two demon cats, she is now a full-time author.

She is a university accredited historian and avid reader of a wide spectrum of genres. She brings her unusual English lilt and humour to all of her writings, no matter the genre.